FIXING A BROKEN HEART AT THE HIGHLAND REPAIR SHOP

KILEY DUNBAR

First published in Great Britain in 2025 by Boldwood Books Ltd.

Copyright © Kiley Dunbar, 2025

Cover Design by Lizzie Gardiner

Cover Images: Shutterstock and Adobe Stock

The moral right of Kiley Dunbar to be identified as the author of this work has been asserted in accordance with the Copyright, Designs and Patents Act 1988.

All rights reserved. No part of this book may be reproduced in any form or by any electronic or mechanical means, including information storage and retrieval systems, without written permission from the author, except for the use of brief quotations in a book review. This book is a work of fiction and, except in the case of historical fact, any resemblance to actual persons, living or dead, is purely coincidental.

Every effort has been made to obtain the necessary permissions with reference to copyright material, both illustrative and quoted. We apologise for any omissions in this respect and will be pleased to make the appropriate acknowledgements in any future edition.

A CIP catalogue record for this book is available from the British Library.

Paperback ISBN 978-1-83656-667-0

Large Print ISBN 978-1-83656-668-7

Hardback ISBN 978-1-83656-666-3

Ebook ISBN 978-1-83656-669-4

Kindle ISBN 978-1-83656-670-0

Audio CD ISBN 978-1-83656-661-8

MP3 CD ISBN 978-1-83656-662-5

Digital audio download ISBN 978-1-83656-664-9

This book is printed on certified sustainable paper. Boldwood Books is dedicated to putting sustainability at the heart of our business. For more information please visit https://www.boldwoodbooks.com/about-us/sustainability/

Boldwood Books Ltd, 23 Bowerdean Street, London, SW6 3TN

www.boldwoodbooks.com

For Nic, who never takes broken for an answer.
Thank you for fixing everything, even after twenty-five years,
With all my love, K, x

1

So many stories begin with a broken heart. This one begins with a broken paper shredder. There will be a broken heart too, of course, only that hasn't quite happened yet, and it's a longer story than the one about the shredder, where it all began.

It was the year 2022 and Charlie McIntyre, an example of the ginger-haired and rosy-cheeked Highland husband, and known to everyone simply as 'McIntyre', was pottering in his garden workshop when there came a knock at its door. Nothing unusual there; neighbours from the small town of Cairn Dhu, and all along this picturesque stretch of the River Nithy, are few and far between, but what few there are stick together and make a point of getting involved in everyone else's business.

That day, his old pal, Sachin Roy, had come from his cottage a fair walk away down near Stranruthie village and was intent on making his broken shredder McIntyre's business.

'Have ye a part for this? I reckon it's the motor,' he said. No 'how's Roz and the kids?' No small talk about the November weather.

McIntyre, however, didn't mind this. He is one of life's fixers and loves nothing more than an excuse to strip down a machine on his workbench and take a look inside.

He is also a renowned hoarder. Only, unlike the hoarders' lives you see sensationalised on the telly, all the old junk he collected in the hope that 'it'll come in handy one day' was beautifully – his wife would say obsessively – organised in labelled crates and tins, tubs and boxes on high shelves all around the huge barn that stands next to their historic old mill house with its working water wheel. Of course it's still working; it's McIntyre's.

'Aye, I've just the thing,' he'd said, and within half an hour, not only had he gone straight to the correct box and put his finger on just the right part, he'd tinkered and welded and dauded (which is a Scottish kind of gentle thump) and got the shredder going again, and he and Sachin were into the Bourbon Creams and Nescafe with powdered milk that he kept out there to save tramping dirty boots into the Mill kitchen.

Even on a cold winter's day, the robins, crested tits and blackbirds around the feeders on the frosty lawn were singing loud enough for the men to catch their sounds over the hum of music on McIntyre's radio. It was, as McIntyre would say, a braw day.

If you haven't heard of this part of Scotland before, the Cairngorms, try to imagine soaring purple mountains topped with snow half the year round, rising from bands of smaller elevations that the hardy hillwalkers who flock here can easily bag before lunchtime. On a very good day there's glaring blue sky, and if you're very lucky, you'll spot a golden eagle gliding overhead, hunting their prey.

If that all sounds too remote and wet-weatherish for you, rest assured, you're never more than a short drive from the more densely populated spots of Aviemore (due west, for the big ski resort, the tourist knickknacks, and the highest gin bar in Scot-

Fixing a Broken Heart at the Highland Repair Shop　　3

land), or there's the Reindeer Centre a wee bit further south. If you come across burly men tossing cabers or the King in his kilt, you've gone too far to the east and you've hit the Balmoral estate and Braemar, home of the Royal Highland Games.

Still curious? Look up any Instagram reel with the hashtag 'My Heart is in the Highlands' or 'I Love the Cairngorms National Park' and they'll bring you straight here and make you wish you were lucky enough to live in this bonny spot like these two do, even if McIntyre's life was a wee bit too cluttered to be considered picturesque.

'What are you going to do with all this old gubbins?' Sachin had said, looking around at the floor-to-beam shelves stuffed with tools, obscure machinery, scrap metal and wood, wires, cables and bits and bobs of all sorts.

'*Do?*' McIntyre held his biscuit mid-dunk.

'When you pop your clogs. Who'll deal with all this... accumulation.'

'I'm fifty-seven and fit as a fiddle,' he'd said, an eyebrow raised. 'A year younger than you, in case you need reminding. Did Roz tell you to say something?'

'*Phwah!* No, no,' Sachin protested unconvincingly. 'But you've enough here to keep the whole of Scotland in spare parts for all eternity. One man cannot possibly use it all.'

'Everything in time becomes useful again.' McIntyre put the lid firmly on the biscuit tin, if Sachin was going to be like that. 'Besides, it's not just me uses it. See yourself? How often are you knocking at my door, looking for a hand?'

Sachin couldn't deny this was true. Now that he'd taken early retirement, passing the storage unit company he used to run with his wife to his adult daughters, he was here near enough every week with some job or other. There was nothing McIntyre couldn't mend.

'And plenty of folks from across the park drop by,' McIntyre went on. 'Only yesterday, I soldered Post Office Pauline's locket chain (he pronounced it sauder'd like everyone else from these parts), and some hiker lassie's dog had snapped its collar out there on the roadside. She waited in that very spot,' McIntyre jabbed a finger towards Sachin, 'while I stitched in a leather patch and a buckle I happened to have lying around. Good as new it was. No, Sachin, you cannot argue this *collection* benefits only me.'

Sachin looked sorrowfully at the out-of-bounds biscuits. 'Right enough. You're a one-man repair shop. You should advertise your services.'

McIntyre blinked and Sachin took this chance to strongarm his old friend. Truth was, he was talking off the top of his head and hadn't given this a whole lot of thought before now, but something needed to change.

'Like that programme on the BBC,' Sachin said. 'People come from all over with their items, and there's a whole team of them fixin' things.'

McIntyre wasn't brushing the crumbs from his overalls and showing him out, so Sachin had taken this as a good sign and went on with his opinions.

Some of it sounded remarkably like Roz speaking. She must have had a word with Sachin at the town's Samhain bonfire and sausage sizzle.

McIntyre knew everyone was concerned about him and the amount of time he'd spend out here since losing his job at the agricultural machinery servicing centre during the first lockdown.

Maybe he *had* taken the redundancy too hard? Roz kept complaining how the twins missed their dad, but Ally and Murray had been living their own lives since they'd finished

Fixing a Broken Heart at the Highland Repair Shop 5

college and Murray only really came home to sleep at that point. Maybe, more truthfully, it was his wife who missed him. McIntyre had tried to gulp away the lump in his throat.

'Open up my repair shed?' he said at last. 'For money? That doesnae sit right.'

He rose, walking round his bench, seemingly to inspect his shelves, one fist bunched at the hip of his overalls, the other gripping his mug. 'Repairs shouldn't cost. Everyone should know someone who can fix and repurpose any number of things, like my dad and his pals and all the mothers across this region, back in the day. Between them nothing went to waste. No,' he shook his head, now addressing the grease spots on the floor. 'You cannae charge folks who want to keep a thing going, who cannae bear chuckin' it in the landfill. There's enough money-grabbers out there!' He was getting het up now.

Sachin had lost the thread some time ago and really should have been getting home to Mrs Roy, if they were going to make it to the pictures in Inverness for three, but he had an inkling something important was happening, so he kept quiet.

McIntyre talked on. 'There's businesses out there making electronics *designed* so they cannae be repaired, devices and gadgets *intended* to turn obsolete within a few years, warranties worth nothing, clothes you wear once and they fall apart. It's all bin that and buy again!'

He'd lifted a hand to a cardboard box marked 'clock mechanisms and spares'. A solemn note was sneaking into his voice. 'Nobody cares about any of this good old stuff. It's consigned to the scrap heap before its time's up, when there's years of usefulness still left in it.'

Sachin was on his feet now too, astute enough to suspect McIntyre wasn't only talking about throwaway objects, but people too. He gripped his now working shredder, shuffling awkwardly for the door. 'I hope I havenae upset you, pal. Thanks anyway for this, and the coffee and biccies.'

McIntyre wasn't upset, though. On the contrary, he was so wrapped up in thoughts of a non-disposable world he barely heard his friend leaving. His mind ticked and his eyes sharpened as he pictured his future.

'A fixing factory?' he was saying under his breath, scratching the back of his head. 'Here, at the mill? No, a community repair hub! It's madness. Is it no'?'

And that was how the idea for the Cairn Dhu Community Repair Shop and Café, famous all across the Cairngorms for its motley band of expert fixers and delicious home baking (not to mention the tiniest wee bit of scandal that threatened to spoil everything), first came into being.

Now that the story of the broken shredder is told, it's time we got to the part about the broken heart; Ally McIntyre's heart to be precise.

2

THIS YEAR, MAY

Ally took one last glance around the repair shop and café to check everything was ready for opening.

Retired GP's receptionist, Senga Gifford, was switching on the tea urn in her little dominion, the café corner, where she held court, helped by her beleaguered younger sister, Rhona, who Senga never allowed to do much of anything other than put the money in the till. A good aroma of freshly baked bran scones wafted from the Perspex display case on the café counter.

Cary Anderson, a local carpenter, barely five and thirty but with an old-fashioned handsomeness about his clothes that marked him as a man curiously out of time, sat at his tool-sharpening station, his foot poised over the pedal of his grinding wheel. He rarely spoke, other than to ask for a fresh cup of tea, but was always smilingly affable and turned up like clockwork every Saturday. Behind him, a poster on the wall read:

NEVER TAKE BROKEN FOR AN ANSWER

Sachin Roy was back too, sitting at his spot in the repairs 'triage' area by the door where he directed clients to the right person and dealt with the paperwork and donations (like all repair cafés nobody pays for fixes here; folks drop a discretionary amount of cash in the jar, and even then it's optional). McIntyre had insisted, since this was Sachin's bright spark idea in the first place, that he surely didn't mind helping out, and his old friend had found he had no choice but to come here, much to Mrs Roy's annoyance, every Saturday since the shop launched, a good two and a half years ago.

Ally McIntyre's mum, Roz, sat with her pin cushion on the back of her wrist beneath her seamsters' banner with its motto 'make do and mend' in embroidered purple velvet like something the suffragettes would have marched under. She was with Willie and Peaches, her young crafting protégés recruited for work experience from the fashion degree programme at their Highland university, both of whom were scrolling on their phones one last time before opening, and both were dressed in their own hand-sewn garments with the look of two fabulous, colourful, patchwork rag dolls – if rag dolls ever interned at London Fashion Week.

Today, Peaches's hair was a wonderful apricot shade with flame-red lengths (the repairers would pass quieter moments taking guesses on what colour it might be the next weekend). These two 'young ones' were adored and coddled by all the elder repairers, especially Rhona Gifford, who'd cannily sneak them cakes to take home with them.

At every station the volunteers waited with their repair equipment (or their cake tongs) ready for action.

Granted, it was a ramshackle sort of a repair shop, furnished almost entirely with the machinery accumulated by McIntyre at

Fixing a Broken Heart at the Highland Repair Shop 9

the height of his hoarding (an abundance of overlockers, welders, lathes, sanders, hoists, bandsaws, clamps, doodads and thingumabobs only he knew the names for). Aside from a few specialist machines they'd sourced from salvage yards or begged as donations, they'd found Charlie already owned much of the hardware and tools they'd needed to launch their fixing venture.

Today there were nine volunteers in total, if you included Ally, though nobody did because nobody was expecting her to stick around. In fact, her day off was the only thing they could talk about this morning, even with the local news crew arriving shortly to record a segment on the global rise of community repair groups since lockdown.

'I'm turning the sign on,' called Ally, hoping to stop the speculation, propping the door open and flicking the switch so the barn flooded with the pink neon light of their Repair Shop and Café logo: a steaming coffee cup with a threaded needle passing through its handle.

'Do you know where he's taking you?' Senga called across the room.

'Somewhere romantic, I bet,' Rhona plucked up the courage to say. 'The Cairn Dhu Hotel restaurant is nice for an engagement.'

Senga batted her down with a tut. 'With all the tourists gawking? Hardly the spot for a proposal,' she asserted, folding her arms across her apron.

'Now, now,' Cary Anderson said softly, but nobody seemed to hear.

'Can you all stop, please. Mum, tell them!' Ally complained.

Roz McIntyre only shrugged helplessly across the room at her daughter.

This is what happens when you open up the family home

(well, its big barn, anyway) and all its goings-on to the whole community. Everyone sticks their noses in.

'There's absolutely no reason to think Gray's going to propose. I don't know where you get your ideas from,' Ally went on, but the flutter in her chest told another story.

Senga took the opportunity to remind everyone that, 'Moira Blain has it on good authority from Jean Wilson who heard it from her cousin, Tony, who's on the hop-on, hop-off tour buses, that Gray came out of the wee jewellers in Aviemore carrying *a tiny bag*.'

Hardy incontrovertible evidence there was about to be a celebration.

'It *is* your anniversary,' McIntyre said under his breath as he passed his daughter, casting an eye into the courtyard, scanning for the news crew.

There'd be clients arriving soon too. They usually started rolling in at the turning on of the sign. Ally sighed heavily but couldn't help following her dad's gaze outside.

Gray was coming at ten, he'd said, so any minute now, and he'd said there was 'something important' he wanted to talk about. That's how all this theorising had begun in the first place.

'We'll probably just go for a walk,' Ally said, refusing to show she too was swept up in hoping, but secretly she *was* hoping, very much.

It had been twelve happy months since she'd met Gray, right here in the shed when he'd brought in his granny's vacuum cleaner to have its jammed rollers freed up. They'd fallen for each other in moments while Ally's dad took the thing apart and Gray approached her with a sly smile and small talk, the dust motes sparkling like glitter in the shafts from the barn's skylight window.

'When a man runs errands for his dear old granny like that,

Fixing a Broken Heart at the Highland Repair Shop

you just know he's a good one,' the repair café sages had agreed at the time, and sure enough, he'd been nothing but charming and fun all year long.

The only problem had been her dad's cooler attitude towards Gray. Sachin – not that it was any of his concern – had agreed there was, 'something we cannae quite put our finger on with that lad. Something sleekit,' which is Scots for something both skulking and smooth.

It didn't really matter what the repairers thought. Ally was having fun and if that fun was enhanced by a little more romance (or even a great big commitment), then that would be very nice indeed. She'd attempted a home manicure last night specially, in case there were surprise engagement announcement photos. Nothing flashy, just a glossy ballet-slipper pink. Subtle, like the butterfly flutter in her chest.

A proposal would mean she was doing something with her life as she approached twenty-eight, other than checking her emails for job alerts and sending out speculative CVs in the hope of getting out of her IT customer support day job and repair-shed-Saturdays rut.

Even her twin brother was helping her from afar. If *he* was taking time out of his schedule to help, it had to be obvious to everyone her career was seriously on the skids. Only last night Murray had sent her a heads-up about a job that was about to be advertised at the charity where he worked in Switzerland.

> Hey you. Just had word from HR one of our Blue Sky Thinking Techs is leaving. We need a twelve month replacement with a knowledge of the sustainability sector ASAP. There's a huge IT skills gap in Switzerland, just look at their visa page. Anyway... I already floated your name to see if it'd be a problem, you applying, being my sis and all. Boss says to send her your resume direct.

This had not been well received. At first she'd laughed, then she'd fallen into exasperated incredulity. A blue sky thinking tech? What even *is* that? Murray had his answer prepped.

> It's just someone who knows how to work the office printer and they can dream up creative communication solutions to assist in the delivery of the charity's projects all over the world.

When he put it like that, it didn't sound so daft. It sounded quite nice, actually. Nevertheless, Ally protested. How could she go to Switzerland? She was always needed at the shed on Saturdays, for a start. And how could she up and leave, moving to a whole new life in a place she didn't know? Leaving Gray for a year, just when things were, hopefully, taking a serious turn.

She'd scoffed and blown at the notion. What a load of nonsense. She'd told Murray all of this, more or less, and he'd rang her immediately.

'Zurich's almost *exactly* like the Cairngorms, only there's less fly-tipping and a few more billionaires, and everybody's carrying those wee Inspector Gadget penknives with the corkscrew and that thing for getting stones out of horses' shoes. I think they're distributed with babies' birth certificates actually...'

She'd cut short his rambling, telling him to be serious for a minute. He couldn't go playing games with her life like this. What had he been thinking, talking to his boss about her? Besides, how could she possibly be properly qualified?

'Hey,' he stopped her. 'You've got the exact same degree as me!'

It was true, both of them had passed the same Environmental Science, Technology and Communications degree, both gaining distinctions. Only Murray had actually put his to good use.

He was still talking. 'What was that thing you told me about how men apply for jobs even if they only have 60 per cent of the qualifications in the job description, and women only if they have *all* of them? You've got to out-bro the bros! You'd be working at the Zurich office with me – well, when I'm there – *and* it would get me out of interviewing applicants because I'd have to declare an interest to HR, and that would free me up to go on the overseeing trip to Mali! Please please *please* apply, sis!'

'All right! As a favour to you, I'll apply.' She'd huffed a breath down the line, even though she'd been smiling too.

Ally never fully understood what her brother did on his trips all over the world, something to do with when a charity shifts a large amount of money to some place far away they send someone from the charity to watch it being spent and get hands-on with the project too. He was always somewhere incredible, doing life-changing stuff. *He* made a difference on a global scale, whereas, last Saturday, Ally had replaced the wires in a faulty battery-operated pencil sharpener. They were in different leagues.

Still, she'd read the job specification and charity mission statement as soon as they'd hung up on the call. The job was all about 'brainstorming tech solutions', creating a more 'sustainable planet for humans and nature', 'scientific co-production', 'dropping in to communities where we're needed most', and lots of other buzzwords about cool office culture, hot-desking and employee perks – presumably to make up for the less than amazing salary.

This was way beyond her experience and capabilities, she told herself. Yet, she'd still sent away her CV with a covering letter at just after midnight, telling herself it was nothing but a favour to her brother, not even wanting to hope she might get into the first round of interviews for a job based in Actual Switzerland.

A thought struck her now. How would she plan a wedding in Scotland if she was galivanting in the Alps for a year?

No! She wouldn't let herself daydream. Nothing had changed yet. Her life was still fixed in its pattern of work, sleep, repair.

She checked her nail varnish for chips.

The repair shop doorway darkened as two people arrived together; a glamorous woman in a long beige tartan mac and a young bearded guy wearing big black headphones with a tablet camera attached to some kind of holster across his chest and a boom mic sticking out from it.

'Charlie McIntyre?' the TV reporter asked, and Ally's dad swept them inside.

They got straight down to business on planning the interview. If McIntyre was nervous, he was hiding it well enough, apart from a pink flush across his cheeks.

'Here's someone else coming,' Peaches said, cocking her head at the crunching on the gravel outside. She was getting invested in the whole Gray proposal idea too – even though her and Willie were new to the repair shop and every inch as much victims of its gossip themselves.

Those uninvolved in the news interview turned their heads

Fixing a Broken Heart at the Highland Repair Shop 15

towards the door... as the grocer, Laura Mercer, pale and bonny and about Ally's age, carried in her basket of milk and loaves.

'How do I get the feeling you're disappointed to see me?' she said, stopping still on the doormat.

'Don't be daft, come in!' Ally said, bringing her towards the café corner. 'It's just this lot, up to their usual nonsense! Don't stand still for too long or they'll have you paired off with Sachin here.'

This was met with a ripple of good-natured laughter and Sachin remarking woefully how his Aamaya might have something to say about him 'taking up with a young lassie'.

Laura had been calling in on her delivery round every Saturday since the very beginning, bringing the café provisions from her mobile pantry. She didn't give much away, usually, but everyone knew she was single because no question was considered too nosey in this place.

'*Actually,*' she began with a sly smile and a lowered voice. This made Senga whip at her sister with a tea towel so she snapped to attention. 'I *might* have met someone.'

'Oh, aye?' Roz McIntyre said. 'When did this happen?'

'Not long ago,' replied Laura. 'I've been delivering bacon rolls to his work on Fridays for a while, and he asked me out the other week. Took me to the Wildlife Park, of all places.'

'Did you see the polar bears?' Rhona asked innocently, only to be shushed by her sister.

'And do you like him?' Senga wanted to know.

'I think I do.' Laura blushed, unloading her basket onto the café counter. 'Early days, mind, but I want him to meet my mum, so...' She shrugged, letting her words tail off into a dopey smile.

'Love certainly is in the air this weekend!' said Roz, winking at her indignant daughter, but keeping her voice low because the first client of the day had arrived.

'Is that so?' Laura turned to Ally with an arched brow, but there was no time for her to answer.

Sachin was directing the customer towards McIntyre. 'Jewellery job,' he called out. 'Lady wants personalised engravings removing.'

The woman, wrapped in a long Afghan coat that looked too hot for the spring day outside and with nicotine blonde hair flowing over her shoulders seemed like she wanted to disappear at the announcement, which was only made worse by Senga enquiring if it was a break-up that had sent her here with her jewels.

'Remove all trace of 'im, eh?' Senga chuckled, before she stopped Laura the grocer from leaving with the offer of a cup of tea. 'Stay a bit, eh? Tell us about this lad you've met.'

Laura gladly accepted and propped herself up at the café counter.

McIntyre was taking a jangling drawstring bag from the customer in the Afghan coat's clenched fist. If anybody had been paying attention to the woman (they were too taken up with Laura's gossip, Ally's upcoming date, and the bustle of the news team getting ready to roll), they'd have picked up on how nervy she was.

McIntyre tipped the contents of the bag onto his work station while the cameraman ordered coffees for him and his colleague.

'Elaine, is it?' McIntyre asked her, inspecting each piece in turn and reading the name inscribed on the lockets and bangles. 'Some lovely pieces here. You sure you want your name erasing?'

'Elaine's my mum's name,' the woman replied in a shaky voice, glancing around the room, and only just spotting the TV reporter. If she was local to the region, she must recognise her;

everyone knew Morag Füssli. 'I want to... give them to my daughter to wear... without the engravings.'

'Well, I suppose that's a repair of sorts.'

'Can we film you working on those, Mr McIntyre?' Füssli said, advancing with her steaming cup and her freshly applied lipstick.

'Machine'll be noisy,' McIntyre warned, 'but it's as good a way as any to show you what kind of thing we can do here.'

'Can I leave?' the woman said, eyes darting around the room. 'Come back for them later?' She didn't wait for an answer, reaching into her pocket for her phone as she headed straight outside, into the courtyard and away.

'Camera shy,' McIntyre remarked to himself with a chortle as he watched her go.

Reaching for his goggles and ear defenders, he settled himself on his stool. 'Ready?' he asked the cameraman, who looked down into the viewfinder at his chest.

'Rolling in three, two...' he said, and Füssli gave McIntyre the nod to start the machine.

As the metal laser hummed and screeched and McIntyre wore away the engraving on the first item, a heavy gold bangle, more people arrived into the workshop, including a slim figure in sports gear. It was Gray.

'That's no kind of proposal outfit!' Rhona was heard to remark to her sister who, for once, had to agree with her.

'Shall we go?' Ally said to Gray as soon as she saw him, hoping to avoid the salacious comments of the volunteers and definitely not wanting them to be caught on camera.

'Sure. Uh, can we take a walk?' he said over the growing noise as yet more people arrived.

The repair shop elders exchanged glances.

'Gray?'

Oddly, it was Laura the grocer who'd called his name, and in such a delighted tone that the Gifford sisters' eyes fixed on her like this was a matinee show at the Eden Court Theatre.

Laura was approaching Gray with a big grin on her face and her empty basket over her arm, her cup of tea left abandoned on the counter. 'What are you doing here?'

It was then that everything started to run in awful slow motion as Ally came to realise what was happening.

Gray was stuttering and staring, looking between the two women. Laura kept chattering on cheerfully, even as her confusion set in. 'I thought you told me you were working this morning?' Laura stepped forward to hug him. Gray took a step back to avoid it.

'You... you and Ally know each other?' he said.

Pennies began to drop around the room. Roz stood up at her sewing station, her eyes narrowed.

'Uh.' Gray was gasping like a fish hauled from the River Nithy on a hook.

Ally watched on, letting him flounder, not wanting to jump to conclusions, but there was no getting around it. This wasn't looking good.

'Are you here to pick up Ally?' said Laura, still trying to smile but looking between the pair in concern.

'Uh, well...' Gray glanced behind him at the open door.

'Laura?' Ally said at last. 'Is this your new man, by any chance?'

Laura, now struck silent, clasped at her wrist where a pretty gold chain set with clear stones sparkled.

That explains Gray's trip to the jewellers, Ally thought. Someone should let Jean Wilson's cousin, Tony, on the hop-on, hop-off buses know. Though, no doubt it would be all across

Fixing a Broken Heart at the Highland Repair Shop 19

their small town before nightfall, regardless. There wasn't going to be a proposal after all.

'Listen,' Gray was saying over the horrid grinding noises from the oblivious McIntyre's workbench. 'I can explain, honestly. Uh...'

'This I've got to hear,' said Laura, coming to stand by Ally's side.

'I'd rather not do it here,' Gray said, warily eyeing McIntyre across the room.

Ally's first instinct was to laugh. It wasn't her dad he had to worry about. Not when the café women already had their sleeves rolled up and were advancing upon him.

Ally was surprised when Laura, who she didn't really know outside cheery greetings while she dropped off the café's provisions, took her hand and led her outside. Gray followed behind.

As soon as they were standing on the gravel in the morning sunshine, he started. 'Look, I was going to tell you I'd met somebody.'

'Exactly which of us were you going to tell?' Laura demanded.

Gray pointed a guilty finger at Ally. She felt it like a knife point.

'Sorry,' he gulped, eyes fixed on Ally, who found she momentarily couldn't form any words.

Laura, however, was having no such trouble. 'Wait a minute. Weren't the café women saying something about a proposal?' Gray took a big step back as Laura squared up to him, all five foot two of her. 'Were you going to ask Ally to marry you?'

Oh God! Why did she have to go and say that? Wasn't this humiliating enough?

Gray shook his head, emphatically. 'A proposal? Jeez, naw! I mean...' At least he had the humility to appear embarrassed once he heard himself. 'Sorry, Ally. I didn't mean it like that. I thought we were having fun, that's all. It was fun, wasn't it?'

Something in his expression made Ally's heart crack. He really believed what he was saying, and she had to admit they hadn't actually promised each other exclusivity. Only, after a whole year, Ally had simply assumed. That was reasonable, wasn't it?

'Oh no!' was the only sound that escaped her lips. The embarrassment was too much. 'Oh no!' she said again.

Laura, however, was only just getting into her stride. Ally wondered if she was actually enjoying this a bit too much. Cars were pulling up into the gravel lot at the front of the McIntyre property. More repair clients got out, all of them craning their necks to get a good view of the unfolding drama.

'So you strung her along?' Laura went on. 'Look at her, Gray. She's heartbroken! Here she was expecting forever and you were taking *me* to see the chuffing polar bears and buying me diamonds!' She struggled to roll the bracelet off her wrist before throwing it to the gravel at his feet. She was definitely enjoying herself.

'It's OK, you don't have to defend me...' Ally began, but Laura wouldn't be stopped.

'What do you have to say for yourself?'

Gray was backing away. 'Look, I'm sorry, all right? I never said we were anything. And you pair were never meant to meet.'

'How many more of us have you got on the go, eh?' Laura called after him as he crossed the car park, leaving the diamonds in the dirt, hastily retreating towards the gap in the stone boundary wall that led to the riverside footpath.

He kept his hands jammed in his pockets and his head down.

Laura saw him off with a barrage of expletives, all highly

appropriate, before turning to Ally who was only just beginning to think of all the questions she'd have asked him had they had an ounce of privacy.

Had he been shacked up with Laura Mercer all those nights recently when Ally could only get through to his voicemail, and later when she'd quizzed him he'd said he'd been visiting his granny?

Hadn't he meant it when he said he was falling in love? All those times in his bed when she'd gazed at their clasped hands in soppy wonder and they'd planned their futures and he'd joked about them having a whole five-a-side team of little Grays? Was it all said in *fun*?

'What a lowlife!' Laura was growling, turning to Ally. 'You're crying! No, no, no! Don't do it. He's not worth it.'

But it was too late. Ally's mortification was complete. Gray, who she'd misread so completely, had walked away, seemingly without a care.

Laura tried to pull her in for a hug but it made Ally bristle.

'I'm fine,' she insisted. 'I'm fine.'

Even more customers were arriving now, some getting off bikes on the drive, some coming on foot from the riverside path, pulling broken-down machines in carts, shouldering sacks, hauling armfuls of old treasures in open boxes, and all of them casting wary glances at the two women.

Ally turned away, swiping at her cheeks. She couldn't bear going back inside and facing the volunteers, or the TV camera for that matter, and staying here to be consoled by Laura – evidently more riled up with the drama of it all than she was heartbroken – was out of the question. So she ran back across the mossy lawn towards the McIntyre family home, fumbling for her key before locking herself inside.

She leaned against the door before sliding right down onto the kitchen's cold quarry tiles.

She'd allowed herself to get carried away on a romantic fantasy, listening to all the old clatterers egging her on, getting her hopes up when there'd been no definite sign Gray felt the same... other than all the lovely dates and the long, lazy Sundays in bed together at his flat, and the flowers and cards and texts and '*I think I love you*'s. He'd looked her in the eyes and seen her, gullible and hungry for love, and he'd lied, over and over again while she ate up his empty promises like Valentine's sweeties.

There, winded on the kitchen floor, while her mum and all the concerned repair shop women knocked to get in, Ally McIntyre made a tearful, bitter promise to herself. She would never *ever* allow this to happen to her again as long as she lived.

3

Exactly a month after Ally's broken heart, the June sunshine was beating down on the repair shop's corrugated iron roof. It was getting on for the end of a long Saturday's fixing, but the locals just kept coming in. The repairers had been markedly busier since their segment was finally aired on the news programme, *Highland Spotlight*, the night before.

Everyone had been amazed. They were only expecting a brief plug in the last news story of the day; the light-hearted 'and finally' story, the cheery antidote to all the awful stuff that had come before it. What they got was a long 'special report'.

McIntyre had been onscreen for all of five minutes. First, he'd been shown working away at his station, goggles on and head down while Füssli's voiceover explained the 'repair revolution' sweeping the planet since Martine Postma launched the very first Repair Café in Amsterdam sixteen years ago and her idea swept the planet.

The volunteers had watched it together on the big telly at the Cairn Dhu Hotel bar and there'd been a hearty cheer when the shot cut to McIntyre standing stiffly in front of the camera outside his workshop explaining why he'd opened up the barn for repairs.

'The throwaway culture we've come to rely on has to end, and it ends with us, grassroots organisations for locals. Our waterways are choked with plastics and chemicals, there are landfill mountains as big as Ben Macdui itself. Even the air we breathe isn't clean. Single-use living is over. We are the skill-sharing, fix-it generation. Our grandbairns'll thank us for it. And we're only a wee part of a worldwide effort to make a change.'

McIntyre's cheeks had turned ruddy as he spoke and his eyes shone. Nobody watching could doubt his dedication to the cause.

Then there'd been some interviews at other repair projects across the Highlands, including a free bicycle repair and toy swap shop in Inverness that was doing a roaring (charitable) trade.

In what seemed like an ill-judged moment, the programme editors allowed the café sisters to have the final word of the show and Senga had appeared on-screen speaking over Rhona while pouring a cup of tea for Cary Anderson who was posing as a customer at the counter.

'A wee cuppa while you wait,' Senga simpered, her eyes boring down the lens while tea sloshed over the rim and into the dangerously wobbly saucer. 'And one of my famous nutty barms?'

She'd grinned exaggeratedly at the viewers, giving an affected tip of her head for good measure. Cary had been opening his mouth to thank her when the segment cut away to Füssli out in the courtyard, signing off.

'The Cairn Dhu community repair shop and café is just one example of concerned residents taking sustainability into their own hands. Will the make-do-and-mend trend continue to grow,

Fixing a Broken Heart at the Highland Repair Shop 25

or are we addicted to our shopping carts and credit cards? Only time will tell, but for now, community projects like this one are flourishing and it's a case of *can do* in Cairn Dhu!'

In the background, just on the edge of the shot, but plain to see for the eagle-eyed, was Roz McIntyre – or the bottom half of her – hanging out of the kitchen window, trying to break into her own home to comfort her daughter who, around about that time on that fateful May day, had been crying herself to exhaustion on the kitchen floor.

Everyone crowded around the bar room telly had pretended not to notice. Ally had been so withdrawn and pale ever since that day, they didn't like to mention it.

It smarted all the more that her humiliation was now immortalised on local TV footage, even if only a handful of people knew the true story of the Gray-Laura-Ally Triangle of Shame. Laura hadn't been back to the repair shed since that awful day, choosing instead to send her business partner with the café's provisions.

Ally had adopted a strict silence on the topic following the break-up and it had made for a tense atmosphere on repair Saturdays ever since.

So long as she kept busy, she could just about contain her bad mood. Which was just as well since the news programme had jogged the Cairngorm region's collective memory that the repair shop and café existed, and so they were now coming to the end of their busiest day's fixing and serving yet.

'Better start telling folk we cannae accept any more items this weekend, Sachin,' McIntyre announced from his workbench where he was showing a young couple how to replace a plug on their toaster. 'Bet you thought this machine was toast, eh? Eh?' he said, waiting for their politely feigned laughter.

Roz and Peaches were hemming a pair of heavy velour

curtains that they'd shortened by two feet, while Willie turned the offcuts into cushion covers, just as the owner had requested, though she hadn't been able to stay to see them make the alterations. She was down the river right now with her toddlers, feeding the mallards.

McIntyre usually liked it when people stayed to watch, learning how to do their own repairs for the future, but he couldn't win them all, and perhaps it was for the best, not having tots tumbling around the floor while Cary was sharpening garden secateurs and saws in a steady stream all day long.

There'd even been an old scythe brought in at eleven which Cary had made a braw job of, sharpening it to a steely shine. The elderly man who brought it in had told Sachin at the triage desk that the scythe had once belonged to his grandfather and the shaft was so worn from use that his granddad's grip had been permanently impressed into the wood. He treasured it, he'd said, and wanted it restored and hanging above his fireplace.

'Each to their own,' Senga had muttered in response as she served the sultana scones and poured the teas with Rhona, both of them in their summer sundresses and pinnies.

The radio had blared out all Saturday long, and everyone remarked on how steamy it was under the baking corrugated iron of the shed's roof. For the first time so far this year they'd wished they had spare money for an air conditioning unit – all except McIntyre who didn't believe in running electric units when you could simply change into your cut-offs and vest. Ally had taken one glimpse at his white knees that morning and tried to talk him out of wearing these clothes in public, but it made no difference, of course. Neither had Peaches's mortified cringing or Willie's remark that seeing 'a ginger Boomer in jorts' hadn't been on his 'bingo card for today'. McIntyre was as stubborn as

Fixing a Broken Heart at the Highland Repair Shop   27

his daughter and had gone about his day not minding the teasing.

Now Ally was hunching over her workbench where she was replacing the little joystick button on a Nintendo Switch while a very invested pre-teen watched on in concern from behind her long fringe as her mum chattered about the cost of buying new tech.

They'd bought the spare button off the internet but hadn't the tools (or the confidence) to do the fix themselves. That's where Ally came in. She was responsible for refurbing computers, laptops, consoles and mobile phones.

It hadn't exactly been part of her life plan to spend her Saturdays in a sweltering barn (excepting in autumn and winter when it was bitterly cold) with her family and a bunch of busybodies, but from day one the shop had needed a 'tech guru' (her dad's words) and surrendering half her weekend meant her parents hadn't asked her for any rent in recent years and she got to remain at home while she 'found her feet'.

That agreement had been reached two and a half years ago just as the fledgling repair shop was first opening its doors and when her IT support centre job had switched to home-working and never moved back. Ally hadn't minded not getting the bus out to the industrial estate every morning and, in the beginning, she'd actually quite liked working half days, answering tech support calls in the comfort of her pyjamas. But working close to home (where everyone had opinions about her love life) was losing even more of its appeal since The Thing With Gray happened.

That's what they called it around the house.

'I know you've struggled since *the thing with Gray*, but there's plenty nice lads out there,' her mum would say. 'Don't you want to get out there again? Start meeting folk?'

Or Murray, her twin, who was so rarely in Scotland he got away with never having had to help out in the shed, would tease her when he video-called, saying, 'He can't be worth the torn face after all this time?'

Ally would huffily shrug it off, or simply ignore them. She was doing fine. Couldn't they see? Doing her customer support job in her dressing gown on weekday mornings then minding her own business in the workshop on Saturdays had become her life, and it was all FINE!

'There,' Ally said, handing back the console so the kid could try it out. 'Good as new.' Granted, she'd had to watch a YouTube demo of how to take the Switch apart but that's how Ally learned lots of things she was attempting for the first time.

Whilst she'd been absorbed in the repair job, the toaster couple had left, taking two of Senga's chocolate tiffin slices to go, and the café's till rattled with coins whenever Rhona slid the drawer shut.

Now that Sachin was turning people away, telling them they'd re-open next Saturday at ten, the shed was quickly growing quieter.

The kid made chirpy electronic music play aloud from their Switch. Willie and Peaches cheered and offered Ally their congratulations. The young girl almost smiled, and Ally spotted a tiny hint of silver braces over her teeth.

'Thank you so much,' the mum effused, having drained her mug and pulled her bag over her shoulder ready to leave. 'What do we owe you?'

'It's voluntary donations,' Ally said, nodding to the big jar behind them on the triage desk.

Sachin caught the words and tapped the glass with his biro.

'You're sure? I can't give you anything for your time?' the mum said.

Fixing a Broken Heart at the Highland Repair Shop 29

'She just said she doesn't want anything,' the girl grumbled, mortified at nothing, the way only twelve-year-old girls can be.

The woman placed a ten-pound note in the jar as she left, singing the place's praises. 'That just saved me a couple of hundred pounds on buying a new Switch,' she told everyone, and Sachin proudly added another chalk mark to the board on the wall.

'She means we just saved another console from ending up in a rubbish dump,' McIntyre called out, as he set about repairing an old coffee machine from the nineties.

'Twenty-two repairs completed today,' Sachin said, sitting back down. 'And a good few quid in donations.'

'And we've a full till here,' added Senga.

'We'll need it for more zippers, and thread for the sewing machines,' Roz chipped in before anyone else could claim it.

'We're almost out of glacé cherries and bicarb for the scones,' Rhona put in.

'Could do with a bit more silver solder, actually. And some paraloid B-72, and some chaser's pitch, come to think of it,' added McIntyre, scratching behind his ear.

There was always something the shed was running short on, meaning donations were immediately ploughed back into the community, just as McIntyre had intended when setting the place up.

Ally had been rubbing away the ache in her lower back from hunching over her workbench and was making her way to the door to turn off the neon sign when two men approached from the courtyard, police officers, both with serious, straight-lipped expressions.

'Um... Dad?' Ally called back into the shed.

'Charlie McIntyre?' the tallest of the men asked. He wore a black chequered cap and a high viz vest over his black uniform.

Ally stood back to let them pass. The smaller, younger man glanced at her with brown, wary eyes. He was dressed in all black and was hanging back a little, letting his colleague take charge.

'That'll be me,' Ally's dad identified himself, pulling his soldering goggles from the top of his head.

'I'm Chief Inspector Edwyn. My colleague here is Special Constable Beaton. We'd like to have a word, sir, about your...' He cast his hand around as though he wasn't quite sure what kind of setup this was. 'Repair business?'

'Anything you want to say, the volunteers can hear it too,' McIntyre replied genially.

'In that case, I'd be grateful if you locked the doors,' said Edwyn.

'Sorry, but what's this about?' Ally chirruped, stepping between the Inspector and her father, her already frayed nerves zinging with alarm.

Sachin was locking them all in, having made sure there were no customers left hanging about the courtyard.

The Special Constable took exception to Ally challenging his senior officer and asked if she'd give his colleague 'a wee bit of space, please, miss.'

Edwyn pressed on, undeterred. 'We've reason to believe that you may have received and processed stolen property.'

This set the Gifford sisters off in vehement protest about how they'd done no such thing.

'That doesnae sound very likely,' Sachin chimed in, and even Cary Anderson put on a show of silent indignation, shaking his head and tutting at the very suggestion.

'What evidence have you got to come in here bandying around accusations like that?' Ally snapped, now facing down the brown-eyed man with a badge on his pocket confirming his name and rank, *Jamie Beaton, Special Police Constable.*

Edwyn was taking a plastic wallet full of images from under his arm, which drew the volunteers in a crowd around him to get a glimpse, except for Willie and Peaches who hadn't dared move and were surreptitiously filming everything on their phones to show their friends at uni.

Roz came to stand beside her husband and, taking one glimpse at the pictures, her face fell.

'Ah!' said McIntyre.

'Ah, indeed,' the Chief Inspector echoed.

In his hands were stills from the *Highland Spotlight* programme that had aired the night before; close-ups of McIntyre's hands and the laser as he carefully erased the engravings on those fine pieces of jewellery the day the news crew visited back in May.

'Elaine,' McIntyre tolled.

'I'm going to need you to tell me everything you can about the whereabouts of that jewellery, sir. Its rightful owner happened to be watching TV last night and spotted her late mother's stolen possessions in your fair hands; some eight pieces of very expensive gold, silver and platinum jewellery taken from the family home in a robbery last Hogmanay.'

'You sound like you think Dad's somehow to blame,' Ally said, her voice surprisingly loud and pitchy, dodging the Special Constable to get at Edwyn.

'Honestly, miss, it'd be best for everyone if you took a step back and let the Chief Inspector go about his job,' Jamie Beaton said, reaching a hand towards her arm but not making contact.

'It's a very serious crime to be found in receipt of stolen goods,' Edwyn went on. 'Deliberately defacing such goods so as to disguise their provenance is also highly illegal,' he added, not looking away from McIntyre whose ears were turning a little pink at the tips.

'Dad couldn't have known they were stolen!' Ally yelped, still trying to dodge Beaton and address Edwyn directly.

'The lassie came back for them, didn't she?' Ally's father said with a gulp, looking to Sachin for confirmation.

Sachin was already way ahead of everyone and was producing his records – thank goodness he was as good a recordkeeper as he was a busybody. 'That she did. See here.' He showed the more senior policeman. 'She collected them the same day she dropped them off, at two thirty to be precise. Left no tip in the jar.'

'So it looks like you owe Dad an apology,' Ally blurted, out of sheer relief, but evidently she wasn't done yet. Angrily, she went on. 'We're trying to do *good* here, but you waltz in like he's some kind of criminal. Did you actually watch the news programme last night? They called Dad a local hero!'

The Inspector turned to his younger colleague and gave him a meaningful nod, sending Jamie into an immediate response.

'If you don't calm down and step back, I'll have to put you in the van for attempting to impede an officer in going about his investigations.'

Ally stared hard at Special Constable Jamie Beaton. He was about her age, a couple of inches taller than her, with dark hair to go with his dark eyes and a clean-shaven, probably-works-out-a-fair-bit look about him. Ally noticed his throat move as he swallowed. 'I'm sorry,' he said in a much lower voice. 'But please just pipe down.'

Edwyn had moved on and was asking questions about CCTV (the repair shop couldn't afford anything like that), and informing everyone he'd need to collect witness statements and descriptions of the woman (Senga and Rhona were clambering

Fixing a Broken Heart at the Highland Repair Shop   33

over one another to offer their assistance), and he wanted to know whether McIntyre had indeed removed every trace of the engravings as that was going to make tracing the jewellery incredibly hard. McIntyre had probably unwittingly quadrupled their street value.

'Engraved jewellery is notoriously hard to shift,' Edwyn crowed as he took out his notebook. 'You must be far more vigilant in future. All of you.' He cast a stern eye around the volunteers.

Peaches and Willie still hadn't moved from their spot in the sewing corner and looked at one another scoffingly like they were hardly likely to be asked to fence stolen curtains any time soon.

'Did you get a good look at the woman, miss...?' Jamie asked Ally, taking her to one side while the café women tried to ply his colleague with baking and coffee, both of which Edwyn refused.

'Miss McIntyre,' she replied. 'I mean Allyson McIntyre. No, just Ally. Umm, let me see, the woman? I... I don't know.' Ally brought a hand to her cheek, trying hard to recall her.

'You were here when she brought the jewels in?' Jamie pressed, with what she interpreted as a soft Lowlands burr, quite posh to her ears. Edinburgh, maybe?

'I suppose so, only it... wasn't a very good day for me.'

'Oh?' He had his pad and pencil poised in his hands.

'I was distracted with... something else.'

'And what was that?' he wanted to know, his expression serious.

'Does it matter?'

He fixed her with a dogged look.

'I was getting dumped, OK? And on what I thought was going to be a lovely, romantic first anniversary, if you must know! It was right there, where you're standing.'

Jamie Beaton glanced down at his heavy black boots and, somewhat apologetically, took a deliberate step closer to the wall, which Ally thought was odd, and possibly a tiny bit endearing.

'Any other details you can remember?' His voice was softer now.

'I think the woman had a long coat on?' she said. 'Beige, maybe. With a furry trim, and embroidered all over. She didn't look like a robber, if that's what you're asking.' Now that she came to think of it, the woman had looked stressed and tired.

'We suspect she was a girlfriend of one of a gang of robbers. If you think there's no robberies in the Highlands just because it's pretty here, you've got another think coming. And criminals can look just the same as me and you.'

This was beginning to feel like a lecture, and Ally instinctively drew back her neck. Who did he think he was? This outsider, fresh from some desk job in the south, no doubt. She wasn't some naïve country bumpkin.

If he could read her annoyance he didn't show it. 'If you saw her again, would you recognise her?' he said plainly.

'I...' Ally began with optimism, before giving it up as a lost cause. 'No, I doubt it.' Her shoulders slumped.

That woman might have been vulnerable or afraid, or at least put upon by some bad boyfriend using her to run risky errands for him. What use had Ally been to her that day? None at all. She should have noticed something was obviously dodgy. She could have helped her if she had kept her wits about her, been smarter, instead of getting in a tizz waiting for Gray to pop the question. But then again, she'd learned recently how she was absolutely no judge of character. Oh aye, *that* she now knew.

Images of how that day had played out returned to her now: that poor woman coming in, her head down as though to hide

Fixing a Broken Heart at the Highland Repair Shop 35

her face; Dad, as proud as punch, working away at the jewellery in front of the camera lens; Gray tossing her aside as though twelve months meant nothing at all.

'Is there anything else you can tell me? Anything at all?' the man's voice broke through her thoughts.

'I told you what I saw,' Ally said, pained, and far too snappy.

Jamie gave her a dismayed look, crumpling his full lips, bringing down his brows. 'Right. Well, if you think of anything, or if you ever suspect someone is coming in here trying to trick you into disguising hot property again...'

'All right! I get it,' she interrupted, gripping her elbows in a defensive hug. 'We'll be extra vigilant.'

Across the room, Edwyn was echoing this warning, going on and on about how they'd be keeping an eye on the repair shop and how, if they so much as removed one padlock and chain from a bicycle or cleaned UV security marker from a laptop, he'd know about it.

'Your friend could work on his dealing-with-the-public-skills,' Ally muttered, watching the Chief Inspector holding forth. 'Isn't that something they teach you in police school?'

She cast her eyes down Jamie's uniform, considering asking if he was still in police school, or if he'd had any training at all. Were Special Constables proper police officers or just well-meaning helpers?

'He's only doing his job.' Jamie was putting his notebook away. 'Trying to keep the Cairngorms National Park a safe place for everyone.'

'Before we spoke to you, we met the news crew,' Edwyn was telling the room. 'We reviewed their footage, looking for images of the woman. Sadly, there weren't any.'

'That's a pity,' said McIntyre.

'I hate to say it,' Jamie all but whispered to Ally, 'but that

Füssli, the reporter? She was on this stolen property thing like a wasp at a picnic. I wouldn't be surprised if you found yourselves back on the telly by bedtime.'

Ally only nodded, absorbing this information. She didn't want to react in case her dad noticed. He could find out this particular bit of news if, or more likely when, Füssli broke it. He'd already had one big shock, and Ally had done more than enough overreacting for one day as well.

It was dawning on her that she'd done it again; made a fool of herself in public. Still, the way that Chief Inspector had spoken to her dad had really been too much. Charlie McIntyre was nothing but kind and helpful, if a little clutter-brained, but his heart was in the right place, and the officers had stridden in here like they were busting the HQ of some Scottish crime syndicate, or at least it had felt that way to Ally in the moment.

She felt herself shrinking. She wasn't good at judging things these days. Her moods were erratic. It wasn't a nice feeling, not being able to trust her own judgement. Gray's parting gifts to her had been low self-esteem and chronic trust issues. She was jumpy these days too. She hated it.

'We'll be off, then,' Edwyn announced.

Jamie Beaton fell in behind him on his way to the door. Sachin ran to turn the key and let the pair out into the sunshine, and the whole shed took a deep breath of the cool outside air.

As he left, Jamie threw Ally a sympathetic smile that made her feel even worse somehow, and later that evening, thinking back, she'd cringed with shame, trying to forget how defensive she'd been under the firm, calm scrutiny of his brown eyes.

4

Three and a half hours after his shift was supposed to end, Jamie turned the key on his apartment door on the second floor of the grey-harled block of flats above the chippy on what passed for a high street in Cairn Dhu. The summer weather hadn't held and the clouds had rolled in making it feel like a dull, damp autumn evening.

There'd been a drug raid planned for an address over an hour's drive away, where a young lad, well-known to the constabulary, had been taking delivery of some suspiciously heavy, dense parcels through the Post Office. A raid was needed to find out if they were one of the few persistent coke dealers living on ordinary streets across the Highlands. The officers had hung around the station waiting for a warrant that never came. Edwyn finally admitted it wasn't likely to happen tonight and told Jamie he might as well go home, especially since he wasn't being paid for overtime. In fact, as a volunteer Special Constable he wasn't being paid anything at all. He was living off his savings now and even they were running dry.

Starving, he'd parted with a fiver for a chip roll and a Fanta and taken his food upstairs. Inside, it was warm and stuffy. At least it felt like summer in here. He'd pulled off his boots, lining them up neatly beside his running shoes by the door. Well-ordered and tidy, just how he liked things.

He ate joylessly in front of a programme about farming that he didn't understand a word of. There'd been something up with the TV since he moved in; it was stuck on the local channel where half the programmes were in Gaelic, plus the subtitles didn't work at all.

He took brisk bites between swigs straight from the can, barely tasting the good, crisp, salty chips. The novelty of living over a chip shop had worn thin a couple of weeks ago, shortly after he'd transferred here, and around about the time he was questioning why on earth he'd thought putting in an application for a post so far from Edinburgh was a good idea.

He'd tried his best with the flat, but hadn't forgotten this was only a temporary, summer home. It had come furnished; if a lumpy bed, wonky TV, drop-leaf Formica dining table and a sofa counted as furnished. There was a kitchen but it was so pokey he only used it for toast and tea.

He tried to work out what the presenter was saying to the farmer, something gripping about hay bales. Even as he stared at the screen he found his mind wandering, dragged back to that repair workshop and the angry Ally McIntyre. She had wild red hair that hung over her shoulders in a mix of coils and waves and there'd been a pink neon light shining from somewhere behind him getting caught in her curls so they glowed an extraordinary violet.

She hadn't been angry, of course; she'd been afraid. Frightened people lash out. Rule 101 of human psychology. The more intimidated she had felt, the more she'd glowered. She loved her

Fixing a Broken Heart at the Highland Repair Shop   39

dad, that much was obvious, and she'd been prepared to stick up for him, and it had all turned into hot fire within her.

He knew that anger too well. He'd been eaten up by it as a teenager. It had got him into run-ins with the Edinburgh beat officers who'd taken him home at fifteen to his shamefaced dad after finding him soused on Buckfast at the cemetery, pulling the heads off daffodils.

'He's lost his mum,' his dad had told the officers on the doorstep, hoping they'd be lenient.

'Sorry to hear that,' the woman officer had said, world-weary and already turning to go.

'He was only four at the time,' his dad had added. 'Took it hard.'

'It was years ago,' Jamie had grunted, cringing, hands shoved into his pockets, cheeks blazing, wanting to cry. 'Hardly relevant now.'

The sanguine officer wasn't moved by any of it. The woman had smiled thinly. 'You keep yourself out of trouble and let us keep on with our real jobs, OK? We're no' a taxi service.'

She'd left with a nod, and his dad had closed the door.

The telling-off young Jamie needed never came. He'd *wanted* a shouting match. Finger pointing. Blame. But his dad didn't seem capable of anger any more. Grief had taken it, along with his waistline, his clean shaven face, and his smile.

The teenage Jamie had slunk upstairs, slamming his bedroom door, momentarily shattering the silence that sat over the house like a tea cosy on a pot long since grown cold.

His dad had tried to keep things going, in his own way. He'd kept the house dusted and vacuumed. He followed the same stew recipe his wife used to make. It didn't taste even a bit the same, but no one said anything. He handed over lunch money every morning at the door as Jamie left for school and his sister, Karolyn, for college. He'd done his best under the circumstances. But they all knew their mum would have done it so much better.

It was the silence at home that had sorted Jamie out, in the end. He couldn't bear it, and he enrolled in the cadets, just to be out of the house. When he was eighteen and too old for cadets, he joined the Army Reserve, then he took a job in logistics at his local barracks and stayed there for a long time, a salary man. Sixteen months ago he'd signed up as a Special Constable based at a station just five minutes from his Edinburgh childhood home, doing a few hours a week in voluntary policing around his work day until recently when he'd quit the barracks and transferred here, just for the summer, until he got to the bottom of this recent bout of restlessness.

Aye, as a kid Jamie had known anger and fear, as well as the impulse to protect others, and it had made him determined as an adult to see the best in people, for the sake of his own well-being as much as theirs. You never knew what someone was going through, so it was best to be kind where you could.

Sympathy – better than courage, better than brawn – was the best thing he could bring to his volunteer policing.

He found to his surprise the chip wrapper in his hands was empty.

He'd done it again, got lost in the quiet, staring, dissociated autopilot that could claim hours of his time, if he let it. He rarely let it. That was where the old Reserves discipline came in handy.

The farming programme's credits rolled on-screen and the music played.

He moved, picking up his hand weights in the corner and building his arms for a hundred reps – the same every night; in the morning he did legs.

Then he took himself to the shower.

Fixing a Broken Heart at the Highland Repair Shop   41

He had found this flat was something of a quiet, muffled sort of place too, just like the house where his dad and sister still lived back home. To avoid the quiet, he played music on his phone and turned the water pressure right up, drowning out the horrible blankness.

In the steam, as he washed, he saw Ally's face again, pale and unblinking, those red-purple curls trailing in a V down her shoulder blades. He should find a reason to go back and see her... No!

He reminded himself of the rules about that kind of thing. Policing 'without fear or favour'. No fraternising with members of the public you have come into contact with during the course of your duties, especially those involved with investigations. He rinsed away the shampoo, thinking how, even if he had asked her to have a coffee with him, Ally McIntyre would probably have laughed in his face.

Hadn't she just been dumped? She'd said it herself. It had happened right where they'd stood. Another reason she was hurting. Another reason to leave well alone.

He was soon taking grey and black tartan pyjamas from the suitcase by his bed. He really ought to have bought a wardrobe or something. Would IKEA deliver way out here?

What if he brought a woman back here? A woman like Ally with sharp eyes? She'd take one look at the sorry state of the place and turn and run.

Socks, needed even in summer, came from the case next. He kept his clothes in an orderly way. The laundrette up the road did a service wash for him twice a week and delivered everything folded neatly. All he had to do was lay it down in the case and close the lid.

Tonight he reached for something under the neat jumpers,

not sure why he wanted to see it again; the first time since he came here.

He pulled the soft, orange-brown thing free; its familiar weight and fuzziness having the same effect on his emotions as it always did.

The stuffed Highland cow looked back at him through its one black glassy eye. Two curved felt horns – one coming away at the seams – framed its silly face. Long ago, when his mum gave it to him, it had a pink, stitched smile but that was long gone. She was worn and bobbled.

His mum had let him name his new cow, or so the lore went, and he'd chosen the name 'Holiday' – and nobody had thought to divert him towards something more fitting like Hamish – and so, he'd made a friend for life. He couldn't remember that first visit to the Cairngorms – the only proper family holiday they'd ever had together – or even the tourist tat shop where Holiday had been bought. Jamie had been three years old.

There were photographs though, also in his suitcase, of him in red shorts, holding his mum's hand at the ski centre where they'd tobogganed on the dry slope. Then they were snapped together on the mountain railway, his dad behind the camera, his sister holding a pink Power Ranger. There was another, capturing them sharing a picnic at the foot of Ben Macdui, and two or three others at various tourist attractions and beauty spots. These photographs were beyond precious to Jamie.

Not one location, when he'd paid them a return visit this summer, clutching the relevant picture, had sparked any memory whatsoever of having been there with his mother, try as he might to stand in the exact same spot, holding up the image, matching the angle and elevation, attempting to conjure up the sensation of his hand in his mum's or the feeling of her smiling down at him.

Fixing a Broken Heart at the Highland Repair Shop   43

The experiments, or whatever they were supposed to be, hadn't worked. Were they his attempt at 'finding' her in the landscape? As though she was still somehow residually there? Even now he didn't want to believe that deluded hope had been the reason he'd asked for the summer transfer to the Cairngorms police station in the first place.

He was a good Special Constable with a proven track record of being calm, observing protocol, and keeping out of trouble. He'd been free to take his volunteering anywhere.

'I really did come here to help out an understaffed force,' he told Holiday the cow, wanting to believe his motivation hadn't been born from delusional curiosity and hope. 'What do you mean, you're not buying it?'

Shaking his head, he slotted Holiday between the tightly tucked covers of his bed, patting her skinny body – she'd lost a lot of stuffing over the years.

He didn't like feeling maudlin, like his dad was. He wouldn't let himself slip into sadness. Making his way round his flat, he poured a glass of water at the kitchen sink and downed it, then he brushed his teeth, before telling his reflection in the bathroom mirror to go to bed.

The noise from the TV caught his attention. He'd left it on, talking away incomprehensibly to itself. The evening news, which was mercifully mostly in English, came from a studio somewhere north of here, and was just winding down to the weather forecast.

There was Morag Füssli, who he'd observed Edwyn talking to that very morning, on-screen now, reminding viewers of the special edition of *Highland Spotlight* where they'd celebrated the dedicated, community-minded Charlie McIntyre. The screen showed stills of the stolen jewellery in his hands over Füssli's appeal for anyone with information about the Hogmanay robbery, along with a description of the woman in the Afghan coat who was 'of interest to police'. The reporter signed off by saying, 'This mishap may spell an uncertain future for the Cairn Dhu Community Repair Shop and Café who can ill afford to be associated with organised crime in the Cairngorms. Can they regain the trust of their community?'

Jamie ran a hand through his still damp hair, picturing Ally McIntyre watching this at home. 'Oh naw,' he said. 'She's going to be furious.'

* * *

That night Jamie Beaton lay awake, listening to true crime podcasts. Usually he was asleep by the end of the second episode but tonight, as he curled up on his side, duvet over his head – a childhood habit – he couldn't help imagining himself back at that cosy, bright repair shop with the smells of coffee and baking, sawdust, oil and rust heavy in the air, and with a fierce redhead standing before him, looking for all the world like she was ready to jab at him, her frustration and fear crackling behind her green eyes.

He told himself to forget her, consign her to the blank region of his brain where his mum also resided, more a feeling than a memory these days; but try as he might, the enchanting vision of beautiful, wounded, fiery-hearted Ally McIntyre would not go away.

5

McIntyre family cautioned by police over fenced jewellery scam

The headline held the whole family transfixed as they gathered around the breakfast table a week after the policemen's visit, chewing toast they had no appetite for.

'Why did you buy the weekend paper?' Roz asked her husband. 'We haven't taken the papers since you finished at the factory.'

'Ach, it'll come in handy for moppin' up spilt oil,' McIntyre tried to joke.

'We weren't cautioned!' Ally objected. 'It was a casual ticking off, if anything.'

'It's the online news you've got to worry about,' added Murray from the doorway, where he was scrolling on his phone. The fact his dad had made the TV news again (and for all the wrong reasons this time) had been enough to bring Ally's twin brother home from Zurich. 'Side bars, click bait, comment sections.'

Charlie McIntyre pulled his own phone from the pocket of his overalls.

'I wouldn't look if I were you,' Murray tolled ominously. 'Why aren't the police trying to find the burglars?'

'I'm sure they are, but until they've actually caught them, the reporters have to find a local angle for the story, and for now that's us,' said Roz, sipping her tea and refusing to read any of this stuff. 'Anyway, I'm just glad to have the both of you home.'

This drew distracted smiles from the twins as they scrolled.

Roz McIntyre didn't play favourites. She had always treated her children exactly the same. If one had got a *Beano*, the other got *The Dandy*. If one had fallen off their bike on the gravel and skint their knee, the other would receive a hug and kisses just as soon as the injured twin was off running and smiling again after being rocked on their mum's lap.

'I had a bit of leave saved up,' said Murray, with a small shrug.

He hadn't actually sat down since he got in from the airport two hours ago, Ally noticed. He'd stood by the door, leaning on the fridge. Maybe he had a car waiting? He was becoming the sort of eco-business dude who always had an (electric) car waiting.

Ally had no excuse for being a teensy bit envious of her successful, jet-setter, probably-raking-it-in brother, even if they had shared a womb, and every classroom they ever sat in, and a degree course and a graduation ceremony. She was still hugely proud of him. She didn't mind too much that he'd outstripped her in the achievement stakes.

And yes, everyone at college had made a big fuss of the fact they were twins. They'd been asked a hundred times, 'Didn't you want to study different subjects?' and 'Aren't you a bit sick of each other by now?'

Fixing a Broken Heart at the Highland Repair Shop 47

The truth was they were pretty similar, academically, although Ally was more practical, more of a fixer, than her brother, and she'd always enjoyed taking things apart to see how they worked; while Murray had more of a talent for understanding how people worked. He was popular, cheery and confident in ways Ally mostly only pretended to be.

Even though they'd applied for the same jobs straight out of college, it was Murray whose career had somehow gone interstellar.

She was happy for him, truly, although his promotion to the Switzerland HQ of the Future Proof Planet global charity had come at a hard time for Ally, straight after lockdown when she'd been consigned to spending her weekday mornings at a laptop in her jammies and wearing a headset, asking confused customers if they could turn their computer off and on again, while he'd been flown business class to his own place with a mountain lake view, its own spa and a steam room, chauffeur, cleaning team and free health care.

Not that she grudged him any of those things. Much.

His job meant corporate sponsor schmoozing and celebrity parties on a gobsmacking level, and Ally didn't really enjoy parties. It's amazing, Ally had observed, how some charities have to do so much of that sort of thing if they wanted to keep up their international reputation and bring in the donors. Though her brother always maintained that their entire spending on fundraising activities, no matter how lavish they appeared, was reaped tenfold in donations which went entirely towards the charity's mission of bringing communities together to sustain their own small part of the planet.

Fortunately for Murray, he loved parties and schmoozing and celebrities. A bit too much maybe, if his sunken eyes were anything to go by.

Ally had missed her brother when he was suddenly far away. Growing up, he'd been her closest friend and her best advisor, especially later on when it came to men.

Murray only dated the most eligible guys in the European sustainability sector these days, and he'd been incredibly picky through college, barely condescending to notice anyone, in fact, especially if they were keen on him. Keenness gave him the ick.

If Murray had stuck around a little longer, he'd have got the read on Gray way before anyone else. He'd probably have told her to dump him. She wouldn't have listened, but that's beside the point.

Still, she was glad for her brother. He worked hard and played harder, and brought in millions in donations for Future Proof Planet and in turn that helped people and communities and ecosystems all over the world.

'Putting the sus in sustainability,' came their dad's voice suddenly. 'That's what somebody called ClimateSceptic11329 says about us.'

All eyes turned to McIntyre.

'I'm reading these comments under our cyber news story.'

'I don't think they call it cyber news, it's just news,' corrected Roz gently.

'Outfits like this so-called repair shop are the reason people can't trust do-gooders, says SusanneF1954.' McIntyre lowered the phone. 'This'll be on the web forever, won't it?'

No one liked to tell him he was probably right.

'You could sue the news organisation for reputational damage,' said Murray unhelpfully.

'Anonymous keyboard warriors posting comments in their underpants on the other side of the world *aren't* the people who matter,' insisted Ally, giving her brother a stern look. 'Half of them will be bots, anyway.'

Fixing a Broken Heart at the Highland Repair Shop   49

'Uh...' Murray got the message. 'Aye, Ally's right. And it won't make any difference here on the ground. Probably.'

'What will you be wanting for tea tonight?' Roz interrupted, doing her best to move things on.

'How about I take you all out, eh?' Murray was saying, before his phone rang and he carried it into the garden, speaking the broken French he'd picked up in Switzerland.

'I think I'll do some nuggets and hoops,' Roz said decidedly, trying to lighten the atmosphere that had hung heavy since last Saturday and the police visit. 'He'll not have had those in a while.'

They all smiled at this, but the truth was they were worried. Cairn Dhu was a whispering place and neighbours liked to know everyone's business while pretending they didn't gossip. The McIntyres hadn't ventured out to the hotel bar to face everyone all week, and nor had anybody called round to extend their sympathies and solidarity after the news report.

'Maybe Morag Füssli's right, and folks will lose trust in us?' McIntyre was saying in a low voice to his wife.

Ally's heart faltered to hear him so worried. Who knew what today would bring at the repair shed?

McIntyre checked his watch with a resigned sigh. 'Well, it's time to open up,' and he was on his feet and out the door.

Ally stood too, stretching in her long, green summer dress with the little white flower sprigs all over; a Y2K vintage bargain from Cairn Dhu's only charity shop, in aid of mountain rescue.

'Just try, OK?' her mum said, catching her off guard.

'Eh?'

'I know it's not easy having Murray home and everything...'

'Not easy eating our way through the Swiss chocolate he always brings with him?' Ally tried, not liking that her mum was picking up on the part of her she was most ashamed of.

'His doing well for himself doesn't diminish your achievements.' Roz's voice was soft, not chiding.

'What achievements?' Ally couldn't help it. She hadn't even heard back from her brother's boss about her application. Even twin nepotism wasn't helping her get ahead.

Her mum cleared the table. 'Oh come on, you're doing well in life. Considering.'

'Considering I was born a girl and Murray has all the added benefits of being a bro in a bros world?'

Roz held Ally in a firm gaze. 'I cannae argue that he hasn't had the breaks.'

'Do you think it's just luck?' Ally appealed.

'I think we make our own luck, but he has put himself out there, and doors have opened for him.'

Ally knew anything she said now would come out in a whine and that was not what she wanted.

She'd put herself out there too. At first. Before it all got so hard and suddenly every place advertising any living wage job was inundated with a thousand qualified applicants.

And it hadn't only been Ally feeling the hard bite of reality. It was a generational thing, she'd concluded, especially if you lived in a picturesque tourist spot like this where local houses that had once belonged to families were now snapped up as extortionate second homes and Airbnbs, and the difficulty getting mortgages without a humungous deposit meant loads of people her age had lost out on opportunities that her parents' generation had.

In an incredible stroke of generosity, Roz McIntyre had inherited the mill house from her grandmother. Ally often wondered how much it would be worth these days, but since her mum never showed any interest in finding out, Ally wasn't going

Fixing a Broken Heart at the Highland Repair Shop 51

to ask. She was simply glad she had a place to stay, and a lovely historic place at that.

It hadn't escaped Ally's notice, however, that recently people her age from Cairn Dhu had been getting promotions or going on holidays, or were organising their hen and stag dos. Some were even moving into homes with proper gardens, starting businesses, and having kids.

Why wasn't she moving on, she wanted to know? Hadn't she worked hard enough? Hadn't she put herself out there with Gray? She'd tried. What did the world want from her before she could level up too?

Murray popped his head around the kitchen door. 'Mind if I hop online and catch up with some work? Sorry I can't help in the shed today. You know I'd *love* to.'

He pulled up a chair at the kitchen table, switching on an expensive-looking black tablet thing that opened like origami and propped itself up as if by magic.

He threw a wink at his sister, out of sight of Roz at the dishwasher, before tapping away soundlessly at the screen.

'I'll bet you're devastated to miss out on checking toddler bikes' innertubes,' said their mother knowingly, but nevertheless kissing Murray on the head as she made for the door. 'Come on then, Ally Cat,' she said, taking her daughter's hand. 'Let's chalk up some repairs; see if we can't get to the one thousand mark this weekend.'

With a fixed smile, Ally left her brother to his work and made her way out into the damp summer Saturday morning.

6

'Nobody?' asked McIntyre, incredulous.

'Not a soul,' confirmed Sachin, looking out onto the repair shop's driveway where the drizzle was turning into heather-and-ozone-scented rain.

Cary Anderson, in a dark slouchy linen suit and braces over a buttoned-up summer shirt, glanced from the McIntyres to the Gifford sisters stationed behind their piled cairn of unsold rock cakes. 'The news's put them off comin',' he whispered, and for once everyone caught his words.

Ally organised her screwdrivers on her workbench. The neon sign had been aglow for three quarters of an hour and the doors propped open, but not one client had come in. This was all deeply unusual, even on a drizzly Saturday.

'And no Willie and Peaches either,' said Roz, all by herself at the sewing station.

'Ah! Here we go!' Sachin announced chirpily, and everyone watched as a lone figure stepped inside clutching a carrier bag rolled tightly at the top with both hands. It was the young Special Constable, moisture caught in his dark hair.

Fixing a Broken Heart at the Highland Repair Shop 53

The sight set off an odd instinct in Ally. Her nervous system sent a burst of chemicals through her, fizzling like a firework upon seeing the appealing shape of him and the placid expression on his face. Before she even knew it had happened, she heard her voice gasping sharply, 'Jamie.'

It seemed to reverberate round the shed, startling a pigeon who'd been sleeping amongst the dusty beams. It made her parents, the Gifford sisters and Sachin all snap their heads towards her in surprise, then their eyes flitted between one another. She caught their smirks, followed by expressions hastily re-arranged into neutrality. Even Jamie must have noticed them suddenly pretending to be far too busy to deal with him themselves.

'Uh...' Ally tried to recover herself, pulling her eyes away from the sheen of light summer rain on tanned cheekbones. 'Do you need something?'

He crossed the shed floor, stopping just before her workbench. She was only now realising that at some point in the last few seconds she'd automatically got to her feet too. Why were all her systems going haywire?

They observed one another.

She flatly refused to speak again until he'd spat out some words. Any words. But he was oddly starry-eyed. She held firm.

After a gulp, he blurted, 'You look nice in green.'

'Oh!' Bewilderment mixed with delight.

'Sorry, I mean... good morning.' He scrunched his face, seemingly scolding himself.

'Morning.' Ally clutched at her elbow, knowing how the others would be listening in to every utterance.

'You're, uh, drinking coffee?' Jamie said, a hand rubbing the back of his neck like he'd sprained it. 'Good, good, uh, do you... like coffee?'

Her eyes fixed on her as-yet untouched café cappuccino on her bench. Was Jamie Beaton asking her out for coffee?

His eyes shot wide open in intuition. 'Uh, no, I mean... I'm just making conversation. Or trying to.' He ventured a nervy laugh.

She couldn't help but be put in mind of that time in first year at high school when Davie Hood was shoved in her direction in the lunchroom by his annoying pals daring him to ask if she was planning on going to the end-of-year disco and, anticipating that she'd (meltingly) say 'yes', he'd been dared to retort, 'well tough, I'm no' goin',' or something similar, and he'd return to his laughing pals as the hilarious hero. Except, she and Davie Hood were the only kids in the lunchroom that knew he really *did* want to ask her, and now he couldn't. She'd have said yes if he'd asked in earnest, but he had to save face with his daft wee gang, who still thought girls were only things to ridicule. So she'd gone along with the whole awful rigmarole of waiting for him to say something as he approached her. In the end he'd fished in his pocket and handed her the fifty pence he owed her for chewing gum and she'd pocketed it in silent relief. He'd returned to the lads to a chorus of clucking chicken sounds. In the end, neither of them had gone to the disco. It was the story of her love life. Near misses and awkwardness.

She looked back at Jamie, not knowing how to act. If he was planning on asking her anywhere it was going to be a great big nope from her.

He was in his uniform again, only this time with a black body armour thing over a tight black T-shirt, with lots of harness-style black straps around his chest and hugging the waist of black utility trousers.

Good arms, she heard her traitorous brain whisper, and she worked hard to fix her eyes on his face.

Fixing a Broken Heart at the Highland Repair Shop   55

'Quiet today, no?' he said, innocently looking around and rocking on his heels.

This was helpful. It felt like bait and she was only too glad to bite; anything to distract from the awkwardness.

'I wonder why?' she answered, accusingly.

Jamie tipped his head before pointing a thumb to the spot between his pecs. 'It's somehow my fault, I take it?'

'Well, isn't it?' she continued, knowing it was unreasonable but she couldn't stop herself. 'You didn't have to tell Morag Füssli about the jewellery.'

'As a potential key witness, we really did.' A line had formed between his dark brows.

Good. Any amount of grumpiness was better than not knowing how to act around this guy.

'You could have done some damage limitation, or something?' she went on. 'Made sure reporters don't go around using words like *police caution*?'

He shrugged. 'I've no control over the news.'

Why did he have to be so calm and reasonable under fire? She was being ridiculous.

'Besides, I'm only a volunteer,' he threw in. 'I don't talk to the press.'

'So are we,' she appealed, indicating the nonchalant (but obviously earwigging) fixers. 'None of us are getting paid for any of this. It's all for the community.'

'Same here,' he said. 'I keep you safe; you keep us in good repair.' He seemed pleased with this, like it was an end to the discussion.

'*Safe*? Have you caught those jewellery thieves yet, or found the woman they were using to get rid of the evidence?'

'Well, no, but we're working on it.'

She had him there. A tiny triumph. 'So why are you here and not out dusting for prints or whatever it is that you do?'

'I mostly just type up reports and make the tea...'

She wasn't laughing along with him.

His face fell once more. 'Chances are, they're long gone by now, moved on to another small town, but I give you my word, we'll keep looking.'

He was so sincere, Ally felt her cheeks burn with shame at her behaviour.

How come he managed to provoke her like this? He wasn't even trying to. Was it the uniform doing it to her? Yet, she'd seen traffic cops and fire officers stopping in for their tattie scones and lattes on repair café Saturdays a hundred times before and, nothing. So why this guy?

He was just some lad with a lilting Edinburgh accent and brown eyes like the cold water of the Nithy burn when it ran slow and languorous in summer. Nothing special. And since The Thing with Gray she wasn't looking for anything else, special or otherwise.

'I actually have a repair job for you,' he was saying, cutting through her thoughts, none of which she hoped were showing on her face.

She watched him open the bag and look inside. He was hesitating like he might change his mind. He lifted his eyes to hers as he reached a hand in.

Sadness, she thought. There was only a tiny flash of it in his eyes, but she caught it. She could feel something in him aching too, could picture him with tears on his cheeks instead of raindrops.

Why was she frightened all of a sudden? Not of him, but of catching these feelings coming off him.

Fixing a Broken Heart at the Highland Repair Shop   57

'It's not tech, is it?' she managed to ask, pleased she'd made it sound so casual.

'No, it's...'

To her surprise, he pulled out a hairy coo, small in his hands, strangely sweet held against his broad chest. The contrast sent her nerves into a grand fireworks finale and she grabbed her bag off the floor to avoid him noticing.

'Then that's definitely not for me. Repairs go to Sachin for triaging first, anyway. *Mum,*' she called over her shoulder. 'I'm off to do some work at the library.'

If she left now she could smarten up her CV and do a job search before lunch. That was her big plan for abandoning her workbench and Jamie Beaton and his plushie, and all this... weirdness. Yes, she told herself decidedly. That would be a good use of her time.

'It's not like anyone's coming in...'

The crunch of footsteps on the gravel contradicted her. Still her feet didn't stop conveying her towards the door. She didn't make it far, pushed back inside by the woman stepping in.

'Ah! It's just yourselves? No customers?' she was saying in a well-to-do voice. The woman was fastening up a golf umbrella. 'I'm Peaches's mother, Carenza.'

Ally recognised the woman from the letting agency signs that were popping up across the region. Carenza McDowell's face, framed with poker-straight white-blonde hair, smirked out from all of them.

Roz had crossed the floor in seconds and shaken the woman's hand and introduced herself before asking if Peaches was poorly today.

The woman straightened her neck and stood tall. 'I'm afraid her father and I took the decision to discourage Peaches from attending today.'

Ally steadied herself. She was staying to hear this, for sure.

'Willie won't be coming either. His mother and I were of one mind. We're members of the same Women in Business association. We talk.'

'And what mind is that?' asked Ally, making Carenza turn to face her.

Still the woman wouldn't be flustered. She set her head at an angle, looking down her fine nose at Ally. 'We wouldn't want them getting side-tracked from their studies, volunteering here.'

Roz made her way to Ally's side and stayed her from saying anything further by gently taking her hand.

'I see,' Roz said. 'We thought they were happy here? And getting valuable work experience.'

'So did we,' Carenza replied. 'Until it became clear there was a... criminal element at work.'

'Oh, now!' Senga huffed from across the shed, coming out from behind her counter.

'News reports, photographs online,' Carenza went on. 'These are things that can tarnish a young person's reputation before they've even completed their studies. Imagine if their names had been printed in the reports. That could follow them around for a long time, and those two are destined for the very top.'

Roz squeezed Ally's hand once more, cutting off the indignant things her daughter wanted to blurt in this woman's face.

'We understand,' Roz said. 'Young people today have enough standing in their way of success without being tarnished with... guilt by association, but you should know we were absolutely absolved of any wrongdoing. It was a case of the repair shop being used by opportunistic thieves. We really had no idea.'

'That's as may be,' Peaches's mother went on. 'But for now, it's best they concentrate on their summer design showcases, I'm sure you'll agree. Anyway, I'd best be off. Lots to do.'

Fixing a Broken Heart at the Highland Repair Shop   59

Roz moved to let the woman leave, gently tugging Ally aside too.

'Tell them we'll miss them very much, especially me,' Roz said as Carenza went. 'They were such wonderful helpers, and they'll leave a big gap at the repair shop.'

'Thank you for understanding,' Carenza said through tight lips, as she opened her brolly to the rain, which was falling even more heavily now.

Ally shut the door. 'Could they not have told us themselves? They're actual adults,' she said to her mum, before turning to face Jamie conveying his toy to Sachin at the triage desk. 'You see? We're two repairers down now and we've an empty shed! You could have done something to protect our reputation. Could have told Füssli to go gentle on us, or given a statement to the press to confirm we were innocent.'

'O-kay,' Jamie said slowly. 'But, with respect, not checking for ownership of that obviously nicked jewellery was a silly thing to do.'

Ally's annoyance swelled once more.

'It's no' the laddie's fault,' Senga put in, only to be completely ignored.

'Ally, listen...' Jamie began.

She turned on her heel and walked out into the downpour, her thoughts barely coherent. She knew it was wrong to blame him. It was wrong to be sullen and storming, but it had to be this way if she was going to shake the peculiar feelings he set off inside her.

After a while spent dodging puddles, wondering why on earth she hadn't grabbed one of the many municipal brollies from the stand by the repair shed door for anyone's use, she reached the library, not registering how the two women at the issue desk hastily stopped whispering at the sight of her.

Calming herself with work, Ally spent the rest of the morning tinkering with her CV and scanning the jobs listings online, taking notes and filling in online applications. She didn't stop until she was starving for lunch. She even let herself look at an online travel profile of Zurich, though she wasn't sure why she'd torture herself like that.

Anyone looking at her would have seen a woman focused on her job search, someone not at all perturbed by sparks of curious feeling still racing in circuits through her body, no matter how hard she tried to switch them off.

'I keep you safe,' he'd said.

He hadn't meant her specifically, but the community generally, she knew that. Yet hearing him say it had set off this strange spark of warmth in her belly, a warmth she'd only ever felt with Gray, right at the beginning, before she'd fallen heart first into catastrophe and learned a hard lesson about how these feelings of excitement and overwhelm (red flags in disguise) could not be trusted.

She worked on, obeying her fears while ignoring her hunger and her deeper instincts and curiosity about the Special Constable who, ever since he'd walked into her life, had heralded nothing but trouble for her family.

7

THAT EVENING

You might have heard the Cairngorms described as Britain's Arctic, and never is that comparison clearer than in the white nights of summer.

At fifty-seven degrees north, on a late-June night, the sun has no sooner melted below the horizon than it is on its return journey above it once more, bringing in an early dawn. The birds barely have time to sleep.

Ally pulled her knees to her chest on the wide stone lintel of the glassless window directly above her home's old wooden water wheel, her eyes set on the sky above her. The rain had blown over hours ago; weather changes swiftly in the Cairngorms.

Now the sky was a sapphire blue spotted with summer constellations while a waxing crescent moon glanced down on Cairn Dhu mountain with its plateau split in two like a broken molar tooth by a wide, ragged crevasse.

The mountain's shape was so familiar and comforting to Ally and her brother, they'd both elected to tattoo the inner side of their left wrists with its outline, drawn in matching heather ink on their eighteenth birthday (when, seeing her poor brother red-faced and puffing at the pain, Ally had become all the more determined to convince the artist it didn't hurt a bit when it came to her turn).

From this angle she could just about make out the ski centre, its snowless slope and chairlift lit up even in the summer season when all that was on offer during the day was dry-run tobogganing and the Ptarmigan après-ski nightclub at the foot of the slope. Many nights she'd gone there with her brother, their college friends (and random backpacking hillwalkers from all over the world) to drink Irn Bru cocktails and talk and dance until closing time. It was a Cairngorms institution.

She pictured the scene over there tonight. While happy people spilled out of taxis, the bar would be getting loud and wild, especially if the lads from the climbing and water sports centres were there with their clients from out of town.

It had been ages since she'd been anywhere after sunset. Gray had always wanted to stay at his place with her – to minimise his chances of being spotted with his other woman, she supposed.

She breathed in the night and blew out hard a few times over. It was difficult to sleep during the Highland white nights. Goodness knows how they cope up in Svalbard in the actual Arctic, and not all that far away, where the sun refuses to set at all for four months in summer.

Nights like these had always kept her out of bed. They made her think. She'd come here to her thinking spot over the water wheel, sometimes dangling her feet over the ledge so they almost touched the pitted, dry, wooden wheel and cogitate her way out of her problems.

She remembered her phone in her hands, and turned to scrolling through Instagram, deliberately searching for the

Fixing a Broken Heart at the Highland Repair Shop 63

profiles of Mhairi, Jo and Brodie, her oldest pals, and thinking tonight she might try sending a few messages saying she was 'just checking in' and hoping they were well. She knew they were busy, she might tell them, pointlessly, but if they had time, she'd be free for a meet up.

On second thoughts, their socials showed them and their partners amidst a whirl of baby scans, flat decorating, wedding photo edits, something called toddler sensory classes, work nights out and ghastly looking 'team building exercises' at the go-kart track, and, to her amazement, there were even a couple of 'first day at nursery school' pictures of little kids she'd felt sure were still only babies in arms.

She hastily sent appropriate reactions, love hearts and 'wows' with lots of exclamation marks and some 'So happy for you guys', but she couldn't ignore the realisation that none of them had been in touch when her family were all over the news or when she'd deleted 'In a relationship with @grayinthegorms97' from her Facebook bio.

She told herself that hers were small, insignificant problems – a local news story and an ex-boyfriend – compared to the grown-up things they were facing. Hell, Brodie and her wife had gone through IVF and had their catering business to run; Jo was soon going back to her corporate job after her second baby, and Mhairi, well, there weren't as many updates from her. She must be happy in the pre-schooler bubble. They probably hadn't even noticed Ally's tiny upheavals. Still, it stung. She hated to admit she was lonelier now than ever.

Could she have done more to keep in touch with them when they moved out of Cairn Dhu to get a foothold on the property ladder in the more affordable new villages? Definitely.

Maybe she ought to have celebrated their successes more, even though she'd sent all the cards and bought things from gift registries and travelled for engagement dos and hen dos and wedding receptions.

She hadn't been able to reciprocate with big exciting invites of her own and, if she was really honest, she'd done her best, at first, to contribute to the baby discussions (which carrying sling is best? Which travel system safest? Where are the best schools and how much do houses cost in their catchment areas?), but it had been kind of hard to relate, if she told the truth.

She put down her phone. It was too late now to get back into their lives, most probably, and if they missed her the way she'd been missing them, wouldn't one of them reach out and tell her?

The cool evening offered no answers. In fact, by the rustling noise coming from the ferns and long grasses on the other side of the garden wall across the low summer river, it sounded like yet more trouble might be coming her way. A clang of metal and some good Scottish swearwords shattered the quiet of the twilight.

'Who's there?' she shouted. 'Murray, are you muckin' about down there?' Not that Murray was the type to take a sunset walk around Cairn Dhu.

'Sorry, who's that?' a voice shouted back; mortified, a bit posh. She recognised it as Jamie Beaton's right away.

A head popped up over the stone wall. Even at this distance she could tell his hair was sticking up.

'You all right there, officer?'

'I fell over a... a roll of barbed wire. In fact... I'm a bit tangled up in it.'

She pulled her lips tight to stop the smile. 'Stay still. I'll get my pliers.'

Part of her expected to find a pair of abandoned trousers knotted in wire over the wall when she got there. Jamie wouldn't

Fixing a Broken Heart at the Highland Repair Shop   65

like her seeing him caught red-handed prowling around her property. He'd be embarrassed.

Yet there he was, trying to lean, nonchalant, on the stones, still very much bound up, wearing off-duty clothes: jeans black and rolled at the ankles; boots, also black with thick dark socks over the top, and a heather coloured Henley, all three buttons done up. He looked good out of uniform too. The realisation shouldn't have stalled her in her progress towards him, but it did, just for a second.

Luckily he was too riled to notice.

'Who leaves rolls of barbed wire on a public footpath?'

'Not us,' she threw back. 'This is Mill House land all the way down the hill to the ski slope. You're on a private path.'

He looked around, neck stretched like a hare scenting wild dogs. 'There's no sign saying so.'

'Isn't this part of your beat? You ought to know whose land you're on at all times,' she said with a challenging smile, even as she kneeled to free him. 'All the locals know not to walk this way. It's boggy further down, even in summer. If a man is lucky enough to get away with his life he could still easily lose his wellies to the mud. Everyone walks the main road to get to the Cairn Dhu Hotel bar.'

'I'm not looking for a drink,' he said, glancing down at the top of her head as she crouched at his feet, working to unsnag him, before quickly averting his eyes with a sense of embarrassed propriety.

Surprised at the teensy lift in her spirits that he might have come searching for her, Ally didn't say what she was thinking: what *were* you looking for, then?

'There you go,' she told him, getting to her feet. 'Didn't need to cut your jeans at all.'

'Right, well, thank you.' His face flared red as she met his eyes again. 'You'll need to tell your dad to get that shifted. It's not safe.'

'I will.' The part of her that had wanted to fight earlier today surrendered. 'Getting late for a walk, is it no'?' she tried instead.

He looked all around, as though hoping for a rescue of some kind. None came, and he sighed at the realisation. With shoulders slumping in defeat he reached into his back pocket. 'I was looking for this, actually.' He showed her a fading photograph of a bridge, his thumb deliberately obscuring the figures in the image.

She peered at the shot, then at him. 'That's the Nithy Brig.'

'That's what one of the crofters told me, but he pointed me in this direction and said it was only a twenty minute walk from the police station, but it obviously isn't. Unless it somehow magically moves locations. It's never where people say it is.'

'How long have you been looking for this bridge?'

'Since I got here a few weeks ago. It doesn't seem to be on any maps either.'

'Maybe us locals want to keep it a secret.'

He crumpled his lips. 'Are you going to tell me where it is?'

'Well, it's not as easy as twenty minutes in a straight line, that's for sure.' Seeing the darkness in his eyes, she added, 'I can take you to it, if you like?'

'Now?'

She looked down at her pyjama bottoms. She'd changed right after dinner but picked out a baggy green jumper to keep away the evening chill (Murray's, as it happened, and nothing to do with Jamie saying she looked nice in green).

'Unless you were busy, of course?' he said, suddenly, darting his eyes to the window ledge where she'd been sitting. So he *had* seen her.

'Busy?' She laughed. 'No, I just sit there when I need to...'

Fixing a Broken Heart at the Highland Repair Shop   67

He tipped his head, waiting for the rest.

'I'll get my boots on.'

'I've got a torch, if that's any help?' he offered weakly.

She glanced up at the sleepless night sky, now tinged with the tiniest green haze of the summer aurora, seen now and then in these parts. 'We won't be needing a torch.'

* * *

'It's along the main road for a wee bit, then across Hutchinson's farm field, over the meadow and onto Nithy burn side,' she'd said, all businesslike.

It was no surprise to pass dog walkers and club-goers as they walked, but after a while yomping along field margins in the wide valley that Cairn Dhu nestles inside, they found themselves alone.

The summer twilight sky, not satisfied with its cloudless display of infinite galaxies, turned greener as the northern lights awakened and fell in barely-there, rippling curtains of emerald.

'Woah!' Jamie stopped dead, eyes lifted to the heavens. 'We don't often get this in Edinburgh.'

Even Ally with all her stubbornness couldn't bring herself to dismiss it as a regular occurrence up here. She stopped too. 'I know. I never get tired of it. Some summers the lights are more active than others; some, we get none at all.'

'Looks like I picked the best summer to come here then.'

He looked for his phone to take a picture, then thought better of it. 'Doubt I'd get a good photo.'

'You're better off just storing it in your memory. Photos can't do it justice,' said Ally, catching Jamie glancing at her briefly before fixing his eyes on the sky once more.

'So, you're only here for the summer?' she said, and this was enough to break the sky spell and get Jamie walking again. She matched his slow pace.

'Temporary transfer.'

She let this sink in. This was good news, surely? He'd be on his way soon, and she could act like a normal human being again.

They reached a stile in the fence, the last enclosure before they hit gradually rising mountainsides, icy-cold lochans and perilous shifting scree leading on to about two thousand square miles of serious climbing and precipitous peaks dotted with dangerous black corries.

'You're a volunteer, you said? How can you afford to live out here?' she asked absently, only wondering if that was a rude question once she heard it on the air.

'Oh, uh...' He stepped up onto the stile and swung a leg over.

'Sorry, I shouldn't have asked.'

He climbed down the other side then waited for her to cross. For a second she thought he was going to hold out his hand to help her but he was balling up his fingers into fists by his sides instead. 'I came into a wee bit of money on my twenty-fifth birthday,' he said, reluctantly. 'Mum's life insurance.'

Ally was over the stile with a jump, her boots hitting the dry ground just as Jamie delivered this bombshell.

She searched his face to make sure she'd understood. The sadness was back. Just for a flash.

'Oh,' she said. 'I'm so sorry.'

'It was years ago when it happened. I was tiny.'

It sounded like something he'd said many times, as though it might make other people feel better for him, as if it made it less awful. For Ally, the fact it was long ago made it much, much worse.

Fixing a Broken Heart at the Highland Repair Shop   69

'Still sucks, though,' he confessed, and that sounded more honest to Ally's ears.

She didn't know what to say, not wanting to push for details, especially when she'd been a royal pain in Jamie's arse since they met. Why should he trust her with the most painful details of his private life?

Fortunately, Jamie was talking now. 'I'm getting my voluntary hours up so I can apply for a regular police officer's job at the next intake, and then it's just the application process and the physical exam to go through.'

'Well, the physical shouldn't be a problem.' The words had jumped right out of her mouth. 'Oh God! I wasn't saying... well, you know what I meant, you're...' She was pointing feebly at his bicep, making things so much worse. 'Are you grinning?'

He barely hid his amusement. 'Not at all.'

They walked on in smiling silence accompanied only by the growing sound of gently trickling water.

'So you're not sticking around at Cairn Dhu station?' Why was she searching for confirmation?

'By the end of summer, I'll be back in Edinburgh. A regular police constable, hopefully.'

'We're nearly at the bridge,' said Ally, quieter now.

Only their boot treads and the grasshoppers chirping on the soft summer breeze broke the silence for many minutes.

'Did your folks get any customers at the repair shed, then? Apart from me, obviously?' hazarded Jamie.

'Three, they said.'

'How many do you usually have on a Saturday?'

'More than we can handle.'

'Ah! Right. Not good, then?'

'Not good,' she repeated solemnly.

'Ally, listen, I'm sorry if anything we did spoiled things...'

Hearing him apologising brought out all of Ally's shame at her behaviour. 'Don't apologise. You couldn't have done anything different. I was being overprotective, and a bit of a dick.'

'I wouldn't go *that* far,' he said, throwing a smile her way.

'You looked ready to cuff me, that first day we met.'

'Hah!' He was laughing again, as they made their way over a path of rolled stones where once upon a time a glacier, never witnessed by human eyes, had cut its way through granite. A few feet away, only a crystal clear trickling burn on a diminished riverbed was left of its waters.

'You were frightened. It's OK,' he said.

She mused on this. 'Being scared is only a reason; it's not an excuse. I'm still embarrassed.'

They approached the ribbons of shallow river. 'It's good to be protective of the people you love. Don't worry about it. And for the record, I'm hardly ever allowed to cuff anyone.'

This made her smile. Then it made her think things she really shouldn't be thinking on an innocent night walk with an upstanding member of the police force.

'Edwyn would have, though,' he slipped in. 'You were this close.' He pinched his fingers to show her.

Their laughter ebbed away as the view opened out before them. Below the Reaper's sickle of a moon, glowing gently green in the welkin lights, arched what remained of an ancient stone bridge, low and long in the landscape.

Ally hung back and let Jamie approach it alone, sensing this was a pilgrimage of sorts and not wanting to spoil his arrival, especially since she'd gone out of her way to antagonise him up until tonight.

She watched him tread slowly into the scene.

Fixing a Broken Heart at the Highland Repair Shop 71

* * *

His breath shaky, he paced around the bridge, easily crossing the shallow rivulets that ran under it. Stones scuffed and kicked out from under his boots.

He held the photo before him as he walked, looking for the exact spot where it had been taken from, nothing else driving him but the need to match up the edges of the image – a tiny window on a lost time – to his own perspective.

There! The curved apex of the narrow, crumbling bridge met with that of the picture. A step or two closer brought the two worlds into perfect alignment and he stood as still as he could on the spot where his dad had raised his old automatic camera to his eye, shutter-button pressing, light flooding through the opening aperture before it snapped shut again, a perfect exposure captured on delicate thirty-five millimetre film.

A child and their mother. The sense of an older sibling paddling nearby but out of shot. Sunlight in flaring white rays hitting the lens. Something that might possibly be a picnic sandwich clasped in the child's chubby hand. The other hand obscured in the mother's as she bends her head, pointing towards the bridge, her mouth open.

Had she been telling the child to 'say cheese to Daddy'? He had no idea.

The mother's arms and fingers are thin, her dress billowing and blue.

Within months she'd be gone and that child would search for her for the rest of his life, even when he wasn't aware that's what he was doing.

Jamie lowered the picture just an inch or two, his eyes fixed on the real world beyond it; the deepest, most innocent part of him willing with all his might for his mum to be revealed behind the fragile paper, still standing there at the foot of the bridge. But behind the photograph there was nothing but stones and shallow water and the summer night.

'What was she like?' Ally's voice at his shoulder made him flinch like a man waking from a dream.

'Uh, I don't remember.'

'There has to be something,' Ally pressed.

He could hear the sympathy in her voice. He didn't usually tell people things like that because he couldn't cope with the sympathy. Sympathy didn't help.

He looked again at the picture. 'She was nice,' he managed. 'Restless, I think. Dad says she was funny and always running around doing stuff. And she was young. She was only twenty-seven here. My age.'

He tried to silence the sound as he swallowed. Hadn't he cried enough? He didn't want to do it here too.

'She looks lovely,' Ally said, a tiny bit closer.

A silent moment passed where Jamie made up his mind to share the few scraps of understanding he had of his mum, partially afraid that if he said them out loud they too might disappear.

'My sister, Karolyn, can remember her better than me. She was six when it happened. She still wears Mum's perfume, says it helps her remember.'

A little more silence.

'What do you think that is, in your hand?' Ally was getting a bit too close now. He didn't want to bristle at the intrusion but it was his first impulse.

'A sandwich, I think.'

Ally looked even closer, her head right by his. 'I don't think it is, you know?'

Fixing a Broken Heart at the Highland Repair Shop 73

'Well, what is it?' This was the closest he'd come in recent years to being cross. He didn't like it, swallowing it down.

'I think it's one of these.' She pulled something from her pocket, wrapped in a bit of paper towel, letting it unfold in her palm.

'Toast crust?' Why on earth was she walking around with that in her pocket?

'Aye. It's for the faerie dog.'

He swung his head to look blinkingly at her. He wanted to tell her he hadn't come all this way to play silly beggars. For a brief moment he considered announcing that he could make his own way back to town from here, she didn't have to stay.

'Faerie dog?' he said dryly.

'While I was changing into my boots, I grabbed the crusts from the kitchen. You have to bring something for the faerie dog when you come to the Nithy Brig. An offering.'

He looked once more at the picture, something triggering within him. Ally passed him the crust and as soon as it hit the palm of his hand and his fingers closed reflexively around it, he knew.

'It *was* a crust,' he said, around the lump forming in his throat.

Ally talked softly, helping him unfold the message that was coming through to him. 'No tourist coming here in the last two hundred years would pass the brig without throwing their crust under it. Everyone round here knows the myth.'

He nodded, the world around him shifting, time slipping. He was moving towards the stone arch.

'It was a big green dog, wasn't it?' he said, surprising himself. How did he know that?

'That's right,' Ally said. 'He needs distracting with a crust or you daren't pass his bridge and walk into the foothills for fear he'll bark three times at your back and, on the third bark, you'll perish where you're standing.' She wasn't holding back on the drama.

'This faerie dog's dangerous, then?' he was saying, his own voice somehow miles away and Ally now just an airy presence, like a voice on the radio.

'Not always. They're protectors, especially of children out there in the mountains. They used to say the Nithy Brig faerie dog will guide a lost child home to their parents. In fact, we were all told at the school about how, once, in the fifties, a lost child who'd been gone for days come home safe all by herself, saying she was brought there by a great big green dog. So it must be true.' Laughter rippled through her distant voice. 'The other tales, I'm no' sure of. But still, you'd better throw your crust for him.'

He turned the hard bread in his hand, fixing his eyes on the dark space under the bridge and the black water glittering over slimy rock.

A billowing blue moved at the edge of his vision.

'Throw it, Jamie, darlin'. Go on, right under the bridge.'

His mum's voice came to him from a locked place, and he threw the crust. He turned, dazed, at the sound of a camera shutter, a cool hand slipping into his – he dared not look down at his empty palm and risk breaking the illusion.

'Well done, my clever boy.'

The voice dissolved away, and he found himself smiling at the picture taken more than two decades ago on this exact spot, and away slipped the daylight and his mum at his side, and into focus came Ally where the feeling of his dad, young and smiling behind his camera, had been a second ago.

'Are you all right?' Ally was asking.

He stared down at the photograph of him and his mother on

Fixing a Broken Heart at the Highland Repair Shop 75

a summer's day offering crusts to the faerie dog under the brig, the moment newly opened up to his understanding.

'Yeah,' he said, having cleared his throat. 'I'm good.' He swiped tears from his lashes.

Ally lifted her phone and snapped a picture of him by the bridge, alone under the aurora sky.

The flash firing woke him further. 'I'm ready to go,' he said.

Ally didn't ask any questions as she and Jamie made their way home, side by side and alone with their thoughts, the faerie dog of ancient, ever-evolving myth having once again re-united a lost child with their family, even if it was temporary, even if it was illusory. Like the northern lights, it was still beautiful.

The aurora dimmed away into sapphire blue and a tiny part of four-year-old Jamie's shattered heart healed.

* * *

When Ally got home that night, after a quiet 'thank you' from a very preoccupied Jamie, who'd nevertheless insisted on walking her to her door, she found her mum still up and sitting at the kitchen table, her sewing glasses low down her nose, her needle poised. On the table before her lay her fabric shears, a bundle of crispy cottonwool and thin slivers of orangey-brown plush fabric.

'There you are. Saw you home, did he?' said Roz McIntyre.

'Yep.'

Her mum knew better than to make any smirking assumptions about why she'd been out walking at nearly midnight with a lad, not after The Thing With Gray.

'He's nicer than I thought. Friendly,' she added, as a sop to her conscience about not sharing things with her mum. Not that there was anything to share.

'Your dad's gone to bed,' Roz said, her eyes still on the little highland cow she was working on.

'Is Murray still here?'

'He's leaving early in the morning.' Roz sighed. 'It was nice while it lasted.'

Ally drew her lips into a sorry smile. Her mum took Murray's absences harder than anyone.

'What do you think?' Roz said, clearly trying to rescue her mood, turning the little hairy coo so Ally could admire the repair work she'd evidently been concentrating on all evening.

It wasn't unusual for her parents to finish jobs outside repair shop opening hours; there was far more work to finish than they could fit inside the ten to five of a repair shop Saturday. Or, at least, there had been until this week. Soon her parents would have their evenings back, if things continued like this.

'I can't sew this little guy up until someone takes a look at this thing,' her mum was saying, holding out a small black object.

Ally advanced, taking it in her hand.

'At first I thought it was a growler,' said Roz.

'Excuse me?'

'Like you get in old teddies? So when it's tipped over it makes a growl sound? But it looks electronic.'

Ally inspected it.

'It's definitely some kind of noise-maker,' Roz went on. 'But it doesn't work any more.'

'It's a little speaker, I think,' Ally told her.

She searched the contents of the old marmalade tin on the dining table for a crosshead screwdriver. Other families might have cutlery or utensils in a jar on their dining table; not the McIntyres, they needed to have tools handy.

Fixing a Broken Heart at the Highland Repair Shop 77

As Ally worked the screwdriver, she asked, nonchalant, 'Isn't this Jamie Beaton's toy?'

Roz nodded and watched on. 'It's been cuddled to death, poor thing. Must be a childhood treasure. I can't put new stuffing in before trying to fix and reposition whatever that thing is.'

Ally opened the little round cover of brittle plastic, carefully placing the tiny screw on the dish on the table reserved for keeping small parts so they didn't roll away and get lost.

'There's a cell battery in here, contact's corroded,' said Ally, slipping into tech surgeon mode. 'A simple chip, and a button to depress to make a sound come out. Wires look OK, but the button's been stuck down for some time, I reckon.'

'Can you fix it?'

'I'll try. It's probably a "moo" sound on this wee chip that activates when it's squeezed. If the chip isn't water-damaged or fried, I might be able to get it mooing again.'

Ally didn't mention how, having watched Jamie sink into some secret dream tonight at the brig, she felt more than usually inclined to re-unite a repair shop client with their beloved item.

She'd seen the difference in him from having experienced whatever it was that had happened to him this evening. There'd been a new smoothness in his brow as they said goodnight, as though he was truly relaxed for the first time since she'd met him. The sadness in his eyes was still there, but there was a glint of boyish brightness too. All of this danced in her mind with the memory of the aurora lights and the grasshopper song from the meadow.

She said goodnight to her mum and placed the whole device in the dish along with the little screw and carried it away to her bedroom, wondering if Jamie Beaton had come to Cairn Dhu this summer seeking more than a bonny part of the world to notch up voluntary hours.

Was he seeking recovery? Repair? She'd been so set upon finding fault with him, as though he was just another broken-down thing opened up on her workbench for diagnostic testing, she'd failed to recognise the same soft, slightly shattered thing within him that she carried inside herself too. They were both a little worse for wear.

She went to bed more kindly disposed to the man with penetrating brown eyes, having caught a glimpse of the sweet little boy within him, but trying *not* to think about how seeing it had opened up a closed-off part of the person Ally had been before The Thing With Gray, and before the rat race went on without her, leaving her behind, underachieving and a tiny bit resentful.

It had instead put her in touch with the part of her that was just a girl; a girl with what was beginning to feel like a very small and slightly inconvenient fondness for her local Special Constable who'd told her he was leaving before the end of the summer.

Not that that was relevant. Not that she looked at her calendar before bed that night, regretfully telling herself there'd be no more night-time excursions or conversations with him. She'd fix his hairy coo and get it back in his possession, then she'd steer well clear.

Ally had no idea that the long white nights of the Cairngorms summer had plans of their own for her; try as she might to navigate her own road safely to autumn.

8

The following week saw a whole lot of wondering whether the repair shed and café's fortunes would fare better come Saturday. McIntyre had retreated almost entirely to the silence of the barn all week long, only strolling home for lunch and dinner (and a gentle scolding from his wife) who was missing their son worse than ever, now that he'd jetted off after his visit. She was too much with her own thoughts to be seriously aggravated by the return of her husband's reclusive habits.

Meanwhile, Ally had tried not to read too much into the change within herself: the little thing that was suddenly insisting she get up early, exercise, shower, do her hair and actually sit at her laptop in a nice outfit for her weekday morning tech support job.

Her shifts online hadn't gone any faster than they normally did, and the clients she was remotely connecting to weren't any less confused or inclined to have lost their logins and passwords or to have installed random, unnecessary malware onto their computers without really knowing why they'd done it, but nevertheless Ally McIntyre was irrefutably happier.

On Tuesday, after the particular battery she needed for Jamie's toy repair had arrived in the mail, she'd spent the evening checking the tiny circuitry, cleaned the corrosion off the battery contact point, and proceeded to make an extraordinary discovery that had made her clasp a hand over her mouth in amazement. She decided to keep her discovery to herself until Jamie was there for the big reveal.

Ally loved repair reveals at the repair shed, when clients were re-united with those extra special projects that might have taken a while to restore, or were items of especial sentimental value. She'd have to wait until a repair café Saturday for that.

They'd had no reason to see each other since their walk to the Nithy Brig, and Jamie hadn't stumbled her way in search of any other local landmarks.

Still, after her morning's work, come clocking-out, and not a second after, she'd rip her headset off and – having checked for email responses to her job applications (there were never any) – decide each day that a walk was what she needed.

On Wednesday, Ally found herself wandering through the town and past the police station, for no reason other than her love of dodging the slow-moving tourists on the pavements and finding every shop stuffed to the gunnels with out-of-towners who'd come in by the coachload. She told herself she had no intention of bumping into anyone in particular, whether accidentally or entirely on purpose.

That's why, when she happened to spot Jamie Beaton in his off-duty gear on the other side of the high street, she hadn't momentarily felt compelled to yell his name and run straight up to him to say hello.

When she twigged he was walking with a beautiful, dark-haired woman – who had her arm looped through his – laughing and chatting, Ally had instead concealed herself

Fixing a Broken Heart at the Highland Repair Shop   81

behind the old phone box, staring after them, something within her deflating like a stray party balloon caught in a hedge.

She didn't know why it hadn't occurred to her before that he'd have a girlfriend and that, of course, she'd visit him on his days off. He had to be working out those muscles for someone's benefit, right? Of course it was a stunning Edinburgh woman, probably with a glamorous girl-about-town kind of job, judging by the seriously cool way she was dressed. She must be a regular visitor to the Harvey Nicks cosmetics department, if her perfectly arched brows and that sheeny red lip were anything to go by.

Ally had skulked away, ending her torture, her cheeks burning redder than the phone box she'd hid behind at the realisation of how close she'd been to nursing a silly crush on Jamie Beaton.

That evening, sitting out on her waterwheel window ledge, the feat of contortionism she put herself through would have impressed even the most experienced Cirque-de-Soleil gymnast. She convinced herself it was *lovely* that he had someone special. A man like him, with a soft, secretive side needed company. They really had looked happy together. She was pleased for him and she was *delighted* for his girlfriend, scoring an upstanding, ambitious, handsome man like Jamie Beaton. Good. For. Her.

And that's how she'd stayed, knotted up in delusion until early the next morning when her brother's phone call made her jump awake.

'Good news, sis,' he'd told her. 'They're going to interview you for the Zurich job!'

9

Please wait for Future Proof Planet to join the video call.

Future Proof Planet knows you are waiting

Murray had let his sister know that his colleagues would join her the next day at 8.45 a.m. on the dot. 'They do everything with the precision of a Swiss engineered watch,' he'd told her before their crackling call cut out. Had he called from Mali? There'd been no time to ask. She'd been unable to reach him again, and he'd left her with absolutely zero nuggets of helpful insider advice and only twenty-four hours to prepare herself for this interview.

Ally's mouth was dry as she sat in front of her laptop now, her hair scraped back and in a knot. She wore one of her mum's suit jackets from the late nineties, olive green, with some red, glossy lip oil she hadn't worn since, well, you know what.

She worried it was all possibly a bit too much paired with her favourite green charity-shop dress with the little white flower sprigs. It was too late now, though. She couldn't shuck

Fixing a Broken Heart at the Highland Repair Shop 83

the jacket off or dive for a blotting tissue in case they joined the call right that second and caught her flustering and regretful.

There simply hadn't been enough time to prepare. Didn't they know she was more of a novelty cuckoo clock type of person than a precision timepiece?

She flicked through the pages of notes she'd made about the charity, finding she couldn't make much sense of them now the time had come.

It had been a bewildering, and depressing, twenty-four hour crash course (minus her work shift yesterday) in the entire environmental crisis. All her carefully researched stats about fossil fuels and the rate of deforestation merged into facts about carbon neutral communities, fines for greenhouse gas emissions, the names of nature conservancy projects – too many to count – the hazards of forever chemicals, and the cost to local authorities of anaerobic digestion waste treatment.

Her heart raced and her vision blurred.

She rubbed her thumbs over the lids of gritty eyes. She should have got some more sleep, instead of cramming like she was about to address the UN Climate Change Conference. Who did she think they were expecting? Greta Thunberg?

They'd take one look at her and see she was an imposter. Why had she told her brother she was up for this?

The screen changed from blue to a red countdown on a white background. *Three, two, one.* Ally fought the impulse to slam the laptop shut and run flat out until she summited Ben Macdui itself. Too late. Three figures appeared on-screen.

'Good morning,' said a model-esque Black woman in a clipped and efficient German accent. She wore heavy beige linen over something cream and simple that made Ally instantly regret her thrifted and borrowed choices even more. 'I'm

Barbara Huber, Future Proof Planet Co-CEO for Strategy Development.'

'Nice to meet you,' said Ally automatically, not sure what Barbara's job title meant, other than she was Very Important.

'And this is Andreas Favre,' Barbara said, indicating the extremely well put together man beside her, also in beige linen and an open-neck white shirt.

Was this some kind of uniform policy? To work there, did you have to dress as though you were fresh from a fashion shoot for some achingly chic, utilitarian eco-brand?

The barely-in-shot, slumped person to Andreas's other side told her it wasn't policy for everyone, at least. This person looked about fifteen and was shrouded in a huge black and white graffiti-print hoodie with extremely large clear plastic glasses and a set of chunky headphones round their neck.

'And that's V,' said Barbara.

'V?' Ally confirmed.

'Summer intern.'

'I mostly fix the printer,' V drawled in a Canadian accent, chewing gum, and looking weirdly spaced out and achingly cool in ways Ally had never been for one second of her life.

'Thank you all for seeing me.' Ally couldn't help but worry that if they had V fixing the printers, why would she even be needed? She tried to concentrate on wowing them. But just how easy was that going to be?

'You have ten minutes. Let us begin,' said Barbara.

Ally shifted in her seat at the kitchen table. Thankfully, her mum and dad had gone for a walk so she could have the place to herself and wouldn't witness any of this. They weren't around to fret over the way sweat was beading at the curly red baby hairs at her temples.

Barbara was talking fast and clear. 'Our donors range from

Fixing a Broken Heart at the Highland Repair Shop   85

governments, major corporations and wealthy philanthropists to private individuals fundraising in their communities, all the way down to school children giving their pocket money. Your application stated you have experience working with cross-sector clients in your repair shop and community café, yes?'

'I uh, I did say that, yes.' Why? *Why* had she said that?

'How do you handle these very different relationships?' asked the beautiful Andreas in a lovely French accent.

'Umm...' Ally tried to think. Nothing but blankness presented itself.

'Can you describe a time where one of your service-users presented some unique difficulties for you, and you resolved the problem?' he pressed.

'Well... there was the time Pigeon Angus drove his Massey Ferguson tractor down to the repair shop and it broke down right in front of the open doors, pretty much trapping us inside,' Ally blurted, hating herself more with every stupid word flying from her mouth.

'*Pigeon Angus*?' Barbara's eyes widened.

V shook their head, openly cringing.

'That's right.' Ally gulped. 'He's a... smallholder.'

That was stretching the truth. Angus was an elderly hill-footer who spent all day splattered with droppings in a hut with his beloved homing pigeons. He lived off his homegrown veggies and stinky roll-ups and was often in the local paper for threatening hillwalkers who strayed onto his land with various antique shotguns which the police seized one at a time, only for him to somehow acquire another.

She was regretting mentioning him now, but it was too late. The interview panel peered impassively at her as she scrabbled for words.

'He's... known to be a wee bit... curmudgeonly. But he

needed our help with his jammed axle so we disassembled the thing...'

'The tractor?' clarified Andreas.

'Yup.' Ally hid another gulp behind a thin smile. 'We, the repair team, took it apart, bit by bit, until it could be rolled away from the shed doors and we could operate the café and shed as normal, and then my dad custom moulded a replacement part...'

She paused as Barbara and Andreas exchanged scrunch-browed looks and scratched sparse notes on paper. Bored, V scrolled on their phone, chewing gum in the most judgemental way Ally had ever witnessed.

Still, she wouldn't be stopped. 'And while Dad was making it, we all took it in turns to drive Angus to and from his hut, bringing him back every day so he could tell us what needing doing on his tractor, and so we could teach him some repair techniques to stop the metalwork corroding further. Mum even made a cushion for the seat, because you know they're just bare metal?' Why couldn't she stop talking?

Barbara moved her lips like she could taste something strange. The man narrowed his eyes. Was he smiling or was he embarrassed for her? The intern smirked down at their phone like they were at home watching a sitcom and not witnessing an underprepared Scottish woman having a sweaty breakdown in an interview for a job she'd known she wasn't qualified for before she even applied.

'So,' Ally swallowed, since no one was talking. 'Angus taught us some things about vintage tractors, and we showed him some new things about metalworking, and we used Dad's specialist skills...'

'To collaboratively repair a man's broken down vehicle,

Fixing a Broken Heart at the Highland Repair Shop 87

which he needs for his livelihood, presumably?' Andreas said, glancing at Barbara.

'It's still working today,' Ally offered hopefully.

In fact, just last week she'd seen his shiny red tractor parked on the double yellows outside the animal feed shop. The traffic warden had been in the middle of writing him another parking ticket (which he'd no doubt crumple up and chuck into the gutter like all the other ones he'd ignored).

'OK, so that's community co-working covered, sort of,' said Andreas, making what looked like a tick in his notes.

'Tell us about your approaches to global strategisation.' Barbara had said the words like they actually meant something.

'Uh...'

This was enough to draw V's attention. 'She means how does the stuff you do have a wider impact.' V was shaking their head again, rolling their eyes at the ridiculous Scottish Millennial who really shouldn't be given the time of day by Future Proof Planet.

'Ah, right, well, thank you, V,' said Ally through a gritted teeth smile. 'I, uh, I suppose everything we do has a global impact.'

She was about to say that if they hadn't fixed Pigeon Angus's tractor he'd have had to buy a new one and that would use up vital resources, and probably energy and emissions importing it, since tractors aren't really made in Scotland now, but then Ally thought how, more realistically, if they hadn't repaired the thing, Angus would simply have let it rot in a field since there was no way he could afford a new anything, let alone a tractor.

'Um...' She felt the cold trickle of sweat down her spine and tried not to squirm. She forced herself to think. 'We, uh, we fix things here in Cairn Dhu and that makes a difference to the whole world because... um...'

Words failed her. How could anything she did here in her small town on the edge of a mountain range in the Highlands of Scotland make even the tiniest bit of difference to the planet? Did repairing, repurposing and recycling bits and bobs in communities like theirs shift the dial on planetary extinction even one teensy, tiny bit? Now that next to nobody was coming to the repair shed (and their youngest volunteers had started to abandon the project) there was surely zero chance of making any difference long term, even in her own town?

'Let us move on, *já*?' said Barbara, cutting through the sound of Ally's heartbeat in her ears. 'If we connected you to a project in, say, New Zealand, where communities were trying to save the endangered kakapo, how could you use your technology skills to enable them to more fully meet their goal?'

Ally searched her memory. Kakapo? The big flightless birds that are so friendly and unsuspecting they were hunted to near extinction? She'd watched maybe two TikToks about them. Could she pull together some semblance of a clever, impressive answer now and save this car crash interview? Andreas, she noticed, had closed his notebook and lidded his pen.

'How I'd help enable the community to save their birds?' Ally asked, and she knew it sounded brainless.

'That's correct.' Barbara's tone was cooling by the second.

Ally couldn't even save her own community of endangered repair experts, and she was related to two of them. How would she reach some remote group and make a difference?

'Well,' she gulped, 'communication is probably key, I'd say?'

'Is that a question or your answer?' Barbara pushed, her voice monotone.

'It's an answer, definitely.' Ally sat straighter. She pictured the empty shed, the neon sign by the open door, the way any random person could come tramping across their yard and into

Fixing a Broken Heart at the Highland Repair Shop   89

their lives, bringing them their problems. She thought of her dad's big, open heart and how he'd created something bursting with hope and purpose, and how it was all about to fall apart around them.

'I think,' she began, words forming of their own accord. 'I think, being present matters to people.'

'Go on,' said Andreas, his head cocked in interest, and also like this was her very last chance to say something that showed she wasn't a complete waste of an interview spot.

'You can't just turn up somewhere and say, *hey, I'm here to fix you and your problems,*' she said. 'You have to be invited, or you have to be *needed*, and you have to be genuinely able to assist. Good intentions aren't enough, I think.'

'OK?' Andreas was nodding. Barbara was listening closely. V was drinking through a straw from a huge water bottle, but at least they were paying attention now.

'A community like the kakapo protectors, just like our local Cairn Dhu townsfolk, would have to see us as some sort of a sign, a *signal*, even.'

'A signal?' V said flatly.

'Yes!' Ally insisted. 'Being there, ready and able to help, properly resourced, with skills and your heart right there on your sleeve with nothing hidden,' just like her lovely dad, she thought, 'is a sign to people that they are better off with you there. It's a sign that you take their problems as seriously as they do, and when they witness caring and co-operation, and creativity and... and *goodness* in action, you're giving out a sign that change can and will happen, and that people are actually pretty decent underneath it all. Because, in the end, we all want to be good people, and we all want to save precious things, don't we?'

'Like the kakapo?' led Barbara.

'Exactly, like the big silly kakapo and everyone who loves them. If you show up for people and you involve them, you're sending a sign that you can imagine a world where change has already happened, and if you can *imagine* that it's already happened, you have a place to start from, and you can work towards it, together.'

She stopped, worried she'd blethered too much, gone too far. She'd got excited and agitated. She knew her cheeks were burning red. She tried to slow her breathing.

'So you asked me how I'd enable that with tech?' she went on, more slowly.

Andreas had opened his book again and was scribbling something down. Barbara sat as elegant as a statue but with a smiling light in her eyes. She was curious about Ally, that much was clear.

'I'd find ways to open channels of communication; meetings, activities – and not just for the organisations involved in whatever the project was that we were working on that day – but involving *their* communities and families and everyone affected. I'd make sure there were virtual *and* face to face spaces to meet, to learn and skill share, and where there was resistance, I'd shine my signal even brighter, really showing people I believe change is possible. I'd distribute tech to those cut off from involvement, find tutors locally to demo how our ideas would work, if needs be, and I'd make sure we were all talking *all the time* and not breaking off, in case the community got spooked and started to doubt we could actually achieve our goals, because that's how some really bloody good community projects break down, by getting spooked and not talking. Sorry. Didn't mean to swear. But it's true.'

Suddenly, it was Ally taking notes of her own. Be The Sign

Fixing a Broken Heart at the Highland Repair Shop 91

That Change is Possible, she wrote. Talk and meet and share and keep everyone on board.

'So,' Andreas was saying, reading from his notes. 'You're saying we need to ideate a world in which change is possible and work towards it as though it has already happened? All while on-boarding as many people as possible across the community?'

'With their hearts open and on their sleeves?' said Barbara, eyes narrowed and assessing.

Ally nodded, and said, 'Well... yes.'

And that was it. After a few cursory words of thanks and dismissal – they had other people to see this morning – the screen went blank and Ally was left looking down at her handwriting, her heart still thumping hard.

Automatically, with no delay, she fired off a quick email about being unable to clock in for her shift, saying she had an urgent family matter to attend to. She hadn't missed a morning's work in years, even during the thing with Gray, so surely they wouldn't mind.

She got to her feet, glad she was already in her trainers. It was five to nine, twenty-five hours until the repair shop and café opened its doors to a make-or-break Saturday.

She knew what she had to do now: send out a signal to as many people as she could reach that she believed change was possible. Small, local change, yes, but if everyone was on board, little communities like Cairn Dhu could send a message to the whole planet.

The door clicked shut on its latch behind her as she ran down the garden path and across the gravel yard and into the street, asking the very first person she saw, 'Have you seen Jamie Beaton out today? You know? The new Special Constable?' She was determined to keep moving until she found him.

10

It was the first Saturday of July and the shed hunkered down among the town houses in the wide green valley beneath great fluffy clouds, bright white against a jolly blue summer sky. Inside the repairers were waiting – and waiting – for their clients to come.

'We may have to face facts,' said Sachin, at once bemused at how people so quickly dropped the repair shop and café like a stone, while simultaneously rubbing his hands together at the thought of potentially getting his weekends back and how much his golf would improve because of it. 'The folk have spoken with their feet.'

'Nonsense,' snapped Senga from behind a towering cairn of fresh chocolate-dipped rock buns on the café counter. 'They'll come back for the cakes, if they won't come for the repairing.'

Even though Senga's delicious rock buns were unmatched in the whole National Park area, nobody seemed very convinced. Nevertheless, they kept their eyes fixed on the doors, willing the morning rush to begin.

'Peaches and Willie couldn't contend with their families'

Fixing a Broken Heart at the Highland Repair Shop   93

disapproval,' Roz said, next to their two empty seats behind the sewing machines.

'Ally not coming either?' Sachin wanted to know, gesturing to her vacant workbench.

McIntyre and Roz exchanged glances. 'I'm not sure where she is,' Roz replied. 'She's been in her own wee world since that job interview yesterday. Barely said a word to us when we did catch a glimpse of her late last night.'

'Came home with her face shoved in her phone,' joined her husband. 'And was out of the house before breakfast this morning.'

'She'll have a lot on her mind,' said the youngest Gifford sister. 'Moving to Switzerland and everything.'

'She didn't seem as confident as you about her prospects there, but thank you, Rhona,' said McIntyre, making Senga jab at her sister with her elbow for making assumptions.

'It wasn't a success, I gather, poor thing,' said her mum, putting the subject to rest.

'Think I'll stocktake the paint stripper and varnishes,' said McIntyre diplomatically.

'I'll help,' said Cary Anderson, hopping from his stool, while the rest of the room fell to thumb-twiddling and long sighs in the silence of the shed.

* * *

At twenty past ten, the postie arrived, making everyone jump to attention.

'Naebody in yet?' he said as McIntyre signed for the order of metalworking supplies he'd been unable to cancel after realising demand for repairs had dried right up.

'Very astute!' tutted Senga with the look of a woman ready to launch a rock bun at the man for stating the obvious.

'I'm sure things will pick up, eventually,' McIntyre smiled placidly, handing back his digital signature.

'It'll be the village meeting that's keeping them,' the postie said, making his way back to the door.

'Eh? What meeting's this?' asked Sachin.

'The polis man's emergency meeting at the school hall,' he said, before disappearing into the courtyard, leaving the repairers exchanging bemused comments.

'Why haven't I heard about this *emergency* meeting?' Senga demanded.

Cary Anderson shrugged blankly. He hadn't heard about it either.

Roz was already on her phone. 'I'll look in the community pages on Facebook. Maybe someone's set up a Saturday event that's taking our clients? Maybe they're *not* staying away on purpose?'

'But a *police* event?' Senga said. 'What could it possibly be?'

'I don't see any mention of a meeting,' said Sachin, also on his phone. 'I'll ring home, see if Aamaya knows anything about it.'

Before his call could connect, voices rose outside the shed in a growing hum. McIntyre was up and at the door in an instant. Footsteps approached and, in a blink, he was swept back into the repair shop by a chattering crowd, headed by none other than Ally and Jamie.

'You're not leaving, are you?' Ally asked her dad with a grin as they were pushed right inside and up to the café corner by the moving bodies still spilling in.

A great gang of people, some of whom had never set foot in

Fixing a Broken Heart at the Highland Repair Shop   95

the shed were here, some from the neighbouring villages, and some familiar faces too: Aamaya Roy was here, delivering a kiss to her delighted husband, plus there was Joy from the laundrette and nosey Tony from the hop-on, hop-off tour buses with his cousin, Jean. The school cleaner was here too. Adding to their number was Reverend Meikle, Pauline from the Post Office, Dr Millen the GP, Ozan the barber, Esma from the chippy with her elderly mum in tow, and so many others, all bubbling with excitement and urgency.

An eager Rhona stood on tiptoes to observe them all over the rock buns.

Peaches and Willie were the last ones to step inside, rounding everyone up like collies shepherding Runner ducks.

'What's all this?' asked McIntyre, his eyes shining.

'Cairn Dhu wasn't going to sit by and watch you struggle,' Willie shouted above all the heads. This was met with a murmur of agreement.

'We've been in the school hall,' added Peaches. She looked delighted with herself in her peach-print dungarees and dyed, acid-yellow space buns.

'Gathering provisions and people,' said Aamaya Roy from her husband's arms.

'For what?' Roz asked, moving through the centre of the group to find McIntyre, slipping her arm around his waist when she got to him.

'For the repair shed's comeback,' said Ally. This was greeted with lots of nods and muttered agreement. 'Because a minor setback is nothing but the set-up for a major comeback!'

'I *told* you!' Senga announced. 'Cairn Dhu could never forego my baking!'

Heads turned towards her.

'And, of course, the repairs are needed too,' she allowed.

Roz beamed at her daughter who was happily watching her invasion unfold, her eyes following the conversation as it bounced around the room.

'Was this your doing, Ally?' Roz called to her.

'It was a community effort,' she said back, and her words were quickly caught up in a surge of voices repeating what she'd just said all the way to the far reaches of the crowd.

'*Tush!*' This came from Reverend Meikle and it silenced the room as though he was beginning an impromptu sermon. 'It was Ally who rallied the whole town. It was her and young Jamie who approached me for help yesterday afternoon, prompting me to ask the school caretaker to open the hall for our meeting this morning.'

'And between them, they chapped on every door in town,' added Esma from the chippy. 'Called in at every business too, and reminded folks that you've been here for them all this time and that if they wanted things fixing, there's no time like right now.'

Jamie had been shrugging this off. 'It was all Ally, honestly.'

What he wasn't saying was that Ally had burst into the police station looking for him yesterday morning. She'd found him sitting behind one of the local officers, Constable Andrew Mason, watching as he typed something on-screen. Ally had registered the strange mood in the room at the time, and the frown on Jamie's brow, before she'd stuck to her plan and begged him to help her.

'You can take him, doll,' the desk sergeant, who happened to be Andrew's older brother, Robert Mason, had said, while Andrew had hidden a smirk. 'He's no' much use to us.'

Ally hadn't understood what that was supposed to mean, and hadn't given it much thought since then, because Jamie had

Fixing a Broken Heart at the Highland Repair Shop   97

immediately gathered up his things and followed her out into the station car park.

'What is it you need me to do?' he'd said, with a focused intensity he hadn't lost all the while they set about their task.

'I see,' McIntyre was saying now to the whole assembly. 'We thought you'd lost trust in us.'

Some looks passed around the room, an awkward acknowledgement that maybe there was more than a grain of truth in that.

A hand lifted in the middle of the group and people stepped aside to reveal Carenza McDowell, Peaches's mother, not quite as shamefaced as perhaps she ought to have been, but with the look of someone here to make amends, if they could.

'Perhaps,' she began, 'one or two of us were of the opinion things weren't quite above board at the shed, and perhaps...' she faltered, casting a glance at Peaches who was filming the whole thing on her phone with a tiny hint of self-righteousness in her smile, 'perhaps some of us were... overly vocal about our convictions. But after a visit from Special Constable Beaton late last night, he was able to satisfy us of some of the broader details of the stolen jewellery case, exonerating the McIntyres, and well... I apologise. It's possible we overreacted when we asked the kids to stay away.'

Roz and McIntyre aimed hurried glances at Senga Gifford with looks designed to make her think twice about saying what was no doubt on the tip of her tongue about this U-turn; that Carenza had made it her business to spread the word the repair shop and café wasn't a reputable or safe place to bring your prized possessions, or for your precious grown-up children to volunteer their time.

Senga harrumphed to herself instead, folding her arms across her bust, none too happy at not being allowed to speak her mind, but she held it in for the sake of community cohesion and her own little café venture.

'So... you're back?' asked Roz, gesturing to Peaches and Willie. 'And Willie, your parents are happy you're here as well?'

'We're back!' they said together, Peaches hopping on the spot excitedly.

'You haven't *all* brought a broken item, have you?' McIntyre asked the crowd.

Aye! Cries went up across the room. Someone shook a box of broken vase shards. *That we have!* Another held aloft a strimmer with a severed cable. *Can you take a look at this?* Another held up a bag of clothes. *And these? If you've time.*

'And we hastily scraped together some donations this morning – materials and ingredients from our own sheds and cupboards,' added Reverend Meikle, shrugging his two carrier bags, bursting with supplies, while Bernice, the Cairn Dhu accountant, offered up a lidless biscuit tin full of bobbins of colourful threads and elastics.

McIntyre had to look down at his feet to keep his feelings from fizzing over.

Ally, however, was smiling, clear-eyed and proud. The community had rallied for her mum and dad. The repair shop regulars were all here and ready to work. They weren't going to be beaten by something as silly as a mistake, no matter how public it was. And it was all down to her belief in her own ability to make a difference. That, and the calm, convincing manner of the man standing beside her with his hands shoved in his pockets in his usual, unassuming way.

She was one second away from thanking Jamie, when Sachin hit play on his favourite Bombay Talkie CD, letting nineties' Glaswegian Bhangra flood the speakers. 'Let's get

Fixing a Broken Heart at the Highland Repair Shop   99

fixing!' he called out, his arms raised, shoulders thrusting upwards with the music.

'Get the hot water urn on, Rhona!' commanded Senga. 'See? I was right to bake those extra bannocks this morning.'

'Form a queue for triaging,' McIntyre instructed, and the bodies slowly moved towards Sachin's desk in the now absolutely stoatin' repair shed (which, for the curious, is a particularly Scottish type of happy bounce).

Jamie was making to leave now, having received a hug from a grinning Roz, a handshake from McIntyre, a chuck on the shoulder from Cary Anderson, and a bag of rock buns from a starry-eyed Rhona Gifford.

Ally only just managed to catch him before he left. Was he honestly planning on slipping away before they could celebrate their success? Was he really this modest? She hadn't even thanked him properly.

Maybe he was in a hurry because he was meeting that girlfriend of his? Ally hadn't dared broach the subject as they'd dashed across the town together, cajoling and assembling, and setting the record straight about the repair shop.

'Can you come back later, at closing time?' she said, snapping her hand away from his shoulder as quickly as she'd tapped him on it.

'Uh, sure.' His face bloomed into an easy smile.

'To get your cow,' she clarified.

'Oh, of course. My cow.' He was nodding fast, schooling his features into seriousness again.

'About five?' she said.

He repeated her words by way of agreement.

Just before she turned for her workbench, having heard Sachin directing her first client of the day towards her, she couldn't help but lift herself onto her toes to give him the fastest, most respectful peck on the cheek. Grateful and friendly, nothing more.

'Thank you, for all this,' she said, stepping away, quickly getting lost from his sight in the bustle.

Although she didn't see it, Jamie watched her go, astonished and frozen to the ground, his fingertips held to the spot where her lips had pressed to his cheekbone.

11

Twenty minutes to five o'clock in the repair shop and the door is closed after their busiest day on record. Scores of repairs were triaged and taken in to be attended to outside opening hours. Many were started and finished today and chalked up on the board, items saved from landfill and taken home to continue being useful (or simply very much loved), until the next time they needed repair.

Now industrious heads are bowed over the last tasks of the afternoon. No one speaks. Cary Anderson and Charlie McIntyre plane wood at the carpentry bench, Cary taking the lead on making the new curved rockers for an old chair that has soothed generations of comfy, dozing folk. Cary perfects the curvature and sands away rough edges. McIntyre mixes his own recipe of two part epoxy with milled glass fibre, stirring the concoction in a pot, perfect for filling gaps. Cary drills in the guide holes and washers. McIntyre paints on the glossy goop where the joins will be. Cary holds the runners in place while McIntyre screws them fast, then the rocking chair is tested in turns by the satisfied repair duo.

Peaches and Willie are taking the hems down on grey school kilts and trousers to extend their wear into the new school year. Willie struggled with the folds on the skirts but Peaches knew the trick was all in the ironing and showed him how to get a crisp, pleated finish with the steam press.

The Gifford sisters are delighted to have a full kitty and not one rock bun or bannock left. Whispering, they set their baking plans for next Saturday. Rhona thinks they ought to try strawberry tarts (which Senga dismisses out of hand as too lavish. What does she think this is? Balmoral?) Undeterred, while Senga wipes down the counter, Rhona whispers to Siri the way Ally showed her how, to add fresh whipping cream to the provisions list, two large cartons.

Roz is sewing the last of the stuffing inside a soft highland cow toy that had been loved to pieces by a little boy who became a bigger boy who couldn't let it go. The little cow's fleecy body, which has had a gentle bath in soapy suds followed by a thorough rinse and dry out, has had its threadbare spots invisibly patched with new, perfectly matching material sourced from an online warehouse way down south. It has a new black glass eye to match the lost original, and a fresh shaggy hairdo of rust brown between its tufted ears which, instead of flopping askew, are now sticking up, alert. Its face, which had lost all its contours and character is back in its original shape with a hidden structure of new boning inside the broad snout.

While Sachin works his broom across the floor in rhythmic sweeps, Ally hands her mother the repaired black plastic speaker with its new battery and advises her where to position it so the now-functioning activation button can easily be pressed through the plump animal's fur. Lastly, Roz stitches back into place a lazy pink smile.

Across the shed, threads are snipped, steam billows upwards

Fixing a Broken Heart at the Highland Repair Shop 103

in warm blasts, clean teacups are stacked and sugar supplies toted up, a chair rocks on creaking floorboards for the first time in a long time, and the big clock on the wall ticks its way past five o'clock.

This is what skill and dedication looks and sounds like when combined with time generously surrendered to saving everyday things.

Ally isn't thinking any of this, however. All she can think of is that any second now, he'll be back and she's hoping this time she can keep a lid on her feelings.

The knocking makes every head lift from their work. Roz, more clear-thinking than her daughter, pulls a yard of purple fabric from the shelves to conceal her latest repair from its owner and slowly the doors pull open and in walks Jamie Beaton.

'Oh!' Ally can't help the sound escaping her as two others follow him.

It's the woman from the other day. The one who'd been holding his arm and laughing. Ally's brain glitches as she sees her grip at his arm once again. There's a man behind them, smiling pleasantly, nodding to her dad and Sachin. He looks a lot like Jamie, just older and world weary.

'Hi, hope you don't mind. I've brought my dad,' Jamie announces. 'He's been visiting me, staying at the hotel.'

'Not that I've seen much of you the last couple of days,' the man says in a gentle way.

'Oh.' Ally fights her own awkwardness to step forward and greet them all properly, realising it was her fault Jamie's missed much of his dad's visit. 'Sorry about that.'

'And,' Jamie added. 'This is my sister, Karolyn.'

'Sister?' Ally pumped Karolyn's hand. 'It's nice to meet you!

Not that it wouldn't be nice to meet you if you weren't Jamie's sister. Obviously. I mean...'

'I'm Roz, welcome to the repair shop.' Ally's mum was stepping in to save her. She still felt the searing flush of red race down her neck, though. 'And this is my husband, Charlie McIntyre.'

McIntyre shook their hands and bid them come to the sewing table.

Even though the Gifford sisters would have loved to stay and observe Ally in her agonies, Sachin was ushering them out of the door saying something about letting Ally see to Jamie without an audience, which all the Beatons and McIntyres overheard.

Once alone, with the big doors pushed shut, everyone was smiling politely, shrugging off the sudden sense of being cloistered in this big cathedral of a repair barn, the anticipation growing.

'We couldn't believe it when Jamie mentioned he was getting Holiday repaired, just like on that telly programme!' Karolyn was saying. 'We cut our wander round the tourist shops short specially to come and see this.'

Roz and McIntyre stood on one side of the table with Ally between them, and opposite her stood Jamie, with his dad's hand on his shoulder and his sister watching closely.

'Is that it?' Karolyn said, pointing to the lump under the cloth.

'I don't know if this was a good idea,' Jamie said ominously, his eyes fixed on it too.

'He was your cow?' Roz asked.

'She, actually,' corrected Jamie with an apologetic, slightly nervous laugh. 'Yeah, she was mine, from when I was wee.'

'You took that cow everywhere,' Karolyn put in, tugging at

Fixing a Broken Heart at the Highland Repair Shop 105

her brother's arm affectionately. 'First day at school, football camp...'

'She even went on that Duke of Edinburgh residential with you,' his dad pitched in fondly.

'And you were sixteen then,' Karolyn teased.

'All right, all right!' Jamie was laughing but it was stiff and pained. He looked at Ally through the embarrassment. 'Holiday was important to me. Still is.'

'Well, she's had quite the makeover,' said McIntyre.

'Do you want to see?' asked Roz gently.

A silent moment passed where all three Beatons breathed deep. Jamie and his sister nodded and their dad tightened his fingers over Jamie's shoulder, his chest swelling in readiness.

Ally lifted away the cloth, her eyes on Jamie's face.

What she saw there, she'd never forget. An expression like she'd never seen before and one so complex and raw no actor could ever replicate it.

Even with his hands thrown to his mouth to cover his emotion, she saw what this meant to him.

Karolyn gasped. 'Oh, that's lovely!'

Jamie let the sight sink in. 'Can I pick her up?' he said.

'She's yours,' said Ally.

Turning the creature in his hands, giving her the softest squeeze, unable to resist the urge to give it the quickest sniff (which made his family laugh again), his eyes melted into the softest of full moons.

'She's exactly how I remember her,' said Jamie. 'Thank you.'

All through this exchange, Mr Beaton stood still as a statue, his lips buttoned together.

'That's not all,' said Ally.

'Hmm?' Jamie was looking the cow directly in the face with childlike innocence.

'I repaired the voice chip,' she said.

'Voice chip?' Jamie looked from Ally to his sister and dad. Both shrugged back.

'It speaks?' said Karolyn. 'I don't remember that.'

'The speaker's been gummed up for some time. Maybe you all forgot?'

'Oh, my,' said Jamie's dad in a rush. 'It's coming back to me now.' He brought his knuckles to his mouth. He looked afraid.

'You can squeeze it, there,' Ally told Jamie softly, 'where you feel the wee hard thing? That's it.'

Ally watched Jamie's fingers move around the fat little cow's belly until he struck upon the button. He had that same look she'd seen the other night, as they approached the Nithy Brig, of a person who was at once desperate to remember some locked away thing and at the same time terrified of what they might discover.

'It's OK,' Ally whispered.

Jamie pressed the button in the deepest of silences and a voice bloomed in the air.

'Mummy loves you, my darlin', happy holiday.'

A sharp hitch in his breath, the kind that becomes sniffs and then silent tears, shook at Jamie's ribs.

Karolyn's mouth fell open in amazement. She put her hand to the toy, now clutched tightly to her brother's body.

Roz and Ally let their tears well through their gladness, and McIntyre pushed his glasses up onto his head so he could pinch at his eyes.

The three repairers hugged each other close and watched on as a family were, to some small degree, re-united.

Only, what came next, nobody expected.

Jamie Beaton's father, Samuel, once big and broad, now wiry and hunched, a man of few words and even fewer smiles, the

Fixing a Broken Heart at the Highland Repair Shop   107

man who had taken on the hardest of tasks – one he'd never believed he was fit for – a man who never once thought about his own grief, prioritising his two heartbroken children, reached for the silly toy in his son and daughter's hands and joined them in pressing the button once more.

When Lucy Jayne Beaton's voice trilled out loud in the room once again, he opened his eyes to the ceiling, his lips twisting apart, and he let out a hard sob that had been waiting to escape for twenty-three summers and he sobbed and cried and laughed and clung hard to his children.

The McIntyres didn't have to look at one another to know it was best to leave them to this moment, so they took their own feelings out into the front yard to share together, convinced more than ever that this work was the most worthwhile thing they could be doing with their spare time.

'Well done,' Roz said as she hugged her daughter. 'Good job, Ally McIntyre, you clever thing.'

When the Beatons eventually emerged from the repair shed, there was a good deal of hugging and hand shaking and a great outpouring of thanks, and the McIntyres happily waved the family away and made their way into the mill house.

* * *

'We'd better be on our way,' Samuel Beaton said to his son, bestowing Holiday back into his hands, still standing in the gravel of the repair shed courtyard. 'It's a long drive to Edinburgh and the roads'll be busy with the weekend traffic.'

'You're going already?' Jamie hadn't been prepared for this. 'Can't you stay for dinner, or something...'

Karolyn already knew what her brother wasn't willing to accept. That their dad had been exposed to a lot of unprocessed feelings in that repair shop, and he was deep in flight mode, wanting to get back to his safe space where nothing ever got talked about.

'I'll take care of him,' Karolyn said, as their dad left the yard through the gap in the wall, making for the hotel car park where their bags were already in the boot of the car.

'We could have had dinner, talked a bit more. I didn't get a chance to say any of the things I wanted to, what with me working so much, then I was helping rally the town all day yesterday. I've got these photographs I wanted to show him, you see? It was just never the right time this week, but now...'

'I know,' said his sister. 'But you know what he's like. I'd better catch up with him. Come here.' She held her brother close. When she released him she surveyed his face. 'You look... lighter. Being here's doing you good.' She patted the cow once more and their mum's voice activated.

This time they smiled without any tears.

'I still miss her every day,' said Karolyn. 'The grief never got any smaller, but I've grown around it, if you see what I mean? It's still in there,' she thumbed her chest, 'but it's deep in there.'

'Whereas Dad is still a big man-shaped ball of grief?' Jamie said, a little wry, a little sorry.

Karolyn nodded. 'But I think he made a bit of progress today, don't you?'

'I've never heard him cry before.' Jamie blinked in wonder, remembering how it had happened.

'I have.' His older sister's eyes were soft. 'You just don't remember.'

Jamie looked down at Holiday, considering something. 'Here,' he held the toy out to her. 'Give it to Dad. I think he needs her now more than I do.'

With all the understanding of siblings united by the

Fixing a Broken Heart at the Highland Repair Shop   109

unspeakable, she took the cow without words. Jamie pulled his phone from his pocket and unlocked the screen, opening the voice note app. When the recording symbol showed, his sister pressed Holiday's tummy once more and Jamie captured the sound.

'Got it,' he said, saving their mother's voice.

'I'll be seeing you, then,' said Karolyn.

This set off a twinge in his chest, the little-boy-left-alone feeling that had once consumed him. She knew this, of course. Her eyes flickered to the mill house behind him.

'You know, you could make evening plans? You shouldn't be on your own tonight.'

'Plans?' he echoed. 'What kind of plans?'

She smiled over his shoulder, lifting a hand to wave at someone behind him.

When Jamie whipped his head around, he caught Ally at the kitchen window, quickly hiding herself from view. And when he turned back to his sister, she was walking away.

'Ask her out, you dingus,' Karolyn called over her shoulder with a laugh. 'Call it your way of thanking her, if you need to!'

Damn his sister and the way she always knew what was going on in his head. He couldn't read her anything like as well.

Left alone, Jamie looked down at his feet, his hands feeling very empty and redundant without the soft fur of Holiday between them.

His brain ticked over. He pictured his flat. Dinner alone on the sofa. Indecipherable Gaelic programmes on the telly. His weights on the floor. One hundred reps. Shower. Hydrate. The same old podcasts, then sleep.

Or, he could turn around and knock on that door.

It took all of one second to make up his mind.

12

The doorman, Big Kenneth, held open the door for Ally and Jamie, giving her a firm nod of approval and a paper wristband.

'Take it easy, folks,' he told them, like he said to everyone he let inside the Ptarmigan après-ski nightclub.

Kenneth would begin his shift here at nine p.m. and end it at two when he'd walk down the lane to the dairy and stock up his milk van ready for his rounds which he, famously, did in his doorman tux. Nobody questioned it round the town. It was just the way things were.

'Will do, Kenneth,' Ally replied, and they made their way up the clanking metal stairs, the walls painted with snowy mountain scenes and dotted with images of the arctic-alpine birds that gave the club its name.

'You ready for this?' she said, stopping before the double doors at the top of the stairs, the sounds of muffled voices and thumping beats behind it. 'Because I can promise you, behind this door will be scenes of absolute carnage and debauchery.'

'Can't be worse than chucking out time in Edinburgh old town.'

Fixing a Broken Heart at the Highland Repair Shop III

Ally's eyes sparkled with the challenge accepted and she pushed the doors open.

Blackness, cut through with icy blue lasers and LEDs criss-crossing the ceiling high above, hit Jamie first. Music, something loud and piercing from back in the day, pulsed through him. The Prodigy, 'Firestarter'. The packed dance floor bounced with wild silhouettes of bouncing braids, arms and spilling drinks raised above heads. Jamie registered in seconds that maybe this was a *wee bit* wilder than the Edinburgh clubs he used to go to (when he was probably way too young for clubs and booze and all the rest of it).

He had to squint in the flashing lights breaking through the dark to keep eyeball on Ally as she made for the bar in strobing, juddering movements like a figure in a silent movie.

She'd hopped up onto a bar stool at the blue glass brick bar that was lit from inside to resemble blocks of sparkling ice.

'They took the ski slope theme and ran with it, then?' Jamie shouted when he reached her.

'I'm getting a cocktail,' she shouted back, not hearing him.

'Order for me as well,' he bellowed, pulling his Visa card from his shirt pocket. 'I'm not up on cocktails.' Was Ally eyeing his shirt? Approvingly, he hoped.

He'd made an effort not to dress like an off-duty cop. The phenomenon was a bit of a running joke at the Edinburgh police station where all the officers clocked off and immediately jumped into black shirts and black leather jackets as though irony wasn't a thing.

He'd gone for his softest slubby white henley, a pair of what Karolyn had advised him were 'nice' dark trousers, and his favourite French-blue chore jacket that he'd had for years but looked after really well. He'd polished his brown leather boots too, suspecting the Ptarmigan had a 'no trainers' policy. A quick glance at the heaving bodies throwing frenetic Keith Flint shapes on the dance floor told him he'd been wrong about that. He was sure he even spotted a pair of Crocs out there.

He settled himself on the stool while Ally got the attention of the bar guy. She ordered something by pointing at the menu then peace-signing that she'd like two, please.

When she was done, she fixed her attention on Jamie.

'Hope you like Irn Bru margaritas,' she shouted.

'I've no idea if I do.'

'They're deadly,' she yelled back.

'Do they make you do *that*?' he said, pointing to the dance floor, but she mustn't have understood as she leaned closer and asked if he danced.

'Course I do.'

She seemed to think for a moment, in two minds about whether she was going to dive in amongst the bodies or not. She chose to prop her elbows on the bar, accept her drink from the bartender and tell Jamie, a little sadly, 'I used to love dancing.'

Jamie paid for the drinks after a protest from Ally and some fencing with their Visa cards to see whose would make it to the card device first.

'I'll get the next round,' she yelled over the noise, slumping a little more, sipping at the thin cocktail straw.

Jamie looked at the salted rim of his luminous orange fizzy drink with its frosted lime floating on the frothy surface and accepted his fate.

It was strong and sweet. He took a second long draught, clearing half the glass.

'Woah! Anybody would think it was you who'd had been run off their feet repairing all day.' She'd shifted her stool so it was nearer to his and she could make herself heard over the new

Fixing a Broken Heart at the Highland Repair Shop 113

song the DJ was playing from the booth at the other side of the floor. Dry ice billowed around their feet.

'I'm still not over Friday when some crazy lady was making me run all across the town calling emergency meetings. I'm kind of worn out.'

'She sounds intense.' Ally's painted red lips curved into a smile as she took the thin straw between them once more. Jamie decided he'd better not stare.

'Ach, she was all right,' he said, making to nudge her arm in a chummy way, but not actually making contact. Good! Professional. Respectful. If anyone from the station happened to wander in here tonight they couldn't accuse him of anything like misconduct. This was a friendly drink, nothing more. He wasn't sure he'd made that clear when Ally opened the front door to him earlier that evening.

'Do you want to do something?' he'd stammered at her doorstep. 'With me. A drink or something. If you want to. Because I do.' He'd definitely winced, because he distinctly remembered Ally stifling a chuckle before saying 'Sure' and throwing in a casual little shrug that said she could take him or leave him. Nevertheless they'd swapped numbers and left one another with a feeling of glowing triumph at the sudden turn of events.

If only Ally hadn't turned up to meet him at the nightclub steps wearing that light cotton pinafore dress thing, with the buttons all the way down the front and the clingy, milky-coffee coloured sleeveless top underneath. Her legs were bare and she had grungy boots laced up around her ankles. *Phenomenal*, his brain had said at the sight.

He had to stop himself now from lifting a finger to touch the swinging, shimmering strand of thinnest silver that hung from her earlobe. Funny how he hadn't noticed her wearing earrings before. The silver shimmer ran down her jaw and touched her neck when she moved. He wasn't going to look at *that* either. He fixed his eyes on hers.

'Hold on, did you just say you'd had a rough day?' he said, genuinely wanting to know what it was that kept cutting her happiness short just when it bloomed in her cheeks. There seemed to be something Ally couldn't help remembering and it was bringing her down. 'Was it that guy you mentioned, the day we met?' he tried.

Her body visibly tightened, just for a moment. 'What?' she very obviously bluffed. 'Are you talking about Gray?'

'Want to tell me about him?'

He could see her swithering. 'You don't have to say anything,' he added quickly. 'Though anything you do say may be given in evidence...'

She nudged him hard on the arm, laughing.

'It's not him, no, but I *should* be arrested!' she said, just as House of Pain told everyone to jump around and a crowd surfer who'd lost a shoe was passed precariously over the dancefloor before getting consumed into its centre like a multiheaded monster eating its prey. 'For crimes against jobseekers!'

Jamie's face must have told her he had no idea what she was on about. Clearly, she had no intention of talking about her break-up.

'I had a job interview yesterday morning, and I was criminally bad. I've been having cringey flashbacks to it ever since!'

'I find that hard to believe.'

'*Hah*! They asked me about globalisation strategies and *I* talked about Pigeon Angus's tractor.'

'Uh, okay?'

'I talked at *length*, like, for an unwarranted amount of time.'

Fixing a Broken Heart at the Highland Repair Shop 115

Her voice strained over the music. 'I'm pretty sure they only interviewed me because of Murray, anyway.'

'Murray?'

'My twin brother.'

Jamie's brows lifted at this. 'You're a twin? Cool! How come I've never seen a brother round the place?'

'He's hardly ever here. He works for the charity that interviewed me. You know, sometimes I forget you're not one of the locals with their noses in everyone's business. Anyway, I felt like they were just doing him a favour.'

He laughed at the nosey thing, but there was that anxiousness in her eyes again. He wanted to fix it. 'It's OK to have someone that knows you vouching for you; it doesn't make it nepotistic.'

'You reckon? Either way, I blew it, banging on and on about nothing. They'll give it to some cool twenty-year-old, or some guy'll get it.'

'What? Just any guy?'

'You know that's how things work, right? I won't stand a chance if there's even one mediocre bloke up for the same job.'

Jamie wasn't so sure that could be true. Ally was amazing for a start. Any employer would be lucky to have her, but he daren't mansplain sexist hiring practices to a woman. Instead he asked, 'Did you really want the job?'

She held herself very still for a moment, thinking hard. 'Truth is, I *did* want it, but I only figured that out as I was watching my one opportunity slipping through my fingers in front of Barbara, Andreas and V.'

He didn't recognise any of those names. He'd remember meeting a V in Cairn Dhu. 'So, not a local job then?'

'Zurich,' she told him flatly.

There seemed to be a moment where she was searching his

face for a reaction. He couldn't help feeling some kind of test that he hadn't revised for was being sprung upon him. He fixed his face into a delighted smile.

'Awesome,' he said, even though something was constricting within him and he didn't like the feeling. The thought of Ally McIntyre leaving for Zurich should not bother him this much. '*Verry* nice,' he said, definitely overdoing it.

She swept her straw around the bottom of her glass. 'Want another?'

He quickly chugged the last of his to keep up. 'Sure.'

All the while, he knew two cocktails was probably not the best idea, but he didn't care right at that moment. Why couldn't he just have something easy and relaxed and happy for once? That's what Karolyn had texted to tell him from the road as he was getting ready earlier. She'd told him to just kick back and enjoy himself for once, underlining the words, it's allowed!

Ally paid for their drinks and they watched the barman shaking and pouring, salting and garnishing. Jamie was feeling more reckless by the minute. To hell with station protocols! Did they even apply to him as a Special Constable? And on a temporary posting at that? And was Ally *actually* involved with the jewellery robbery case any more? Even if they *said* they were keeping an eye open, his senior officers had plenty on their plates policing the illegal parking and congestion on the high street at school run times, and Pigeon Angus kept everyone on their toes with his latest firearm certificate infractions. Those jewels were long gone, and the robbers too, more than likely. Case gone cold. What was stopping him enjoying Ally's company?

'Just popping to the loo,' she was shouting, hopping from her stool as an ancient Electric Six track blasted from the sound system, shouting, 'Danger, High Voltage!' at the clubbers.

Fixing a Broken Heart at the Highland Repair Shop 117

If the song could be interpreted as a subliminal message for Jamie, he was determined not to pay it any attention. He was already resolved to make Ally happy if it was the last thing he did tonight.

'Cheers,' he told the barman as he lifted his fresh drink to his mouth. He was enjoying himself.

* * *

One breakthrough per day is more than enough for a woman, but the Highland white nights were set on educating Ally one more time. Not contented with reminding her of her strengths in leadership and community-building today, they were set on offering up a reminder of what a waste of time mourning a broken heart had been these last few weeks.

As she stepped out of the bathroom, there stood Gray. Or rather, he was leaning on a column in the corner. She recognised the lean first. It was his sexy, tell-me-all-about-yourself-you-fascinating-creature lean. There'd be some poor woman faced with that rolled shirt-sleeve and Lynx Africa doused armpit. Who was he trying to seduce this time? She let herself take a quick peek as she passed.

It had been a thunderbolt at first, seeing Laura Mercer's upturned face grinning at him. They were still seeing each other? After all her blustering and bracelet-chucking?

Ally crossed the dance floor, forcing people to part for her like a pissed-off Moses, and lifted herself back onto the stool, taking the straw between her teeth automatically.

'Are you OK?' Jamie asked.

'Uh...' she thought hard. 'Actually...' Was she OK? She mentally patted herself down, checking for injuries. Nerves? Pretty calm actually, now the surprise had worn off. Brain? *Not* running a montage of lovey-dovey moments during which Gray had looked at her in the wolfish way he was currently sizing up Laura. That's progress, she told herself. Heart? Honestly? Fine.

She lifted her drink to Jamie, feeling like she was waking up from a long sleep. 'I am OK,' she said, surprised.

He touched his glass to hers.

'In fact, I'm in better shape than I thought I was.'

He didn't understand, but he was going with it. 'Cheers. Here's to being that.'

N-Trance was now blaring from the speakers and a whole laughing, singing Highland club crowd made post-ironic big fish and little fish with their hands.

Jamie downed his drink and set the glass on the bar, wiping his mouth. Ally copied him, her chest filling with lightness.

A wicked look had passed over his face.

She cocked her head, enquiringly. 'What?'

He was moving his hands, forming little boxes. 'Oh no,' he was saying, his smile growing. Ally watched him as he rose to his feet as if under the DJs control. 'It's happening,' he said, his arms jerking harder like a nineties raver.

Ally threw her head back in a laugh and stood too, mimicking his movements, making a big cardboard box in the air in front of her.

Grinning madly, they danced to the edge of the crowd and let the lasers claim them while the clubbers sang about being set free and pointed fingers in the air, not one person caring how they looked. They were young and cocktail-fuelled and it was Saturday night, and as Ally and Jamie laughed and sang in each other's faces, both of them knew this was, more than likely, definitely a date now.

* * *

Fixing a Broken Heart at the Highland Repair Shop   119

Later, after chucking out time, when the street had cleared and the ski slope lights were switched off, Ally and Jamie sat side by side on the Ptarmigan steps, tinnitus setting in.

They'd switched to drinking water at some point but not before they'd charged their cards with enough cocktails to power a lot of high energy retro dance moves. Ally hadn't laughed so much or danced so hard in her life. Her body had absorbed every beat and was now enervated and delightfully buzzing.

'You know?' Jamie said, tipping his head towards Ally's again. 'Switzerland is kind of just an overpriced version of the Cairn-gorms, anyway.'

He'd said it out of nowhere. Had he been thinking about the possibility of her leaving? Was it playing on his mind? She observed him, his hair messy, the buttons of his Henley undone, revealing the kind of lightly corded neck Ally could imagine running her lips over. Had she shocked him with the revelation that she quite fancied a job in Europe? Had he wanted her to stay? A part of her hoped so.

'Oh, it is, is it?' She slurred a tiny bit when she said it, and they both laughed.

'Sure.' He shrugged. Was he comforting her or trying to convince her to stay? Not that there was any chance of her being offered the job, but she decided to go with this and see where it was taking them.

'What does Zurich have that Cairn Dhu doesn't, eh?' he said.

'Uh, a choice of more than one hairdresser, maybe?'

'Hey!' he complained, touching his fingertips to his recently shorn nape (which Ally *absolutely had not* thought about, wondering if it was as velvety to the touch as it looked). 'Ozan's a master with his clippers!'

'I'll give him that,' she said, snapping her eyes away from

the bristly soft areas over his ears where Ozan had indeed worked magic, 'but you can't argue we couldn't do with a proper pizza place or a takeaway,' she tried. 'Other than the chippy?'

Jamie wouldn't be bested. 'You must be forgetting the Cairn Gourmet Sandwich Van in the lay-by on the bypass.'

'Hah, OK, what about an actual clothes shop?'

'What's wrong with Kilt it! on the high street?'

She blurted a loud laugh at this. 'I'm sure it's fine if you're going to a ceilidh. What if you just want a pair of jeans?'

'There's the charity shop,' he said, triumphant. 'Anyway, that's what the trains to Inverness are for, I suppose? To whisk you away to the malls.'

'Doesn't Switzerland have the most affordable and efficient transport systems in the world?' she countered smugly. '*And* I'd bet good money on Zurich having more than one place to go out at night.'

'I'm pleasantly surprised by the Ptarmigan,' he said, glancing behind at the locked doors. 'It's the only nightclub I've even been to where entry includes a free morning's skiing, if used within six months, and,' he peered at the band on his wrist, 'one complimentary slope slushie?'

'I always get blue raspberry,' she quipped.

'You ski?'

'Not really, but I won't pass up a free slushie. I'll be in the dry slope queue at ten tomorrow to claim mine.'

He beamed back at her, making her warm all over.

'You really haven't been inside the Ptarmigan before?' she said. 'On a date, or anything, since you arrived?' she asked in quite an obvious way, but they were both a few too many margaritas deep to feel any awkwardness now.

'I've stood outside plenty, when I was on duty, helping drunk

Fixing a Broken Heart at the Highland Repair Shop   121

folk into taxis at two in the morning, but I've never gone in. No dates, or anything.'

They fixed eyes; his earnest, hers probably lit up with stars, if the way she felt was anything to go by.

'What about you?' he asked.

'Me? Me what? Are you asking about dates? God, no! Not since...' She let the sound of the milk float puttering past and a 'night, folks' from Big Kenneth in his tuxedo jacket take up the spot where Gray's name would have been. She didn't want any part of her ex interfering with this nice, easy feeling she had.

They both waved at Kenneth as he went.

'Another thing Zurich must have, that we don't have here?' she said. 'A dating scene.'

'Ah! Right! You've got me there. Unless there's a dating agency on the high street? *Mountain Mates*? *Macdates*? That one's a drive-thru.'

'Oh God, stop,' she laughed.

'*Highland Flings*?' he persisted.

'I think you like it here more than I do,' she said.

This calmed them a little.

'I can't lie; it's no' so bad. It has been an adjustment, mind, living and working here. The whole Cairngorms has a population of just eighteen thousand...'

'And Cairn Dhu probably accounts for about five hundred of those,' she interrupted.

'That's being generous. Are you counting the sheep population in that number? Naw, policing's definitely different here, with people dispersed across towns and villages and the crofts. Some of the calls that come in are from barely accessible places. God knows how you'd reach them in the snow and ice of winter.'

'That's what the mountain rangers and rescue service are for,' she said. 'Must be strange after Edinburgh.' She felt a little tug at her heart at the thought of bustling, lively Edinburgh pulling him back home again, where he belonged.

'There's about five-hundred-thousand-odd-folk to police there. You're no' kidding; it's *very* different. Not that they let me do much policing here in Cairn Dhu, mind.'

'What do you mean?' Ally wondered if it had anything to do with that snotty officer from yesterday, the one who'd been rude about Jamie at the station, telling her she was welcome to take him since he wasn't doing anything useful anyway. She remembered the other officer smirking too.

She didn't know what they had to smirk about. They were the Mason brothers: one from the year below her at school, the other from the year above; and both as daft and acned as the other, back in the day. If they thought they were any better at their jobs than Jamie, they'd better have another look at themselves.

Jamie hesitated once more, before folding like he'd held this in for too long. 'I don't like to complain, not when I'm an infiltrator at the station.'

'Infiltrator? You mean volunteer? There to help out? Lighten the load?'

'*Pfft!* You need to tell that to some of the team. One of them said I was a hobby bobby. It's OK, I'm not bothered, it's just frustrating.'

Ally watched him, fighting the urge to reach for his hand where it rested on his knee.

'Sometimes I feel a bit... undervalued,' he went on. 'I mean, Chief Inspector Edwyn's all right, when he's around. He's my supervisor, the one who'll write my recommendation when I apply to be a full officer. He teaches me stuff, shows me how the systems work, that sort of thing. He's decent like that. But some of the team don't want to make use of me.'

Fixing a Broken Heart at the Highland Repair Shop 123

'But why?'

'It's hard to explain, but being a Special, some Regulars can find it hard to trust someone they might only see coming in to volunteer two or three times a week, depending on shift patterns, and they're not all going to welcome everyone with open arms, especially an outsider from a Lowlands constabulary. I get it. They can't trust me fully. It's hard to trust outsiders when you're a cop. The ones here stick close to their own.'

'You wouldn't act like that though, would you? In their position?'

'One day I *will* be in their position, hopefully. You never know, maybe I will?'

Ally scrunched her nose. 'Naw, I can't see it. You'd include everyone.'

'You don't want some volunteer coming in and messing up a big case, though. Especially the investigating officers.'

Ally nodded. 'Like the ones looking into the jewellery robbers, you mean?'

Jamie didn't respond.

'Can't talk about it with a civilian, right?' she said, nodding in acceptance.

'I used to dream about being an investigator in Edinburgh,' he said, dodging the topic.

Ally went with it. Anything to make it easier for Jamie. 'Like something in an Ian Rankin novel?' she said, smiling.

'Aye! That'll be me.' He mimed turning up a shirt collar and lowered his chin, scowling.

'Is that your John Rebus face?'

'Like it?' He broke into a smile again.

'You've got the job!' Ally said, and in their laughter it felt like a good idea to stick out her hand for him to shake.

'Cheers very much,' he said, shaking hers, his cheeks pinker than before.

It took a second for either of them to realise they were still clasping hands. Ally's eyes fell to where he held her.

Decidedly, he didn't let go. A squeeze of his fingers told her he wanted to stay linked like this. When she looked at him again, he asked, 'This OK?'

A nod from her, a smile, possibly slightly dazed, and Ally relaxed her arm, letting him hold her hand, her wrist resting over his knee.

'Back there,' Jamie cleared his throat, gesturing with his head towards the club. 'Was that guy your ex, by any chance?'

Ally drew her neck back. 'You saw?'

'I'm good at observing things, kind of goes with the badge and radio.'

'Got it.' They were still holding hands. His thumb rubbed in ticklish circles over the soft root of her thumb. Electricity seemed to spark there and it made it hard to think straight. 'It, uh, it was my ex, yeah. With his girlfriend.'

'Ah. Sorry about that.' He seemed to think about this for a moment. 'I mean, I'm not *super* sorry that he's out of the picture, but I'm sorry if it hurt.'

Why was he able to make her feel nineteen and giddy like this? And where did he get his confidence? He just said what he meant. It was lovely.

'Actually,' she said, shifting her body to face him better, their eyes locking. 'I wasn't hurt at all.' She stroked her thumbnail around the inside of his curled palm, hoping it sent Jamie into a dizzy butterfly-filled state too. 'I thought I would be sad if I bumped into him, but actually I was happy.' His pupils pinpointed down to tiny dots. She was doing that to him.

Fixing a Broken Heart at the Highland Repair Shop   125

'You were?' His voice was breathy. His eyes sank to her lips. He swallowed.

'I think I thought he was as good as it was ever going to get for me.'

His eyes were back on hers. 'God no, you deserve the best of everything.'

'I'm coming to agree with you,' she said, her lips curling, showing the tips of her teeth. It was enough to weaken him completely and, seeing the way his eyes swooned shut, her whole body answered his and she leaned in, almost closing the space between their mouths.

In the danger zone before their lips touched, she asked if this was OK? And before he could finish telling her it was more than OK, they were together. It wasn't gentle or tentative, but a needy, urgent kiss that turned Ally's brain blank.

Something breathy escaped Jamie's lips, halfway between a sigh and a moan. Lips warm, palms now gripping shoulders and arms, drawing each other nearer. She was probably supposed to break away at some point, act cool and demure, lower her eyes, blush or something, but that would have taken more strength than she had, so she kissed him deeper, on and on, as the constellations crept across the sky getting slowly consumed by the horizon.

After untold breathless minutes, Jamie laughed lightly against her mouth, but didn't pull away. 'I can't stop,' he told her, before trailing his parted lips devastatingly slowly over hers from one corner of her mouth to the other, slowing the whole world right down to just this one sensation.

Blankness, goodness, everything perfect in its rightness.

Jamie must have asked if he could kiss her neck, because she'd definitely said yes to some whispered thing and his lips were pressing all along her cheekbone, then pinching around her ear. Ally's core softened meltingly.

When he paused, holding his mouth by her earlobe, his breath upon her, the sound of him setting off sparks in every neural and nervous pathway within her, her breath hitched, waiting.

When at last he pulled her lobe between his lips, consuming the spot where the metal bar and butterfly of her earring penetrated her flesh, her inner muscles glowed hot with wanting. This guy knew exactly what he was doing, and it didn't feel like it was from practice, but from instinct, because together their chemicals were combining and reacting in the best way possible.

If this kiss was an experiment to see if Ally could really like this guy, all her findings so far pointed towards its success. As he kissed into her neck, hard then softer, alternating the pressure, shifting between sucks and soft pillowed kisses, she let herself lean into him, her eyes opening drowsily.

They were making out like teens on the steps of a nightclub while the sleepers dreamed in their beds. She should go home. Soon, the birds would begin their morning song. But as Jamie brought his lips to the soft dip under her jaw, nothing was going to pierce the bubble forming around them.

Except, Ally's eyes caught movement in the distance. She blinked softly, letting it come into focus. A figure, alone, wrapped in a long coat, arms folded. Jamie drew his lips to the soft pulse of her temple. She could barely see straight, let alone think, but something troubling made its way to her as the woman approached. She was wearing high-heeled boots but had the heels lifted off the pavement, silencing her steps. The woman hadn't spotted them yet.

Ally tapped both hands at Jamie's shoulders, waking him

Fixing a Broken Heart at the Highland Repair Shop 127

from the kiss too. She cleared her throat, finding she had no voice, just a croak.

'Someone coming?' Jamie said, dopily, turning his head, his eyes heavy-lidded.

They watched as the woman turned down a passageway between the low-rise blocks of seventies flats set amongst the birch trees, lawns and scattered wheelie bins on the other side of the road. The woman had a black eye.

Ally peered harder before she disappeared from their sight. 'That was her!' she hissed.

Jamie was alert again too, rubbing his fingers over his eyelids. 'Who?'

'That was her, the woman who brought the stolen jewellery in!'

Jamie sprang to his feet. 'You're sure?'

'Sure I'm sure. Same coat, straggly blonde hair, everything.'

'Stay here.' He stepped off the pavement, crossing the road in her direction.

'What are you doing?' she hissed back, but he didn't hear. He was skirting after her, just as quietly as she'd been moving through the dewy dawn light.

Ally sat, just like he'd told her. Hugging her knees, she was suddenly cold. Torn between alarm that Jamie was possibly on his way to apprehend a suspect all by himself, and her sneaking amusement and delight that they'd kissed until morning. A shudder rippled through her as her body remembered the sensations.

Absolute silence descended. She pulled out her phone. No messages, no missed calls, nothing since she'd texted her parents at half eleven to say she'd be staying out late, she was still with Jamie. A thumbs up from her mum with a reply of 'have fun, stay safe' sent in acknowledgement that she was the cool one of the parenting pair, or she was at least trying to be.

Ally's thumb hovered over the keypad.

Should she ring the station? There was no sign of him coming back. He'd told her to stay here, but should she have followed?

Then footsteps, and she dropped her shoulders in relief. He was running back over the street towards her.

'I lost her. She disappeared somewhere among the flats,' he was saying, already unlocking his phone screen. 'You OK?' he checked, before he dialled and held the phone to his ear.

'I'm fine. Did you notice she had a black eye?'

He nodded, eyes widening. 'I did.' The call went through. 'Hello? It's Special Constable Beaton reporting potentially suspicious activity in the Ptarmigan flats area of town.'

Silence as he listened to his colleague down the line. Ally watched him stifle an eyeroll at something he'd heard, but he pressed on. 'A woman, white, mid-forties maybe, long coat with fur collar and trim...'

'My mum called it an Afghan coat,' Ally told him, wanting to be helpful.

'An Afghan coat. One black eye. Out alone and passing between blocks one and two, possibly going inside one of the buildings. That's where I lost her. Positively ID'd as the suspect handling stolen jewellery in the repair shop case.'

More silence. Jamie shifted his weight from foot to foot, holding a hand to his brow, growing agitated.

'The ID was from Allyson McIntyre,' he said, having been prompted. 'We were outside the Ptarmigan...' He was interrupted. 'About five minutes ago.'

Something that sounded like tinny, crow-like laughter came over the speaker. Even Ally heard it from a few feet away. Jamie

brought the phone back to his ear. 'Are you sending a team...'
Again, he was interrupted. He listened, his face falling. 'Right. I
won't. Yes. I said I won't.' He let his hand fall to his side as
whoever it was hung up the call. 'Shit.'

'What is it?' Ally staggered to her feet, not sure if she should
put a hand to his arm to calm him. They'd kissed, but what were
they now?

'That was Robert Mason. He called me "Taggart" and told
me to leave the stakeouts to the big boys.'

'Uh? So, they're not coming to search for her?'

Jamie's face told her everything she needed to know.

'Come on. Walk you home?' he said, turning, hands stuffed
back in his pockets.

Ally could do nothing but follow him.

Pink bands of morning light, blushing at the memory of the
night before, streaked the navy blue horizon as the pair made
their way silently through the slowly waking town.

'Who's Taggart?' Ally asked.

It was enough to make Jamie, who'd been lost in his rumina-
tions, break into a wry smile. 'No idea,' he said, jutting out his
elbow, hand still in his pocket, and she gripped on to him as he
saw her to her door in the cool of the Sunday sunrise.

13

Ally slept for a long time and woke up desperate to tell someone what had happened the night before.

Murray was in Mali, possibly. Would he even be reachable? No one in the family had heard a peep from him since he notified Ally about her interview appointment. Worth trying a text at least, she thought.

> Murray. I don't know if you're overseas and not getting messages. I haven't had any from you either, by the way, in case you've been trying to reach me. I just wanted to tell you about things here. Nothing big, just stuff. So don't worry or anything. Travel safe, A x

Still under her covers, she read her message over, thinking how juvenile it sounded. Her brother was off working on some huge charity project and she wanted to squeal at him about a kiss?

She deleted it. Not something she'd have done even a couple of years ago when she'd have sent it and waited for him to ring and demand every last torrid detail before imparting some of his dating wisdom upon her.

She didn't like to think what not telling him about Jamie meant for her and her twin these days, but the sneaking worry they too had grown apart while she'd stayed still in Cairn Dhu played at the back of her mind as she typed a new message.

> I know you won't get this for a while, but I'm thinking about you. We're all fine. Have fun in Mali! Miss you. A x

She let the message fly from her phone, and turned to wondering what Jamie was doing. They should have made plans for dinner or something when they were at her door this morning as he'd seen her safely inside the sleeping mill house. They hadn't kissed again on the step, which she wasn't going to read anything into. He'd been upset about things at work. It was understandable. So she'd wait, and listen for the doorbell. There was no way he'd stay away now. Not now it was clear they had this special connection.

The weather changes quickly in the Cairngorms. One minute you can be buying an ice lolly in your shorts and sandals, the next you can be ankle deep in a flash deluge with rainwater running in a river down the main road. Some days, you can start a hike sweating in seventy degree heat and come back down the mountain to frost on the foothills. Locals are used to these drastic shifts, having lived with them all their lives, but outsiders can be caught unawares in these extremes. Last night had been mild and balmy; today a storm was brewing. Jamie Beaton, however, was about to be taken by surprise by more than fluctuations in the temperature this morning.

Chief Inspector Edwyn's office at the back of the station was austere and unpleasantly lit with garish strip lights. His certificates and awards hung framed on the white emulsioned walls alongside a picture of him surrounded by his wife and kids from long ago. He was the very image of the upstanding copper Jamie wanted to become.

Edwyn was on his feet, pacing, while Jamie sat in front of the desk. Not a good start, whatever way you look at it.

'You pursued a suspect alone, having spent the evening drinking in the Ptarmigan?' he asked in a serious tone.

This was a side of Edwyn Jamie hadn't had directed towards him before. The angry side.

'Well, yes, sir, but I'd sobered up by then.'

Had he really? The way he remembered it was pretty hazy, but that had less to do with the alcohol still in his system and more to do with what it had felt like kissing Ally McIntyre.

It came back to him now. The faintest memory of the soft scratches of her short fingernails as she caressed his neck, both her hands at his throat, her fingertips moving over the shorn areas of his short back and sides like she'd loved the feel of him there. She'd done it a few times, each time letting her fingers tangle in the longer hair at his crown, her touch setting off dizzy sensations. He'd ran his hands along her arms until he could hold her hands in place back there, their fingers lacing in his hair...

'You were with young Allyson McIntyre, am I right?'

'Yes, sir.' He snapped out of the memory. Was he really in trouble over this?

'A key witness in a robbery investigation.'

Yep, he was in trouble.

Fixing a Broken Heart at the Highland Repair Shop   133

'That's correct, sir. It was her who made the ID, positively linking the woman...'

'Special Constable Beaton. An off duty, voluntary officer cannot and should not follow any suspect on foot, especially while under the influence of alcohol.'

Jamie lowered his head. 'Is it only the drinking that's the problem, sir?'

Edwyn's jaw jutted. 'What do you mean?'

'Was I wrong to be out with one of the McIntyres, sir?'

Edwyn searched for an answer, grumbling as he thought. 'Well, there's no especial rule against socialising with members of your own community, of course.'

'But dating someone?'

'Normally, this wouldn't be a problem.' Edwyn must have seen it on his face, the hope. 'Except in this case, Allyson is, as you yourself acknowledge, an identifying witness.'

'Right.' Jamie's shoulders dropped. He tried to sit straight again but couldn't quite draw himself up.

'*Discretion* has always been an important quality in a trainee officer,' Edwyn began, a touch of sympathy and condescension in his voice.

'Yes, sir.' Where was this going? Was he saying it was OK to see Ally if he was discreet about it? How exactly would that work? Sneaking about? Keeping it secret?

'That's all,' said Edwyn.

'Oh.' How could that be all? Where was the advice? The dating line drawn to help Jamie maintain the Thin Blue Line of authority and respectability?

'Dismissed.'

He was on his feet. 'Yes, sir.' With more questions than answers, Jamie made for the door. 'Sir?' He turned. 'We'll search for that woman with the black eye?'

'You won't,' Edwyn answered. 'The Mason brothers are abreast of the latest intel. Let's leave it in their capable hands.' Edwyn's mouth drew into a thin smile before he sat down at his computer to get on with his important work.

Crestfallen, Jamie left the room and made his way into the office area where Andrew was busy working on a screen. They didn't acknowledge his arrival so he sat at the empty desk and waited to be assigned a job to do, thinking long and hard how, with one kiss, a few drinks and an ill-considered foot chase, he may well have blown the good opinion of Edwyn and the entire application process to become a regular officer.

14

While the gale raged on all the next day, bringing chilly, whipping rain in from the east, everyone in Cairn Dhu stayed close to home. The shops didn't open and the buses didn't run. A few phone and power lines were brought down by toppling ancient trees. Nobody dared set foot on the mountains. Chimney smoke from the remotest crofters' cottages spread sparsely across the range where it was whipped up and away in the winds. The birds hid in the hedgerows and heathers. Everywhere fell quiet except for the heavy gusts beating at the windows.

Jamie hadn't called Ally. Her brother hadn't replied to her text. Her friends hadn't acknowledged any of her comments on their socials from days ago. Her mum and dad were watching TV, cuddled up on the sofa, enjoying the chance to stop and relax. Ally's work systems were down, so she couldn't even do her day job. Everyone seemed to have somewhere to shelter and something to do, except for her.

The hiatus of the gales gave Ally time to think. One thing she wasn't going to do was slip back into her dark mood of late spring. She'd come too far for that and, yes, having an incredible time with Jamie was *partly* responsible for the great big boost of confidence and adrenalin she'd been surfing, but she had also gone a long way towards turning a corner on her own too.

Seeing Gray and Laura had helped. She'd faced the moment she'd dreaded since the break-up and, to her surprise, upon seeing him there in the club, gangly and oblivious, being dumped by Gray hadn't felt like a huge loss, a thorn in her heart, or even a devastating betrayal, any more. He'd looked, well, kind of grey. The hold he'd had on her was gone, those big desperate feelings she'd nurtured for him sapped of all their strength and colour.

Laura was welcome to him: welcome to his long monologues about his work, his bland taste in practically everything from food to fashion. She was welcome to his shifty ways. Ally tried and failed to remember one interesting thing she'd ever heard come from his mouth. She must have been in a bad place, wanting to tie herself to someone like that for life.

Sure, spending time with Jamie might well have helped her reach this realisation quicker (the contrast between the two men could not be starker), but the curious little buoyant feeling within her was her own doing.

She'd achieved so much recently. She'd successfully brought the locals round in their attitudes to the repair shop – and if she could convince snooty Carenza to allow her precious baby, Peaches, to return to the repair den of iniquity, she could convince *herself* she wasn't completely without talents.

Plus, she'd helped the Beaton family take a big first step towards healing their unspoken grief when she'd re-united Jamie, his dad and sister with Holiday, and by extension, their beloved mum.

That feeling of having made a difference through making a

Fixing a Broken Heart at the Highland Repair Shop   137

repair was increasingly deeply rewarding; not something she'd really understood until she saw it for herself written on Jamie's face.

If she could do these things, she could do more. She could build on these feelings.

As the storm buffeted the Cairngorms that wild and moody Monday in July, Ally took action, directly messaging her three closest friends from back in the day, asking if they fancied a catch-up, saying she was sorry she'd been out of touch lately, she'd got a bit stuck in a rut. She'd love to see them and meet their kids properly.

It was risky. They could reply *where the hell have you been?* and tell her to get knotted. They could be indignant at her lack of interest in their lives recently. There was also a chance they might simply ignore her, too busy to meet up with a singleton friend from the past with whom they had nothing in common now they'd moved on, leaving her behind.

Sure, she knew she also had feelings she needed to put aside; self-pity at having been forgotten, at not being enough for them now they had families and she didn't.

If she valued their old friendship, however, which she was sure she still did, she thought she could bridge the distance that had kept them apart, or at least she could try.

It had taken all of sixty seconds for the replies to start coming in.

BRODIE

> Oh my god Ally!!! We've been meaning to get in touch. Can't believe we haven't seen you since the wedding! Hold on I'm adding you to the group chat.

A notification appeared and Ally accepted the invite.

JO

Ally! How are you??

ALLY

I'm good! Are you all OK? I've missed you guys.

JO

We've missed you too. I'm tagging @MhairiSears so she gets the notification. She needs to see this.

BRODIE

She's in this group but ghosts us lol

JO

She's super busy with Jolyon.

Jolyon was the only one of the friend group's kids she'd actually met beyond naming parties and Christenings back when they were wee woolly bundles in their parents' arms. He'd been the first baby born in the gang, just before lockdown.

Ally had met up with Mhairi and her husband, their Jack Russell, and little Jolyon in his pushchair for fresh air walks when restrictions first lifted. She'd held the little guy in her arms and smelled his new baby loveliness. When restrictions tightened suddenly and everyone was confined to their houses yet again, she'd sent him presents and FaceTimed with his mum. Jolyon was the only kid she'd ever held or got to know in any real way. He was gorgeous, never cried, barely made a sound, in fact, and was always contented. The perfect baby.

Somewhere around about Jolyon's third birthday Mhairi had grown distant in her DMs. Ally could have made more effort, she knew, but she'd taken it as the sign it was, that Mhairi was happy with her new mummy friends, the pre-school crowd. Too busy for Ally.

Fixing a Broken Heart at the Highland Repair Shop

BRODIE

We should meet up!

ALLY

We definitely should.

They'd said the same thing in their Christmas texts when the whole Covid nightmare was coming to an end. They'd repeated it when she'd bumped into Jo that time in the big Tesco, but it hadn't happened. It was just one of those things old friends say.

JO

How about a Friday? 18th July?

Ally's heart jumped. The happiness surprised her, even though reaching out had been her idea in the first place.

BRODIE

I can actually do the 18th!

Maybe for once they'd pull it off and get together? This felt good.

ALLY

Fine with me. Where? At the Ptarmigan? Like old times?

Ally wasn't absolutely sure she wanted to go back there any time soon, however. It would fall short, compared to Saturday, no matter how good it was.

BRODIE

Lol, nope. I was thinking morning coffee? Gillie's in playgroup from 10-3. I can drive over to Cairn Dhu, park at Luce's mum's. @MhairiSears can you do the Friday? We haven't seen you in like 2 years!!

ALLY

You guys haven't met up either?

That was a revelation. She'd thought they'd been wrapped up in a mummy bubble together.

JO

It's been way too long since I saw any of yous!

And so the chat went on, drilling down to the finer details of the women's availability. Ally would be working until one o'clock that Friday so could only meet after then. Jo had one hour between a paediatrics appointment with her eldest, Alfie, and something called a 'Keep in Touch' afternoon at her office near Aberdeen. She was nearing the end of her maternity leave for her second baby. She thought she might be able to drop the kids at her mum's so she could arrive child free and 'actually drink her coffee hot for once!' Brodie would be bringing little Gillian along unless her wife happened to be working from home that day, meaning she might be able to 'sneak out on her own!' too.

It had been eye-opening as to how fiddly the logistics were just to get out for an hour. Their plans now hung on Mhairi answering and being able to come to meet at the Cairn Dhu Hotel bar at precisely one fifteen on Friday the eighteenth.

They'd left the chat open for her reply, signing off with kisses and, once Ally had taken a shower, she'd come back to see Brodie and Jo had shared comedy Gifs of harried mums speed-

Fixing a Broken Heart at the Highland Repair Shop   141

drinking espressos which she thought had to be a good sign that they were looking forward to this meet up. Not finding the Gif thing all that amusing (it must be a bit sad, mustn't it, rushing everything all the time?) she nevertheless responded with a laugh-crying emoji, her heart bouncing with excitement that yet again her proactiveness was paying off.

This felt good, and in direct contrast to the dark skies outside. The howling winds blew on while Ally rubbed her hands together over her laptop. If she could orchestrate a friends' reunion after absolutely ages, and in no time at all, what more could she do?

She'd opened a new document and had begun typing 'Repair Shed Community Event Ideas?' at the top of the page when the doorbell rang.

* * *

Jamie had been as taken aback by the increasingly high winds sweeping through the wide Cairn Dhu valley as he'd been by the crushed feeling within him.

He'd been on a high after the breakthrough with his dad and all the incredible emotions the reunion with post-makeover Holiday had brought about for him and his family. Added to that, his night out with Ally had made him feel like he was soaring, but now here he was having been (albeit informally) reprimanded and having lost a lead on a suspect, making his way through the tempest to Ally's door, his head and heart in the very eye of another kind of storm.

She answered the door out of breath, like she'd sprinted to answer it. She still seemed full of excitement, which made this all the worse, knowing what he was about to do.

'Oh no, what?' Her face fell from a picture of expectant joy to worry, like she'd suspected a hitch was coming, just not this soon.

Once inside, standing in the kitchen, it hadn't taken long to explain how, for now, perhaps it was for the best if they tried to keep things strictly friendly since, morally, he was hanging on a shoogly peg (which is the Scottish version of skating on thin ice, only much, much more fun to say, usually). He risked compromising the investigation for his colleagues if he kept seeing her while she was technically still a witness. Even if Edwyn hadn't come down hard upon him, he'd got the message that what they'd done at the Ptarmigan was definitely frowned upon.

Ally protested how she knew fine well the Mason lads had dated girls whose brothers and uncles and fathers had run-ins with the police. 'They were putting it about all over town and *they* didn't get into trouble at the Station.'

'That you know of,' he'd replied. 'Maybe it's different if you're full time, and a local,' conceded Jamie. 'Whatever the rules are, I don't think we should do it again.'

Ally seemed to be keeping an ear open for her parents listening in over the TV game show from the living room before she spoke, lowering her voice to clarify, 'What shouldn't we do again? Run after criminals? Or kiss each other?' There was still something playful in her eyes, an inner light he hadn't yet extinguished.

She'd stepped closer as she said it. Too close. Jamie inhaled the wave of her freshly washed hair and her body lotion and it kickstarted something running low in his belly like an engine and he'd had to hold his arms to his sides like he'd done in the Reserves during a 'turnout' inspection, or else he'd have grabbed her there and then, pulling her close.

Her lips looked softly pink and plump, somehow even more

Fixing a Broken Heart at the Highland Repair Shop 143

inviting than when they'd been unable to stop themselves on the steps of the club.

The wind whistled down the old mill house's kitchen chimney and rattled the front door behind him. He had to get out of here or he'd fold like laundry. 'I can't...' he began, drowsy with wanting her. 'You understand what a gossiping place Cairn Dhu is. Word spreads so easily. Carenza McDowell managed to convince the town the repair shop was a hotbed for criminal activity in the space of a few days!'

'Well, her plus a news programme *and* the same news article re-posted everywhere online,' Ally countered.

Jamie persisted. He'd come here to make his point and he wasn't going to fail now. 'If we were spotted like this, even just talking as friends, it could be... misinterpreted.'

Ally stepped back. 'I'm sorry,' she said, shaking her head, looking annoyed with herself. 'I don't want anything getting misinterpreted.' Her voice had a tiny spike of bitterness in it, but it was soon quashed with the sympathy she seemed to have running through her. 'Look,' she sighed, 'the last thing I want is to ruin things for you, with your application and everything, of course I don't.'

She'd stared hard at him, eyes moving over his face. She was trying to act cool but it was clear she was steeling herself for what was, basically, goodbye.

She gave a forced smile, and there came an awkward moment where she reached for the latch to send him on his way, and for a split second he thought she was reaching for him, and he'd been about to say 'screw it' and risk it all for another hard kiss, but, caring woman that she was, not wanting to ruin his chances at becoming a full police officer, she hauled the door open, struggling with its weight against the wind.

She let him turn and walk out.

'I'll be seeing you around,' he tried, and the weak words were caught in the wind and carried away.

'Okay... bye.' She slowly closed the door on him, still smiling thinly like a consolation prize winner.

From the other side he heard the latch clunk into place.

For a short while he just stood there, staring at the barrier between them, fighting the urge to knock again, before resolutely tugging up the zip on his jacket.

'Shit.' He let his head hang. 'Shit.'

Hunching in the raging air, he trudged slowly back to his empty flat.

15

She'd hit snooze on her alarm three times already, except now her phone was making a different sort of sound. With a horrible jolt of realisation it dawned on her there was a persistent video caller waiting for her to answer. Upon peering closer at the screen through crusted eyes, she recognised the name Andreas Favre. The guy from Future Proof Planet was calling her out of the blue! Like the capable, confident, *can-do* grown-up she'd pretended to be at the interview, and even though she was only in a hoodie over her Scottie-dog pyjamas, she clicked 'accept call' before the cortisol hit any harder and she chickened out.

Andreas appeared, beautiful and sleekly blond, looking like some tanned tennis pro or someone in a toothpaste advert. He was in front of a vast window with a magnificent Alpine vista behind him. How did he get any work done with a distraction like that?

'Andreas? Hi!' Possibly a bit informal? She wasn't sure what tone to go for.

'I apologise for calling you without emailing first,' he said in his lovely French accent. He wasn't quite as composed as he'd been at the interview, she noticed. 'I am happy to tell you, you are proceeding to the second round of interviews for the role of Blue Sky Thinking Tech.'

'I... I am?' She couldn't help showing her amazement.

'Yes, of course. You impressed us with your passion. The way you spoke about community and hope aligned closely with our values here at Future Proof.'

'Really? I'm...' she was going to say she was astonished but bit it down. 'That's great news. Thank you.'

He was all business now. 'You need to drill down to practical matters in this round. You are required to present a real-world community project scenario.' Ally scrabbled for a pen and paper, making a show of efficiently taking notes, nodding, agreeing; all the while, barely registering what was required of her. 'It can be any project you wish, but one you have been practically involved with, or one you'd like to roll out in the future. Outline the real-world steps you would use to bring the project together, showing how you use technology as a means to your project's end. I'll have V email the full instructions over in a minute.'

'It can be anything at all?' said Ally, her brain racing.

'Anything. One word of advice? No tractor talk.'

She smiled in response to the sweet quirk of his lips at this. Stuffy, chic Andreas was capable of having fun after all.

'HR will email a choice of interview dates.'

'Got it.'

So Future Proof Planet actually wanted to see her again? Her. Ally McIntyre, the one-time recluse, working from home, pyjama-dweller with the chip on her shoulder.

'And, uh, Ally, I wondered...' Andreas was faltering. She wasn't sure what to make of the change in him. He cleared his

Fixing a Broken Heart at the Highland Repair Shop 147

throat. A finger loosened his white collar as though it was suddenly tight. 'We were wondering how your brother was doing?'

'Murray? Uh, he's fine, I guess.'

'Only, he left so suddenly.'

Ally blinked.

'Did he get home safely?' Andreas pressed, his smile thinning.

'Home? I haven't heard from him since he went on the Mali trip.'

'Mali?' He looked a little sickly.

'You're frightening me, Andreas. Are you saying he's not in Mali, and he's not in Switzerland? When do you think he left to come back to Scotland?'

'Murray left home... I mean, he left a charity event late on Friday after... a heated discussion. He, uh, took an unauthorised leave of absence, I believe. I assumed he'd taken a car to the airport that evening, going back to Scotland?'

'You're saying nobody's seen him for days? Sorry, Andreas, I should get off this call and ring him. I have literally no idea what you're on about. He definitely didn't come back here. He'd only just *been* in Scotland!'

'Please...' Andreas leaned closer to the screen. 'It will be for the best if you don't mention to anyone that you and I discussed your brother's absence...' he scrambled for words, '...for privacy law reasons?'

'*Hmm.*' Ally knew when something was off. Was Andreas calling back all second-round interviewees, or had he wanted an excuse to ring her and ask about Murray? 'I'd better go,' she told him. 'Thanks for letting me know about the presentation.'

'No problem. If you hear from Murray,' he added urgently,

'perhaps you'll be good enough to let me know? No need to mention it to anyone else in the office, or at the interview.'

Ally nodded her agreement, newly cautious about this guy's motivations and wondering whether he had more to do with Murray's absence than perhaps a mere collegial relationship gone awry?

She left the call and immediately rang her brother, getting directed straight to his voicemail.

She wasn't going to panic, yet. He'd be fine. He always was. He'd said he had some annual leave to use up, didn't he? Knowing her brother, he'd be taking some time out on a bougie beach. Maybe he hadn't been selected for the Mali trip and was sulking? But disappearing without permission? From the job, the travel opportunities, the apartment, the gym, and all those other company benefits and glamorous perks? He'd have to be mad. That, or something really bad had happened.

'Call me back as soon as you get this,' she told his voicemail.

No, she wouldn't panic yet.

It's not like he hadn't gone to ground before. There was that time in college when he pretended his heart wasn't broken over a dreamy pop-idol-looking guy who worked behind the campus sandwich bar. The guy who'd been the reason he came out at a particularly memorable Sunday lunch at home, during which he'd barely said a word, building up to it, while everyone except him devoured their mum's celebrated mushroom wellington. As the chocolate gateau was being dished up, he'd at last blurted it out, surprising precisely no one.

He'd been greeted with hugs and gentle words by his mum and dad, and a proud smile from Ally who'd known all about what he'd planned that day.

He'd done it, not because he felt he had to, but because he wanted to tell the people who mattered most about Wulf. That

Fixing a Broken Heart at the Highland Repair Shop **149**

was his name. Sweet, blond Wulf, who made a mean prawn Marie Rose with iceberg on buttered granary.

There'd been a brief period of elation, in which Wulf had come over to meet the parents, but then it sort of fizzled out, inexplicably as far as Ally could see, for no other reason than they were both twenty-one. Ally never got the full details, other than, for her brother, it had been love.

That had been the beginning of Murray hiding out at random mates' flats, doing nobody knew what, not coming home to Cairn Dhu for weeks at a time. He'd never forgotten to message Ally every now and then, though, to let her know he was OK and to catch up with her news.

After they graduated, he'd hopped straight up the career ladder, his long absences becoming a way of life for the twins, both of them remaining connected to one another like a planet to its moon, always knowing where the other was, reassured by the cellular-level gravitational pull that meant a part of them remained at all times aware of the other's location, two satellites transmitting data, sending out tiny blips into the cosmos for each other.

Thinking again, her concern deepening, Ally messaged him.

> If you don't send me some sign you're OK soon, I'm telling Mum and Dad you've gone AWOL and you KNOW they'll go full mountain rescue search dogs and spotlights on you.

> Speak to me. Or else I'll seriously start to worry.

She watched the message go. The word 'delivered' floating beneath it, and then just as she predicted, the little tick that showed he'd read it. He was alive. A blue thumbs up appeared as further proof of life. That's something. She watched the screen, waiting for the text bubbles that said he was replying. None came.

She'd have to be smarter to draw him out. Then, thinking even more, she typed again.

She baited the trap with something irresistible, something he surely couldn't help biting.

> Andreas is worried too.

16

The station had been oddly quiet. There's nothing like howling gales and a whole mountain range shutting down to wipe out petty crime.

Chastened ever since Edwyn's words of warning and following a few more days' 'banter' from the Mason brothers, during which they called him the name of every TV detective they could think of, Jamie got on with his work.

'Get the kettle on, Miss Marple. Milk and sugar in mine, cheers,' Robert had quipped.

'One more thing, Columbo,' Andrew said. 'Printer's out of paper.'

When Jamie had accepted he definitely wasn't going to be sent out on anything interesting, at least while the town emerged from the aftermath of the storm, he'd settled down to filling in his application pack for the next intake of full officers in Edinburgh.

The eldest Mason brother had seen him absorbed in typing and quipped, 'Hey up, *Murder, She Wrote*, sticking to paperwork, are we, instead of apprehending suspects when under the influence?'

He'd accepted their comments with the good-natured demeanour he hoped they were being said with, trying not to mind them too much. It was all part of the job for him now and it sharpened his resolve to be recruited into the force full time and on full pay.

Sometimes, as he was documenting his experiences as a volunteer on the application form, giving reason after reason why he fit the bill as a member of the Old Bill, he'd found himself distracted by the windows rattling, the rain running down the pane, and it would set off something wistful within him, and in spite of himself, he'd remember Ally leading him through the long grass to the Nithy Brig. He pictured her red hair against the emerald glow of the aurora night sky. He'd see her sitting on that ledge over the waterwheel, framed in old stone, staring up at the stars and how he'd got so distracted gazing up at her he'd walked straight into that barbed wire.

If he really let himself slip, he'd replay the way they'd kissed, hearing all over again her breath at his ear and the sounds he'd coaxed from her, delicious gasps and sighs. Just thinking of them sent shudders bolting down his spine, each time waking him from daydreaming, and the screen would come back into view. He'd return to completing the form, a little more reluctantly with every involuntary excursion into those deeply imprinted memories of Ally, hitting the keys with a dogged determination to control himself. This application had to be perfect. He had to get out of here, far away from temptation, and soon.

* * *

Fixing a Broken Heart at the Highland Repair Shop   153

Days later, and Jamie's flat could not have been neater. His clothes were folded. He'd scrubbed the kitchen and the bathroom. His bedsheets were tightly tucked like he was back at cadet camp. He'd grocery shopped, worked out and hydrated. Still, he couldn't get his mind off her.

He'd stumbled across the repair shop and café's new TikTok account. If 'stumbling across' means deliberately going in search of any para-social way he might get a glimpse of what Ally was up to – just to check she was happy and not too hurt by the way he'd led her on then dropped her like a stone as soon as his job was at stake.

What he'd found were a series of extremely well edited and distinctly quirky videos about the repair life, made by Willie and Peaches. Any one of them could be used in a multimedia student portfolio. In one, he caught the briefest sighting of Ally at her workstation while Peaches showed the shop's followers how to embroider a kitten face over a hole in a jumper to hide it.

'Good as new,' the text onscreen said. Behind it, Ally was hunched and focused on fixing a fault in someone's robot vacuum, the glimpse too short to gauge her general mood.

It was the uncertainly of it all that was getting to him, that and the simple fact he missed her. She'd been in earnest when she'd told him she wouldn't dream of doing anything to endanger his application. She hadn't so much as sent him one message. She was as good as her word and nothing but respectful. Somehow that made this all the more agonising.

Edwyn hadn't exactly tapped the side of his nose that day he'd delivered his warning to Jamie. There'd been no *wink, wink, if you catch my drift* about his attitude to Special Constables fraternising with local women involved in unsolved cases. Jamie had left that office knowing Edwyn was leaving it up to him and his sense of discretion whether or not he continued to see Ally.

If it had been more clear-cut, he might know better how to conduct himself. Maybe then he could meet her for a friendly cup of coffee and he wouldn't be missing her like this? Though it troubled him that if he were seen to be being indiscreet or reckless one more time, it could be the thing standing between him and a career in the police.

He'd done the right thing cutting contact with Ally, hadn't he? It wasn't mere selfishness, on his part, right? He knew for sure that he didn't want to lead her on and get close with her the way he desired, only to find out he was being sent away in disgrace. That'd hurt both of them, and it'd break him, for sure.

Ally couldn't possibly feel as deeply as he felt for her. That'd be crazy. If he'd been surer of her feelings, if they'd had more time to explore them together, maybe then he'd have been able to tell Edwyn it really wasn't any of his business and that his intentions for Ally McIntyre were nothing but right and proper, even if they were mixed up with wanting her hard in his arms and soft against his lips as well... No, he'd done the best thing for everyone concerned. He'd caught it before it got out of hand.

That didn't stop his brain cycling back through this conundrum time and again, replaying his cowardly words with Ally, the way he'd tried to let her down gently. He hated himself for it.

It had been enough to have him filling a water bottle, jumping into his running shoes and dashing out into the ten o'clock twilight, dodging the puddles and slowly rolling cars. He wasn't much of a runner, but he'd read somewhere that pounding feet on a pavement in a steady rhythm could recalibrate the entire nervous system. It was worth a try.

As his running shoes carried him out of Cairn Dhu and onto the long stretch of pavement that ran alongside the main road, past the shut-up sandwich van in the lay-by and out to where the valley widened, he concentrated on the sensation of

Fixing a Broken Heart at the Highland Repair Shop 155

pounding the tarmac, the jolting impact, the good hard thump of his rubber soles.

It was good. It was working. His heart pounded too. Chemicals released all through his musculature, seeping from his brain, letting Ally out from where she'd tormented his thoughts. He sweated, clammy and hot, in the cool of the July evening. He'd release her as best he could, leave her out here. Maybe, if he ran for long enough, he could actually sleep well tonight?

Before he knew it, he had crossed the bridge over the bypass and was entering the new housing estate. His legs weren't tired. The agitated, restless feelings that were fuelling him showed no signs of wearing off. He'd not turn back; he'd keep running. All night if he had to.

Out along the foothills skirting Ben Macdui the air was clean and damp, heather-scented. The mountain loomed dark to his right, a great monster of immoveable granite and slipping scree.

On he ran, until he found himself entering another little village, not one he knew. Flats and terraces, gardens and a few closed shops. Cars lined the residential area as he paced through it, a good looseness in his hips, a lightness in his head. Maybe he was getting a little tired now? He drank from his bottle and the coolness brought his temperature right down. His pace slowed, he halted under a street lamp, bent to rest his hands on his thigh muscles. They were burning in the best way.

Nothing troubled him now. His brain was quiet. The street was quiet. In fact, the whole village was quiet. He looked around in the half light. No sign of a pub where he might treat himself to a pint before running back. Nothing but lights behind closed curtains and pigeons settling down on the roofs.

He turned, thinking a walking pace was enough for now, enjoying the night, and that's when he came face to face with –

no, almost bumped straight into – a woman with a fading yellow bruise under her eye.

'Sorry,' she said quietly, dodging out of his way.

'It's you?' he said, still getting his breath back, sweat on his eyelids. He swiped it away.

The woman walked briskly by, her head down, pulling her long coat around her. He turned, noting the rip in the fabric under one arm.

'Wait, please!' he called.

It was enough to start her running, barely fast enough to get a few metres before he was by her side, his hand stilling her.

'Get your hands off!' she said, still trying to walk away.

'Please, just talk to me. You're hurt? Has someone done this to you?' He pointed to the rip where white lining showed through the beige outer layer of her Afghan coat.

'Are you a copper or something?' She still tried to shake him off.

'Volunteer Special Constable,' he admitted, knowing if she was going to talk to him, he had to be on the level.

'Not a copper then,' she concluded. The heels of her boots clicked loudly as she walked. Jamie stuck by her.

'We can offer you protection. If you just tell us who gave you the jewellery you took to the repair shop that day.'

This almost stopped her in her tracks. He read her hesitation as his way in.

'Whoever's using you for fencing or trafficking, we can put them inside, move you to a new area. Get a fresh start.'

She tutted, a wry curl at her lips. All the time her eyes stayed fixed on the pavement. She upped her pace. He matched her.

Jamie would have to take a punt if he was going to make progress. 'Whoever did this to you,' he indicated the tear at her

Fixing a Broken Heart at the Highland Repair Shop   **157**

coat, but just as easily could have pointed to her eye, 'can't be worth protecting all that much, can he?'

Silence. She made a sharp turn down a side street. There was no road sign to help orientate him. They passed a small playpark with two swings swaying ghost-like in the breeze, and a set of monkey bars over a rubbery red surface. At the end of the park she made another sharp left. She wasn't going to lead him to wherever she'd been going. She was trying to lose him. Both of them knew he wasn't giving up.

Edwyn's voice rang in his ears. He should call for assistance. But how? If he did, she'd start running again, then he'd have to apprehend her.

'All I need is a name, and I'll leave you alone, I promise.'

She jolted to a standstill. Now she looked straight at him he saw how blue her eyes were. They were shot with weary sadness. At first he'd guessed she was in her mid-forties. Now, though, he wondered if she were much younger.

'You've nae idea what you're asking,' she said. 'Even talking to you in the street could get us in big trouble. Gonnae just leave me alone, for both our sakes?'

Hers was a familiar accent. Maybe not Edinburgh, but near enough.

'What part of Mid Lothian are you from? Or is it East Lothian?' he tried.

She laughed, exasperated. 'None of your business.' She walked on for a moment before turning sharply up a path between two front gardens, then passing deeper between the terraces, coming to a stop in a dark dead end flanked by unlit back yards on either side, both overgrown with tall shrubs and weeds.

Even in the low light her eyes were strikingly baby blue.

Aware she'd brought him up here so they couldn't be seen or heard, he whispered. 'Just a name.'

'You know I cannae dae that.'

'He'd be in the back of a van within the hour. He'd never know it was you. I'd make sure of that.'

'Would you?' she hissed back, incredulity in her voice.

'The Chief would. I can absolutely guarantee it.' Before she could waver he added, 'It's a whole gang, isn't it? Not just your fella, but there's a network, right? Just tell me the ringleader. A name, or the HQ, and I'll let you walk away. Or if you like, before we're even knocking their doors down, we'd have you in a safe house miles from here.'

'I cannae leave the area.' She said it so quickly, Jamie drew his chin in.

'Because you've someone keeping you here?'

He knew the MO of groups like the one he suspected had this woman in their thrall; he'd seen it repeatedly in training. Overwhelm a vulnerable woman with gifts and goodies, whatever she wanted, just enough to reel her in. Then ask her for help storing something for a mate. Then before she knows it there's a package needs picking up, or some man needing a place to sleep for a while, keeping a low profile. If she objects, she's reminded that they know all about the one thing more precious to her than anything else.

'My lassie,' the woman admitted with a dejected sigh. 'She's at her granny's for now. Things have been chaos at my place. She cannae be missing school.'

'We can keep her safe too.'

She didn't believe him. She pulled a vape from her pocket and its little light shone blue as she inhaled then blew out a bloom of foul-smelling vapour. Jamie stayed close. He'd grab her if she decided to run now. His phone was in the pocket of his

Fixing a Broken Heart at the Highland Repair Shop **159**

jacket. He willed it not to ring before remembering he'd switched it to silent around the same time he was running out of Cairn Dhu, having given no one any indication of where he was going. He didn't even know the name of this village, but all he had to do was dial the central line and they'd pinpoint his location and send an unmarked car for this woman.

'I'm Jamie,' he said.

The lights from the only vehicle to pass by briefly lit the night and were gone again. She'd stepped back further against the bushes, the light on her vape going out. If she was this jumpy, the guy she was involved with had to be nearby.

'Where were you going tonight? Are you on another job for them?'

'No, I was not,' she said, like this was somehow offensive. She unrolled the bag she was holding. Jamie took the opportunity to slip the phone from his pocket. Bringing the lock screen to life with a tap, there was enough light coming from it to illuminate the contents of the bag. He peered in.

'A... music box?' It was pink, decorated with ballet slippers and with a small gold latch and hinges.

'A jewellery box, for Shell.'

'My sister had one just like that when we were wee. It had a ballerina inside, on a little spring.'

The woman rolled the bag closed again. After a beat, during which she pulled at the slipping shoulder of her coat, she said, 'I haven't done anything for that bastard since he did this.' She turned her face to him as though he somehow might not have noticed the bruising.

'Did you get it seen to, in hospital?'

'As if.'

He let the silence fall, not wanting to risk saying anything more about how escape was possible if only she'd give him something to go on.

Probably let down at every turn, she had no reason to trust anyone, least of all him, a sweat-drenched off-duty volunteer. He didn't even trust himself at this point. Edwyn would be furious that he still hadn't let the station know what he was up to right now. His prevaricating would not look good on the incident report.

The cool was getting into his damp clothes. He tried not to shiver but she noticed anyway.

'You're frozen,' she remarked.

'I'm fine. Don't worry about me.'

He let her think, could see the turmoil written across her face. She held the bag tighter in her fist.

'Just one name?' she said.

Jamie nodded. He opened his palm, showing her his phone, now dark and in locked mode again. 'Say the word and I'll get things started. You'll be with Shell and her granny in a hotel miles away before he knows what's hit him and his pals.'

Her eyes were wild with the possibility. Her irises burned into his as she got closer to agreeing. He daren't say another word in case he blew the fragile trust between them. Maybe he was good at this after all? Sympathy, kindness, the things you needed to be a good officer, things he'd got in spades from his mum and dad and his big sister. He knew instinctively how to do this stuff because the thought of this woman living in fear for her little girl moved him more strongly than any desire to stop a bunch of violent thieves operating.

'I...' she began, fear on her face, but she was cut off by her phone ringing loudly inside her coat. Flinching, she rushed to pull it free.

Jamie saw on the screen the name 'Franc.'

Fixing a Broken Heart at the Highland Repair Shop   **161**

'It's him,' she said, staring at it. 'I have to answer in three rings.'

'Do it then,' Jamie urged. 'Be calm.'

She had the button pressed and the phone to her ear as soon as his words were out.

She said nothing, only listening for a moment. Jamie could make out a man's gruff voice, sharp and splintered. She held the phone a little away from her ear as he spoke louder. He wanted to know where the fuck she was.

'I'm visiting the bairn,' she said. 'I told you I was.'

She held her voice so firm, Jamie actually felt proud for her. She glanced at him for reassurance and he nodded back.

'Twenty minutes, I promise,' she said, taking the phone right from her ear and letting Jamie hear.

'You'd better be, Livvie Cooper.' He was driving. Jamie could make out the engine sounds. 'I've some pals coming round, wanting a look at you. An' you'd better come in smilin' this time.'

Jamie was definitely out of his depth here. What kind of situation was this woman, Livvie, in if she was expected to extend her hospitality to a bunch of strange men she didn't know in her own home? She was in dire need of refuge.

'I'll be there in a wee bit,' she was saying shakily, pressing the phone to her ear again, turning away. Jamie read it as her not wanting him to hear any more of the man's instructions. She was ashamed.

The voice on the line said something else that Jamie couldn't catch and the call ended.

She checked and double checked it was hung up before she said anything else.

'His name's Francie Beaumont, and he's just down the road there... in my flat. I don't know how many others there are.'

Jamie stopped himself asking if there were often others. How many men were being brought in to 'have a look at her'?

'What's the address?' Jamie said, opening his phone up.

She hesitated, gulping hard.

'It's all right. We're going to help you, tonight. I'm calling a car. We'll pick up Shell and your mum on the way, and we'll get you out of here before anything else goes down. OK?'

She was nodding, her eyes huge circles, her mouth set in a grimace.

'He's bigger than you think,' she said, and Jamie knew she wasn't talking about his stature.

'Can't be bigger than the police, no matter the network. We'll sort it.'

Another car was rolling by. Jamie heard it pass along the next street down, the one with the playpark. Something uneasy and urgent was stirring in him, some instinct that something wasn't right.

The car was turning at the end of the row and doubling back on itself, only on this street now.

He only had to look at Livvie to see she was making the same connections. She turned her phone in her hand, looking at it like it was a ticking bomb.

'Livvie? Does Franc have a location app linking your phones?'

The car lights grew brighter, the slow roll of tyres telling them the driver was crawling the streets looking for her. Jamie took her phone from her hand and tossed it as hard as he could over the hedges and shrubs of the row of back gardens to his right. He heard it land with a knock against something hard about four gardens down. He pushed Livvie right into the bushes behind them, but it was too late. A black car blocked the footpath they'd turned up.

Fixing a Broken Heart at the Highland Repair Shop 163

Jamie pressed the direct line number on his phone. It clicked through.

'Ops,' the woman said.

'One officer, one civilian woman, this is a Zero Zero,' he had time to say; the request for GPS tracking, immediate assistance, and comms silence, before he clamped his mouth closed and whipped his phone out of sight.

The car door opened and a wall of man, all in black, ascended from the driver's seat.

'It's him,' Livvie hissed.

Jamie had one second where he was still shrouded in the darkness, undiscovered, during which he could shove his phone, still connected to the muted call handler somewhere in Glasgow, into Livvie's coat pocket, in the desperate hope that they were already working away at their computers, locating him on their maps, alerting the nearest units to attend an undisclosed, multi-service emergency. He'd need unbroken signal on his phone for them to find him. All he could do was pray for five bars of connectivity as the man lumbered towards them.

'Who's this wee gnaff?' said Francie Beaumont, before deciding he didn't really care who Jamie was, he was going to thump him anyway, and as he brought down a thick fist hard onto the top of his skull in a brutal caveman swipe, Jamie heard Livvie beg, 'No! Franc!' just before he felt the impact that compressed his neck painfully down between his collarbones.

Feeling, rather than thinking, how weird it was that the ground was coming up towards him, Jamie's brain conjured an image of a woman with red hair standing in the glow of pink neon light. Then the tarmac flattened him and the night turned pitch black and deathly silent.

17

Friday the eighteenth of July at one-fifteen, and Ally was on time.

There'd been a last minute change of plan when Mhairi Sears finally appeared in the group chat to say she couldn't make it to the Cairn Dhu Hotel restaurant, what with her husband having the car that day, so they'd rearranged everything to meet near her newbuild estate on the other side of the motorway. It had been fields until lately, and was now houses with a purpose-built health centre where they'd recently moved the community midwife's office, physiotherapy, the health visitor, and the dental surgery. Plus there was a small co-op farm shop and a café at the centre of the complex.

Ally had borrowed her mum's old Citroen to get there after her work was done for the morning and now she was the first one here.

The place had a municipal hospital coffee-shop vibe, all very new and clean, but plasticky and impersonal. There was a rainbow mural on the wall made up of kids' handprints, and a glass display counter with cling-wrapped rolls and individual

Fixing a Broken Heart at the Highland Repair Shop 165

scones on paper plates with mini jam jars and clotted cream pots.

She took it upon herself to order the tea, confident they'd all be gasping for a brew. One thing they all loved was tea. So she paid and carried the tray and big silver pot and four mugs to a vacant table with low sofas right at the back and waited, reading leaflets from the rack about breast feeding support, baby vaccinations and talking therapies for men, feeling oddly out of place amongst the groups of elderly people too early for their appointments and the mums huddled over coffees while babies slept and toddlers caused havoc in the little soft play area in the window.

Why was she nervous? These were her friends from way back. She knew them better than anyone on the planet, other than her own family, and they knew everything about her.

They'd been through it all and had the photographic evidence to prove it, from primary school wonky fringes and skewhiff bunches, through pre-teen, gappy-teeth Christmas ceilidh dances in their party dresses, to high school performing arts club and jazz-hands big numbers and nervy solos, as well as a memorable prom night where Mhairi's awkward first date with a Cairn Grove Boys' School lad turned into an engagement at twenty-two and baby Jolyon not all that long after.

'You all right?'

The voice, happy and loud, broke through her thoughts and she was in Brodie's arms in an instant, the air being squeezed from her. Brodie had always been exuberant like this. Motherhood had done nothing to diminish it. In fact, she seemed brighter than ever.

'Luce's sorry she couldn't come too, she's on tax return duties today.'

'Wow,' Ally said, stupidly, still a little dazed by this reminder of Brodie's whirlwind energy. 'How is the catering business going?'

Brodie swept a dismissive hand. 'Amazing, but I'm not here to talk about work. How are you?'

They sank onto sofas opposite each other. If Brodie wasn't going to fill her in on the business, what on earth were they going to talk about?

'Um, I'm great,' Ally said, thinking how it was true in most regards, apart from the one that really mattered. Her heart was splintered yet again. But she couldn't say any of that. 'I'm applying for jobs, and planning some fun stuff for the repair shop, trying to grow its reach, you know?'

'I don't know,' Brodie grinned, leaning forward. 'Why don't you tell me all about it?'

The jolt felt like sitting in the passenger seat of a sports car going from nought to sixty in five seconds. Brodie was using her extrovert powers to draw her out of herself, but where was she supposed to begin after not talking for ages? It felt weird and artificial, even though Ally's face was fixed in a grin too.

'Well, I'm thinking about pulling together a special event at the repair shed to help out Mum and Dad...'

Brodie cut her off, spotting someone approaching from the door. She was on her feet and making a lot of noise, welcoming Jo.

Ally watched them hugging and Brodie effervescing with excitement, feeling like she was experiencing this from somewhere outside herself. She took in the contrast between Brodie, all casual dungarees, boots, undercut and brown skin glowing with lotion and summer, and the blonde expensiveness of white, curvy Jo who'd arrived in a cloud of Tom Ford perfume with a full face of make-up like she'd just come from the beauty

Fixing a Broken Heart at the Highland Repair Shop 167

counter. She'd always looked immaculate like this, and she'd always leave her perfume scent on Ally's clothes.

Now Jo was hugging Ally and saying, 'Thank God' she'd got the teas in already, she was 'gaspin'!'

Brodie poured out the milk while Jo shoved in on the sofa beside Ally.

'No Mhairi, then?' Jo said, propping a huge red leather bag with flopping straps on the table, after checking the surface for stickiness.

'She'll be late,' Brodie said, matter-of-factly. 'Should I get us some cakes?' She didn't wait for an answer, bounding off to greet the lady at the till like she was an old friend before loudly ordering, 'One slice of everything.'

'Mhairi's not the type to be late?' said Ally, confused.

'I'll be surprised if she makes it at all,' replied Jo.

'Really?' Ally's heart sank further.

'She's cancelled on us at the last minute on every meet-up we've arranged.'

Ally watched as realisation hit Jo that she'd just let on the girls had been organising meet-ups without inviting her.

'Not that we've met often!' Jo added. 'I haven't seen Brodie since her Christmas party.' Ally told her face to stay frozen in a smile. She hadn't been invited to any Christmas party, had she?

'I mean, it was more of a last-minute drinks kind of thing.' Jo's perfectly set, flawless make-up was no match for the flush of panic at her cheeks.

Ally felt sorry for her. 'I'd have been busy, probably,' she said, letting her off the hook.

'Yeah, you seem like you've been so busy,' Jo said, just as Brodie cut them off again, bringing a big plate of cake and a fistful of forks.

'So, how are the kids?' Ally said as they sat.

Brodie nodded as she shovelled in a bite of red velvet.

'Good thanks,' Jo said, a placid smile forming. She hadn't lifted her fork and Ally knew she wouldn't take a single bite of cake because of her white work outfit.

Was this whole thing going to be stilted and slow? Why wouldn't anybody actually say something real and interesting about themselves?

'And Luce is OK?' she tried, before looking to Jo. 'And Gus?'

'Luce is great,' Brodie said, her eyes still on the fork as she conveyed some of the Victoria sponge to her mouth.

'Gus is busy. You know,' said Jo.

Ally really didn't know. Were the girls holding back because she'd left it too long getting in touch? Was this the payoff for a phenomenal lack of effort recently? They didn't trust her with their private lives any more?

Back in the day, she'd heard it all. A blow by blow account of the first time Jo had slept over at Gus's place, and Brodie hadn't exactly been reserved about her relationship with Luce when they'd first got together and there'd been an awful love triangle with another girl Luce was seeing in Glasgow. The friends had had to rally round to comfort Brodie when it looked like Luce wasn't choosing her but this other woman, and then they'd listened to a detailed breakdown of the way they grew closer over many months of avowedly being 'just friends', and then suddenly it was all on again and they were living together at Brodie's place. And God knows, she hadn't held back then with the eye-opening details of assisted insemination attempts and the rollercoaster of emotions and hormones as they tried and failed and persevered over and over until Brodie gave birth to their longed-for baby, Gillian.

'How's Gray?' Jo asked, and Ally almost dropped her fork. 'Oh! *That* good?'

Fixing a Broken Heart at the Highland Repair Shop 169

'Yeah.' Ally scrunched her nose.

'I'm sorry to hear that,' Jo said, her fingertips touched to Ally's knee in a flash of pearly varnish.

'I'm honestly OK about him,' Ally reassured them, and it was true. What she really wanted to do was blurt out how she'd promised herself after Gray that she was never getting hurt again, but she'd somehow forgotten her vow and let herself get carried away over a hot, brown-eyed trainee police man, and now that was over too – before it had even really got started – and it was making her miserable. But she'd be damned if she was going to sit here and talk about a man, or rather about the single kiss she'd shared with a man. Not when she was supposed to be a grown-ass adult with a life of her own.

Jo sipped her tea, trying not to spill any on her afternoon at the office clothes.

'So, what *is* a *keep in touch* day?' Ally asked.

'I was going to say you're brave wearing white with a baby and a toddler running around,' Brodie added admiringly.

'I changed two seconds before I ran out the house, or my dress would look like that.' Jo pointed to the painted handprint art on the wall.

'You're getting ready to return to work soon?' Ally clarified.

Jo's eyes clouded with something wistful. 'Yeah. Full time as well.'

'Think of the commute!' spouted Brodie. 'That's precious time all to yourself. And working lunches in nice places, and actual adult conversations!' Brodie was enjoying painting this picture, but Jo's smile wasn't quite reaching her eyes.

'I guess,' Jo said, smoothing her dress over her thighs.

'*But...?*' Ally prompted, hoping this would be the breakthrough from all the distance and posturing. Were they actually going to talk about something real now?

'I'm *so* sorry I'm late!' came a voice, making their heads turn.

Mhairi stopped before them. Jolyon was passed out asleep in a buggy that his legs seemed too long for. 'I couldn't get him out the house.'

Brodie and Jo exchanged the quickest glance that Ally didn't know how to read, before all three of them hugged their friend in turn. Ally felt Mhairi shaking as she pulled her close.

'You OK?' Ally said.

Mhairi only nodded and dropped onto the sofa beside Brodie.

'I can't believe we're actually all together in one room,' Brodie enthused, pouring Mhairi's tea and pulling the plate closer to the new arrival so she could inspect the cakes. Mhairi seemed to be having trouble taking her eyes off Jolyon.

'He's getting big,' Jo said, following her gaze.

'Too big for that buggy?' Mhairi said quickly.

'What? No, I wasn't...' Jo was panicking. 'I just haven't seen him in a wee while, and he's got so tall, that's all.'

Mhairi looked close to crying.

'Doll, what's up?' Brodie said. *Doll.* Ally hadn't heard her say it in ages.

'Just some woman at the primary school trial session the other day. Said he was too big to be in a buggy at all.' Mhairi pulled her mouth shut like she'd said too much.

Ally wasn't sure how old some kids were when they got rid of their buggy, but she felt sure it couldn't be anybody else's business and she told Mhairi so now.

'Yeah, fudge her. What does she know?' said Brodie, reining it in since there were kids everywhere.

Jo, however, was looking at where the boy's feet touched the café linoleum. Mhairi caught it.

'He doesn't like to walk far,' she explained. 'Just drops to the

Fixing a Broken Heart at the Highland Repair Shop 171

ground and cries. It's just easier with the buggy.' Her voice trailed off.

'It's OK,' Brodie said, her hand on Mhairi's arm. 'You don't have to explain yourself to us. God knows, it's hard enough raising a kid without people being judgy about your choices.'

Jo nodded vehemently. Ally too, for what her opinion on parenting felt worth.

'I'm not sure it is a choice,' Mhairi said in a shaky voice. 'Just something we have to do or we'd never get out the house.'

Everyone looked at their friend with sympathy. Ally had never seen her like this. She was in jeans and trainers and a big sweatshirt hoiked up at the sleeves. Her hair was mousey brown and hanging over her shoulders instead of her signature honey highlighted bob she'd had since they were twenty-one.

'Anyway, let's not talk about me. How are you, Ally?'

Even Mhairi was deflecting conversation away. Were they really stuck with this small talk? Ally couldn't stand it. If they were going to get anywhere she was going to have to take a hammer to the reserve that was trapping them all like flies in setting toffee.

'Honestly?' Ally began, her voice soft. 'I know I've been crap at keeping in touch. If I'm truthful, I've been completely stuck since Covid times. I'm working from home in a job I could do in my sleep. I'm trying to help Mum and Dad with the repair shop in case Dad slides back into depression and hides out in his shed by himself at all hours like he did when he was first made redundant, and I'm worried about Murray because he hardly talks to me any more and he's gone all stuck-up and Swiss and I'm pretty sure he's been shagging one of his work colleagues and things are bad for him but he won't open up about it. In fact, I don't even know where he is right now, and yes, Gray cheated on me, and I'm trying to rebuild my life one little thing at a time, and I wanted to start with you lot because you're such a big part of me, and I've really bloody missed you, but most of all, I've missed myself and who I was when we used to hang out and,' she gasped for breath and realised she couldn't help what was about to happen. She was going to cry.

Brodie had her hands to her cheeks in amazement.

'And I just want to say I'm sorry for hiding away. It's not because I didn't care. It's because I thought you might not need me any more with your jobs and your kids and your lovely homes and everything being perfect and...'

'Perfect?' Jo all but spat the word. Her eyes were round like they'd been when she was a kid. 'You think our lives are perfect?'

'Well, maybe not perfect, but many, many more steps ahead than mine, and...' Ally wasn't doing a good job of explaining herself. Everyone looked hurt.

Brodie was leaning forward, having abandoned her cake shovelling. 'Sure, we've got our dream baby in Gillian,' she said in a low voice. 'And the catering business is beyond busy but we've expanded to a point where I barely have time to shower! And me and Luce haven't had sex since we got shitfaced at New Year and even then I can't actually remember it! So no, things aren't perfect, even if it looks that way.'

'Oh!' Ally's shoulders slumped.

'New Year? Try March last year!' Jo threw in.

'What? Since you...' Ally's eyebrows must have shot up.

'Honestly, I can't remember; we have to have done it when we made Seren but I don't remember any times after that. Gus is *literally* never there, even when he's working from home, he's completely wrapped up in his job. Things... things aren't perfect, guys.'

'Shit.' Brodie's mouth hung open. 'Why didn't you say something?'

Fixing a Broken Heart at the Highland Repair Shop 173

'Why didn't *you* say anything about you and Luce, or about the business?' Jo countered.

Brodie accepted this without appearing too wounded. 'Good point. Are you and Gus really struggling?'

It took a moment for Jo to answer. 'I don't know. What I do know is I'm supposed to be in the office in an hour for the first time in six months and my boobs are leaking and my dress is cutting into me, and all I want to do is go home and wrestle Seren off this new au pair Gus has hired. She barely looks old enough to look after herself let alone a baby.'

Jo dabbed a napkin under her perfectly underlined eyes, as close to sobbing as she'd allow herself to get in public.

Ally was in the middle of reassessing everything she'd been thinking about her girlfriends these last couple of years.

'Well...' Ally began, trying to compose herself, but with tears running down her face in public, something she'd normally never do, it was too late now. 'Why didn't we talk about this stuff?'

'Because,' came Mhairi's quiet voice, 'it's all so... isolating.' She smiled sadly towards her sleeping boy before smoothing his lovely golden hair off his sweet pudgy face.

The three friends watched Mhairi, waiting for more.

'What?' Mhairi said, once she noticed, looking between them.

'You're the worst of all of us!' Brodie said, injecting some jokey lightness into her voice, though her brow was crumpled.

Mhairi's expression cycled through indignation, before falling to shame, then utter defeat. 'You guys... how am I meant to tell you how hard it's been when you're not supposed to complain about it all?'

'Says who?' Ally asked.

The three mums pulled the exact same world-weary expression and said in wry unison, 'EVERYBODY'.

'And there was you fighting for baby Gillie,' Mhairi continued. 'Going through all the tests and injections and the worry of assisted insemination. And, Jo, you make it all look so easy, juggling kids and working in the city and you and Gus looking busy like some Instagram power couple. And, Ally, I couldn't burden you with my stuff when you're young, free and single. You're going on dates and working hard.'

All three were huffing dismissively, telling her this was 'rubbish', laughing at the very notion they had their lives together or they were too self-absorbed to relate. And yet all three were throwing guilty glances too, acknowledging that maybe there were grains of truth in all of this. Mhairi, however, was finally getting this off her chest and she couldn't stop herself now if she tried.

'And my life is so boring and child-admin heavy, I can't even bring myself to repeat it to anyone! I've done nothing but try to get Jolyon an appointment with the Speech and Language Therapies people for the last three months and *will* they answer my messages? No, they won't. Or I'm at home worrying that he's still in nappies when he's supposed to be starting primary school in August, and asking myself why does he only eat yogurt and breadsticks? How can he be getting what he needs to grow? And where the hell's my mother when I need her? In a timeshare in chuffing Alcúdia with her new man! And exactly *how many* smug parents and nursery assistants have to casually let me know that my baby's missing key milestones, unlike *their* four-year-old who's already signed up for NASA space camp or something, but *not one* of them actually offers to bloody well *do something* and help me!' Mhairi covered her face in her hands and fell into stifled sobs.

Fixing a Broken Heart at the Highland Repair Shop 175

Ally, Brodie and Jo had their mouths open and eyes searching in a *what just happened?* way, only for a moment, before they were on the move and draping themselves over their crying friend in a group hug that drew the attention of the whole café.

'OK,' said Jo, releasing herself from the weepy bundle after a moment. 'Just a sec.'

She got her phone from her fancy handbag, rang through to a number in her contacts list and explained she couldn't get in to her keep in touch afternoon, she was going to have to reschedule, and they weren't compulsory anyway so what were they going to do about it? Then she hung up, a look of utter relief on her face, and she lifted a fork, handing it to an astonished Mhairi, before taking another for herself and cutting a great wedge of cake, not caring about the crumbs.

'Right,' she said. 'Start from the very beginning, Mhairi, and then we'll do the same. No one leaves until we're right up in each other's business!'

And that was how it all came out; four friends, two rounds of tea and cake, and the great unpacking of the last few years of absolute chaos, anxiety, surprises, celebrations, and disappointments.

It was an unburdening. Everyone listened, nobody judged, and four friends found out more about one another in that one afternoon than they'd discovered in twenty years, and Ally McIntyre had to lay down the chip on her shoulder that had told her she was the only one feeling under-supported, misunderstood and overwhelmed with everything, learning that even her most 'together' friends struggled with many difficult things they had for the most part kept to themselves. And all before their childcare duties resumed at teatime.

Afterwards, Ally chugged her way home in her mum's old

car, thinking hard all the way, because – just like her dad – she knew a good idea when it presented itself to her. It was meeting the girls again that had really focused her vague plans to do something even bigger than her and Jamie's big emergency meeting when they'd both swung into action and brought the community together to recover the repair shop's reputation.

All she had to do now was bring everyone together again, an easier prospect now that she knew how to do it, and she would put on a Cairn Dhu event to go down in the history of the repair movement as the biggest ever seen in the Highlands.

She'd need help. From everyone, Murray included, wherever he was, and yes, the police station, and Jamie too – if he was still allowed to be in the same room as her without turning morally corrupt in the Force's eyes.

It occurred to her as she drove that maybe the whole 'I want to see you again, but I'm not allowed' thing that he'd spun her might be nothing more than an excuse, a way of letting her down gently after coming to regret how they'd got so close so quickly that night at the Ptarmigan. She rubbed a hand over the twinge in her chest where her seatbelt pressed against her. Hadn't he missed her at all? She hadn't even spotted him patrolling the high street recently. It was like he'd disappeared.

No, she'd set to work on her big repair plans and do her best to rope him in. There could be nothing in the rule books about them working on the same community cohesion plan together, surely? As colleagues? That way, maybe she wouldn't have to live with the ache of missing him quite so much.

He'd been serious when he'd said he had to keep his distance. Still, a message would have been nice. How could he stay away from her, even if he felt just a tiny bit of how she felt about him?

She'd shaken those thoughts away as she got out of the car.

Fixing a Broken Heart at the Highland Repair Shop

Friendship (and temporary friendship, at that; Jamie *was* leaving soon) was all she could ask of him, and she'd have to make peace with that sooner rather than later for the sake of her great big idea.

If she was quick, she could finish plotting it all out on her laptop and capture the plans circulating in her head, making use of it all in her Future Proof Planet second interview preparation. The interview was in a couple of days and this time she'd wow them.

She wasn't going to leave her friends out of her plans either, not after they'd reconnected today. Heck, she was going to rope in every parent in a thirty-mile radius if she could, and their parents too! But first she had to convince the repair shop regulars that she could pull it off. With a bright ember of conviction burning within her, she pulled on the handbrake outside the mill house.

She had work to do.

18

The next day, before the shed opened to the public, Ally was ready, clicker in hand. The slide deck was loaded and displayed on the screen she'd rigged up. The chairs were set out in a semicircle in front of her workbench.

After Sachin, the volunteers had arrived in twos; the Gifford sisters, her parents, then Peaches and Willie, leaving only Cary Anderson who came in last and by himself as always.

Ally had deflected their intrigued comments until everyone was sitting, happily taste-testing Senga's new sweet, crumbly tablet squares with walnut chunks that were being passed around in a greaseproof wrapping and everyone had agreed this had to be her best tablet yet.

Ally began, advancing through her slides, showing them images of their town overlaid with alarming statistics she'd got from government and charity websites detailing the extent of the loneliness epidemic sweeping rural parts of the country. She talked through them as she clicked.

'One in seven people report being lonely either some or all

of the time,' she was saying, and this was met with a good deal of agreement and concern from her listeners.

Cary Anderson listened in characteristic placid silence and yet no one in the room would have guessed he'd have counted himself amongst that number of lonesome, isolated Highland residents suffering for want of a companion.

'What a shame for them,' Rhona had said, unable to imagine such a state of affairs, while her sister informed her wisely that there were 'plenty folk without the good fortune to have an older sister to stay with'.

Ally went on outlining her plan. 'More than anything,' she was telling them, 'we need to reach isolated people.'

'The crofters?' said her dad.

'Yes, partly it's for them,' Ally confirmed.

'And some of the rangers on the mountains? They can seem lost when they come down into the town, as out-of-place as a yeti,' said Sachin.

'Why not? But I'm thinking about the people who might not *look* isolated, but actually are. People like I was, if I'm honest. People working remotely, living virtually, stuck socially or financially...'

'Ally...' her mum said, her mouth turning down at the corners.

'I don't feel so stuck *now*, Mum. Not now I'm making all this stuff happen,' Ally hurried to comfort Roz who, it was only just dawning on her, hadn't fully understood the extent to which her daughter had felt left behind and overlooked, which is precisely why Ally had to do this.

'It's too easy to assume a person is OK,' she went on, 'when underneath they're screaming out for help. Take my friends, Jo and Brodie. They appeared to me like they were racing up all the ladders society has propped up for them, but it turns out they were discovering the ladders are covered in grease and they couldn't stop themselves from slipping! Then there's another pal, Mhairi, who's feeling even more cut off than them. No family nearby, no support network. We need to reframe how we think of this repair café – it could become a place where we restore broken connections as well as fixing broken things.'

There were murmurs around the semi-circle, nods and notes taken. Ally took this as a good sign and talked on, changing slides. 'And we have to be properly accessible too, literally and financially, with a website listing our events, and we need comfy places to sit...'

'Are we talking... expanding the café?' Senga cut in.

'Probably, yes, but if that's not an option, at least letting more people know we provide a warm, welcoming place, even if they don't have spare money for their coffee and rock buns.'

'Free buns?' Senga's lips pinched in protest.

'I was thinking more of a *pay it forward* scheme, where people can choose to pay for their own drink and put money in the till for someone else's, someone who's not feeling so flush that week. Loads of places are doing it, look it up; some places call it *suspended coffees*. And we could have some items on a *pay what you want* arrangement.'

'We've wanted to try doing toasties?' Rhona put in, wiggling in her seat with eagerness.

'Pay what you want toasties?' Senga wasn't convinced.

However, McIntyre was determined to prevent the wheels coming off his daughter's presentation. 'You are the best baker in the Highlands, Senga. Increased footfall will only spread that reputation further, and more than make up for any shortfall in ingredients costs to subsidise a few freebies.'

Senga looked like she might object, but then fell to thinking. 'I *am* a fine baker,' she said, cannily.

Fixing a Broken Heart at the Highland Repair Shop   181

'No disputin' that,' said Sachin, crumbs on his lips from the tablet.

'I *could* pass those baking skills on, you know?' said Senga, always amenable to praise. 'In a baking basics class?'

'How would that work without ovens on site?' said Sachin.

'Oh! Sweet traybakes they could mix here and take home to cook?' suggested Rhona.

'Or you could use our kitchen?' said Roz, inspired. 'The range fits six shelves. Sharing it for a few hours a week couldn't hurt.'

'And I'd help,' Rhona practically bounced. 'I'd have made a braw home economics teacher, if I'd had the chance.'

Senga, for once, pulled her lips into a smile of understanding for her too often overlooked wee sister.

'Once a month, then?' Senga asked Rhona, securing a nod of agreement, before turning to McIntyre. 'If you think we can afford the extra ingredients?'

'We'd budget for it,' said McIntyre.

It was actually working. They were on Ally's side.

'Any other suggestions?' she tried.

'I could add automotive skills to our offering?' said McIntyre. 'A sort of *learn how to change a tyre and do an oil change* sort of thing? One-to-ones or small groups, out on the driveway. Reckon that'd be popular.'

'That would be *so* helpful,' Ally said, her voice bubbling with happiness. 'I've no idea how to do those things so there must be others like me.'

'There we go, then. Decided.' McIntyre stretched his legs and crossed his ankles.

A hand lifted in the semi-circle. All eyes turned to the quiet and unassuming Cary Anderson. He'd listened patiently to all these ideas and seemed to be striking upon one of his own, if the gleam in his eyes was anything to go by.

'Yes, Cary? Go on...' Ally prompted gently.

'Well,' he began, his voice so scratchy and low the repairers leaned in and fixed their faces in concentrated listening. 'I learned carpentry from my grandad. He'd been an apprentice at the old sawmill at fourteen and was a foreman at forty, building house frames and floorboards and fitting cabinets and stairs, the lot. Half the builds in the old estates were Grandad's, and then my dad followed after him as a draughtsman, but who's teaching the kids these skills?'

'There's a definite skills gap on the horizon if we don't teach young people these things now,' Ally said, hoping this meant he was about to volunteer more of his time.

Cary thought for a second before saying, 'I could build a few workbenches with woodworking clamps, at a child's height, and teach the beginnings of it all; measuring, sawing, sanding, joining, if you can bring in the younger ones to learn it?'

'A woodworking kids' club?' said Ally.

'Is it a daft idea?' Cary asked, his handsome brows crumpling as doubt struck and he slipped into silence again.

'No! It's a brilliant idea! Let's try it,' McIntyre jumped in. 'I'll help with that too.'

This set off a little ripple of applause. This was going better than Ally could have dreamed.

'I could host a sewing circle?' Roz said.

'Or a design masterclass?' added Willie. 'Your creative darning repairs are the best I've seen, Peaches.'

His fellow fashion student accepted the compliment with a huge smile. 'I don't mind showing people how to do those. Easy,' she told the group with a shrug. 'I already demonstrate Swiss

Fixing a Broken Heart at the Highland Repair Shop   183

darning techniques and Japanese Sashiko embroidery on our socials.'

'And I can easily teach anyone how to crochet a granny square,' chimed Willie.

'That's true, he can. He taught me in, like, ten minutes,' Peaches concurred.

'We could call ourselves the Highland Happy Hookers!' shouted Rhona, lifted to her feet with inspiration, before realising it didn't have quite the right ring to it and lowering herself sombrely into her seat once more, Senga greeting her with a kindly pat on the knee.

'We could do with some kind of recruitment drive for new repairers generally,' concluded Sachin, who'd been listening carefully to all of this.

'That's exactly what I'm proposing,' said Ally.

'So... what we're talking about is opening the barn up for these...' McIntyre circled a wrist looking for the vocabulary.

'Mixers?' tried Sachin.

'Community classes?' tried Cary quietly.

'Skill shares?' Peaches suggested.

'Welcoming, safe spaces, and... everything you just said!' Ally was grinning again. 'That's *exactly* what I'm saying, and not just on repair Saturdays, but on other days of the week too. For people of all ages and backgrounds and from all over the region. So what do you think? Should we try it?'

'No harm in trying,' McIntyre said.

'We'd need more space for all that,' came a voice that made everyone whip their heads around to face the doorway.

Murray dropped his bag from his shoulder and stepped inside.

'You're here!' Ally gasped in relief at the sight of him.

Roz had crossed the floor in a second to hug her son.

'That I am.' He looked exhausted, like he'd travelled a long road. Roz ushered him into the circle, finding him a chair.

'Are you on leave again?' Ally asked, not wanting to give away the things she'd gleaned from Andreas, at least, not in front of everyone. 'Are you staying?'

'If you'll have me?' he said sheepishly.

'This is your home, always,' said their dad, leaning across to pat his back.

'You were saying?' Ally fixed her twin with an intent look. 'About us needing more space?'

Murray was sitting down, unzipping an expensive looking sports jacket. 'From what I caught of your brainstorming exercise, if you're going to host all these events, and you want them to grow, you'll eventually need more floor space.'

'That's what I was saying,' tutted Senga.

'An extension to the barn?' Roz didn't look too sure. 'That would be a lot of work, and expensive.'

'If you applied for funding, you might secure a small sum to expand at the back.' Murray pointed into the depths of the shed behind the café where his dad's collection of parts and spares were stored on their tall shelves. 'If you had someone with experience in writing funding applications...' he tailed off into a cunning smile.

'That's Murray's job settled, then,' Ally said before he could back down and run off to Europe again.

'Let's not get ahead of ourselves,' Murray stopped her. 'We have to prove there'd be a demand for these new services. You can't just turn up in a community and do things to it. You have to be needed and offer something that'll have a measurable impact.'

'That's why we need a great big repair café open day to

Fixing a Broken Heart at the Highland Repair Shop 185

launch our plans so far and to field local opinion, ask folk what they want and need from us.' She hit a button on her laptop and a slide materialised that made Roz clasp her hands in delight. It read:

Cairn Dhu Community Repair Shop and Café, Open Day, Saturday 9th August, 10 a.m. – 6 p.m., come along to our Skills Share recruitment drive and Societies soft launch. All welcome. Always Friendly and Free.

'You've got it all figured out, sis,' said Murray, and the whole shed agreed.

'Not everything, I don't,' she said meaningfully, peering right at him. There was still the small matter of her brother going AWOL from work to get to the bottom of.

'Uh, right, well...' He stood. 'If we're finished here, I'll, uh, get unpacked,' he said, hiking a thumb towards the exit, shouldering his bag.

'And that's the end of the meeting,' Ally blurted at lightning speed, following in the wake of her brother as he dashed for the door. He wasn't going to get away with disappearing and reappearing on a whim like this, especially if he reappeared seemingly without a job, and without telling her at least some of what had happened.

But as the twins reached for the door handle and yanked it open together, they were halted by a great big body in black, his hand raised to knock.

'Allyson McIntyre?' said PC Andrew Mason.

'Andy, we went to school together, you know who I am. What are you wanting?'

He dropped the formality immediately. 'It's Jamie Beaton.

He's in the Infirmary, assaulted while attempting to apprehend a suspect late at night in the Garten Valley. And he's asking for you.'

19

A ride-along in a cop car would, Ally had always imagined, be laced with excitement and intrigue. On the hour-long drive to the Infirmary, however, it was all Ally could do to sit still in her seat. At least Andrew had let her ride in the front. Calls were coming in over the radio, but he didn't respond to any of them. It transpired he was technically off duty.

'Doin' a favour for a pal,' he'd said when pressed, and Ally had wanted to ask what kind of 'pal' he thought he'd been when he was mocking Jamie at every opportunity, but she kept her mouth shut as they made their way through the mid-morning traffic, passing the occasional tractor and many, many caravans holding up the road.

Andrew didn't seem to know much about Jamie's condition, or he wasn't letting on. Which was worse.

Ally felt just as she had done the few times she'd flown on family package holidays to Lanzarote or Majorca when she was a kid. After take-off she hadn't dared let herself nap or read her graphic novels, wouldn't even leave her seat to go to the loo, because she felt somehow the pilot needed her to lend her powers of concentration to keep the plane in the air. So she'd sat, bolt upright, hands clasped tightly over the rests, keeping an eye on the wing, willing the plane to stay up in the air. That anxiety however, that exhausting channelling of willpower, was nothing compared to the sixty minutes she spent in that police car.

Jamie was asking for her. He wanted her. She had to get there quick and hope he was holding on and not thinking she wasn't coming to him.

'Can you not put your foot down a wee bit?' she'd wailed eventually, seeing the building queues of traffic as they got closer to the city.

'All right,' Andrew said, feeling himself a hero. 'Hold on to your seat!' He flicked the sirens and lights on and Ally watched as the cars parted for them all the way down the carriageway.

* * *

Ally hadn't known what to expect when she reached the ward, but it wasn't an armed officer at the door of Jamie's room. She'd shown her ID and been ushered in.

Chief Inspector Edwyn stood in the way of the bed, his back to her. Robert Mason stood up as she came in.

She peered at the white bed, the drip bag and tubes, Jamie's hands pale over the blue waffle bedcover, his chest and throat exposed through the chequered hospital gown. His lips were parched and he had a great big bandage over one side of his brow with a red, stitched gash showing around its white edges. The deep brown of his eyes deepened further when he saw her.

'Ah, and here she is,' said Edwyn, stiffly. 'Your friend's arrived. I'll file your statement back at the station. Robert, take over as security watch from Officer McNally at the door.'

Fixing a Broken Heart at the Highland Repair Shop   189

'Yes, sir,' said Robert, before turning to tell Jamie he'd be right outside.

'Mind and get some rest,' Edwyn told the patient as the door closed.

Left alone, Ally wasn't sure how to act. A monitor clamped over Jamie's finger charted his heart beats and oxygen levels on a screen attached to a trolley by his bed. It beeped reassuringly every few seconds.

She wanted to sweep across the room and hold his bruised face in her hands and kiss the web of red scratches on his cheekbone. But she stood stock-still at the end of his bed.

'You came,' he said simply.

'You asked for me.'

He tried to nod, winced, and let his head press back into the pillow. The green line on the screen spiked then fell sharply again. It was enough to get her feet moving.

'Come here.' She fixed his pillows, thinking how this felt like a movie and not her real life at all. 'If I asked what happened, would you tell me?'

A smile formed at the edge of his mouth. 'I don't remember much of it. The Garten patrol unit found me knocked out in a back alley, the suspect long gone, along with the informer. They said I'd been out cold for hours.'

'Christ! Who did this to you?' Her hand twitched with the impulse to touch the padded bandage over his lovely brow. Would he tip his head and rest against her hand if she did?

'Francie Beaumont. Heard of him?'

Stumped, Ally pulled a face.

'No reason you should have, but the constabulary have known him a long time. Small time crook but persistent, and slippery with it.' His voice broke into a crackling cough. Ally offered him the water glass, and even though Jamie's arms seemed fine, he sipped from it like a helpless man.

'Where is he now?'

'In a cell,' Jamie said, letting his eyes close for a moment. 'Him and nine of his pals will be paying a visit to the High Court.'

'Nine!'

Jamie still hadn't learned his lesson about the stiff neck and attempted a nod.

'*Tshh!*' He inhaled sharply.

Ally slipped her hand under his jaw and cradled his neck. He was cool to the touch.

'Stop trying to move!' she scolded him. 'Silly thing.' All she could do was smile, even though it was patently unfunny seeing him in pain. Yet, he was all in one piece and smiling back at her.

'They were traced back to a property half a mile from where I was found. Recovered the stolen jewellery too,' he added, his eyebrow lifting as he told her the good news. 'Along with a fair few other things linking the gang to robberies all over the central belt and enough coke to get them custodial sentences for intent to supply alone.'

'Wow! So you're the hero of the hour then?'

'Hardly, I just about got handed my own heid to play with.'

Again, they laughed. It was grim and absurd, but he was in a warm bed, in the arms of the NHS, and with Ally's thumb softly stroking his cheek, even when she told herself she really shouldn't.

'Thank God you're all right. How on earth did you know where to look for this...' She'd already forgotten the guy's name.

'Francie Beaumont? I didn't. It was all an accident, if I'm honest. Or a coincidence? Either way, I ran right into the woman who brought the stolen jewellery to the repair shop.'

'No!'

'Yep, and she gave me enough to go on to get a positive ID on the man who assaulted me, and she said one or two other things, enough to add coercive control to his list of charges.'

'Oh no, that poor woman. Is she in a cell too?' The alarm must have registered on her face because Jamie brought his hand to hers at his cheek.

'No, no, it's OK. She's safe. She's the whole reason we caught the gang. I slipped my phone with its GPS switched on into her pocket before Francie got the chance to lump me, and she led us right to their door.'

'You might well have saved her life,' Ally guessed.

'She saved herself,' he countered. 'By confiding in a safe person.'

He *was* a safe person. Ally's heart swelled with the certainty of that.

'She's with her mum and her little girl right now, getting the support she needs.'

'Jeez! A little girl? Will they be kept safe?'

'Edwyn assured me they would be. Livvie's already made her statement and that will be more than enough to send them all down, so far as I can make out. She was very vulnerable, by all accounts, and with no way out.'

Ally couldn't stop her eyes welling. She dropped her head, remembering the woman that day, skulking into the repair shed, then seeing her again with a black eye in the middle of the night going who knew where.

'She won't even have to go to court,' Jamie pressed, rubbing at her hand reassuringly. 'She'll never see any of them again. Edwyn gave me his word on that.'

Ally absorbed all of this, hardly able to see her way through the tangle of feelings and all the potential other outcomes that could just as easily have happened. They were lucky to have got out alive.

'And are you going to be OK?' she said, breaking from him for just long enough to pull up a chair so she could sit.

They clasped hands against the blue cover.

'The docs said I could be discharged in a few days. They had to check for concussion and brain bleeds, but so far, they seem happy with me. Ally...' he grew suddenly serious. 'I won't be allowed to work for a while, and then I'll have to make up my required voluntary hours, and then my transfer will be over. I'll be heading home to Edinburgh.'

Her heart quickened like it wanted to burst. What was he saying?

'I wondered if...' he paused, wetting his cracked lips, 'you wanted to spend some time with me? Now the case is closing?'

'Oh!' Ally hadn't even thought of the ramifications of all this for the pair of them. She hadn't even dared to hope things could change.

'Edwyn thinks it's all right, does he?'

'He was the one who told Andrew to bring you in. I was asking for you when they found me, apparently.'

'When you were barely conscious?' This shouldn't be an image that conjured up joy, but hearts are funny things and Ally's was drumming a tattoo in her chest.

'So they tell me.' He was smiling a cautious smile, trying not to move his jaw too much. 'Ow!' He whipped his free hand to his face.

Ally rose to her feet again.

'So, you're asking me *out* out?'

'I am.'

Party cannons shot confetti in her cerebral cortex while news banner ticker tape simultaneously ran the headline *this guy is leaving soon; so don't get too carried away, missy,* but all Ally could do was laugh at the dizzy thrill of it all and lean over him as gingerly as she could so as not to hurt him, pressing a hand into the hospital mattress to steady herself. The last thing she saw before closing her eyes was Jamie looking helplessly up at her, his eyes glazed with wanting.

She pressed her mouth to his, the kiss shutting down all the noise in her head and the siren and traffic sounds from the road outside. She kissed him softly, loving the scratching sensation where his lips were dry. He exhaled shakily, melting down into the bed, his hands holding the backs of her arms, encouraging her, pulling her closer, the urgent hunger of their kiss sending the green jagged line on the monitor soaring off the charts, and Jamie Beaton forgot all about being in pain.

20

Ally and Jamie stood side by side at the foot of the path looking up at the green-blue granite elevation of Cairn Dhu in the distance. The mountain, shaped like a ragged molar tooth and topped with the lightest powdering of snow even in summer, lifted into a hazy sky. Leading up into the mountain was a wide boulder-strewn pass, almost always in shade, that leads hikers on deeper into the range and a week's serious hillwalking before you'll lay eyes upon a driveable road or a pub again.

'Just a gentle trek, right, for an hour or two?' Ally said, checking again that Jamie felt recovered enough for this.

It was the first day of August, and bright and cool. He'd stayed in hospital, sleeping mostly, for another few days, just to be sure, before holing up in his flat for a few days longer, with the district nurse calling in to change his dressings. Some of his old pals from the barracks had come up to see him too, once word got around Edinburgh what had happened.

Ally had stayed away, partly because she was so busy planning the repair shop open day, and partly because she knew Jamie needed to rest and he would already be beset with neigh-

Fixing a Broken Heart at the Highland Repair Shop 195

bours bringing him stews and whisky, Lucozade and shortbread (all a convalescing man needs, apparently – and who's to argue with local wisdom?)

Jamie, his bandage now gone, with a scar across his temple already turning sheeny silver, showed Ally the route on his phone app. 'Five hours' round trip, at most,' he confirmed. 'Easy-peasy.'

When he'd suggested they go out, she'd thought it would be just that. A nice dinner somewhere. A drive with a view and a fish supper at the end of it. But a trek, albeit a modest one, hadn't once crossed her mind. When he'd told her his intentions over Messenger during his recovery period, she'd had to take a moment to process why she felt the tiniest bit disappointed. Then, just as quickly, she'd dismissed the feeling. She'd landed in trouble having just those sorts of feelings over Gray; hoping for romance and commitment when what she really needed was to be known by someone and in turn to understand them. Whether that was truly possible with Jamie, she wasn't sure. Not when the clock was ticking on his return to Edinburgh.

She tried not to think about that. She was here now and so was he. That in itself was pure luck, given that he'd spent the night out cold on the pavement down an alley only recently. The fact he was standing beside her at all was miraculous. That was more than enough.

Two buzzards wheeled in a widening gyre high over the scattered downy birch trees and low shaggy junipers now thick with silver-blue berries – that unmistakeable juniper fragrance already filling their nostrils.

Jamie searched for the tattoo on her wrist. 'You love this mountain, right?'

'Love looking at it,' she told him.

Ally's boots hadn't known what was happening this morning

when she'd reached for them at the back of the cupboard. They couldn't remember the last time she'd taken them onto the hills. Her parents and teachers had made sure she knew the passes well enough as a child, but in recent years – the pyjama years – Ally's connection to the hills had severed and she hadn't known she'd missed it until this moment.

To get into the pass they'd have to walk through the gently rising open moorland, a sea of stone and purple heather before them.

A stag bellowed in the hills somewhere. Jamie's eyebrows shot up at the sound. He looked beyond delighted.

'*Am Monadh Ruadh*,' Ally said to herself, awe in her voice.

Jamie faced her, questioning.

'These mountains weren't always call the Cairngorms, you know? Their ancient, Gaelic name is *Am Monadh Ruadh*. Russet rounded hills.'

'Hah.' Jamie was impressed. He fixed his feet all the firmer on the dry earth.

They fell quiet, letting the mountains hear their old name invoked again.

A band of walkers, clearly set on many days' climbing, passed by, head to toe in Gore-Tex and neon nylon, huge packs on their backs, determination in their strides. They greeted Ally and Jamie the way all adventurers do; talking of the weather, and checking for mountain news in passing.

'Quiet on the lower elevations this morning,' one of them said in a Geordie accent.

'Gonna be cloudy out there,' said a second.

'Doing the thirty K to Lairig Ghru?' another wanted to know.

'Just a picnic in the pass,' Ally confessed with a shrug and a smile.

'And home before evening,' Jamie added.

Fixing a Broken Heart at the Highland Repair Shop   197

With a wave and well wishes, the group tramped on.

Jamie watched them go, then smilingly glanced down at his own clothing; basically his running stuff with a fleece and a thin waterproof jacket on top. 'Are *we* experienced hikers? No,' he said to Ally. 'But are we good map readers? Also no.'

'But we've got GPS and a flask of tea, so...' Ally shrugged, mirroring Jamie's lightness of mood. 'Lead the way.'

They moved off, at half the pace of those serious walkers already making good headway over the gently rising heath. Jamie and Ally followed what's known as one of the many 'community paths', busy year round with locals and dog walkers out for the day.

Young wrens flitted between the scrubby trees, chittering their noisy songs. A robin emerged, not long out of his summer moult with his fresh fluffy grey feathers and a lingering bare patch in his red breast. He eyed them with curiosity as they passed.

Ally and Jamie exchanged all kinds of observations and small talk while the going grew gradually rockier and the sounds of gently tumbling waters increased. They crossed a new wooden bridge over crystal clear runnels, water that had filtered through mountain rock on its way down into the valley.

'Do you have the same feeling?' Jamie asked as they stepped into the first sparse signs of the pine wood that skirted the foot of the mountain.

Ally started in surprise. The feeling? That she was walking beside a person she could happily walk alongside forever? She wasn't going to admit to *that* feeling, that's for sure. 'What do you mean?' she said, trying to stop her voice turning pitchy.

'That everything here has been around way longer than we have, and it'll remain after we're long gone?'

'Ah, that feeling!' She let herself laugh. 'Your brush with the reaper has made you dowie.'

'Dowie?' asked the lowlander.

'You know? Wiser, but maudlin?'

'I can assure you I'm just as daft and just as cheery as I've always been. Well, maybe I'm a wee bit cheerier recently.' This was accompanied by the hint of a meaningful glance at her.

She hadn't noticed at first but Jamie was offering a hand for her to take. When it dawned on her that's what was happening, she found her own hand, entirely of its own volition, jumping into his. The sensation of touching struck them silent again.

It was good. It was absolutely right.

Through the thickening patches of bowed old spruce they passed. Most of the trees had branches only on their leeward side and were bent from having weathered squalls since they were saplings, their windward trunks entirely bare.

Hoping not to betray their shared awareness of the electric crackle between their clasped palms, they pointed out the bracket fungi on the trees and the mushrooms around the roots. They swiped midges away, spitting and blowing their way through the irritating, nipping clouds of hungry beasties. They froze at the sight of a red squirrel twitching and scratching only feet away and didn't move a muscle until it had gone.

When they left the trees they found themselves in the shadow of the mountain, still a distance away, but they were already in the pull of its gravity, that strange mountain magic that makes frail human beings want to strap water bags to their backs and spikes to their boots and tackle heights only the eagles should know.

Jamie consulted his app and pointed their way up a long flight of granite steps – neither of them could tell whether they were mountain-made or put there by man.

Fixing a Broken Heart at the Highland Repair Shop   199

Ally fought the urge to ask if they were nearly there. She thought of the cheddar sandwiches in her bag and hot milky tea and the prospect of a cosy picnic, but Jamie announced there'd be at least another three kilometres' clambering before they hit the area earmarked for their rest stop.

'It's steeper than I thought it'd be,' she told him as he helped haul her over big black jutting rock steps.

A green figure emerged up above them on the stones, and he waved them down from a distance.

Ally narrowed her eyes to focus his face. 'It's one of the mountain rangers. Don't know who, though.'

As he drew closer she made out light brown hair and a scruffy beard spoiling what was probably a handsome, and young, face beneath it all. He'd be handsome if he wasn't scowling, that was. A quick, amused glance from Jamie told her he was reading this man's grumpiness too.

A patch embroidered into his moss-green fleece bodywarmer told them his name: Finlay Morlich. Not a name Ally was familiar with.

'What brings you onto the pass th' day, folks?' he asked, his accent as thick as his beard.

'We're doing a bit of sightseeing,' Jamie told him.

'*Hmm.*' Finlay cast a glance down to their feet, not liking what he saw, evidently. A pair of amateurs.

'Are you out patrolling?' Ally asked.

'Always,' Finlay answered primly. 'Making sure folks ken what they're taking on.'

Ally had to turn and look behind them to stop herself chuckling. That's when it struck her how high they'd climbed. She nudged Jamie. 'Look how far we've come!'

The clustered grey roofs of Cairn Dhu down in the valley were matchbox small.

'See? You've covered mair ground than you thought,' Finlay said. 'It's easily done if you're no' used to the range. Are yous turning around now, headin' hame?'

'Not yet,' Jamie told him. 'We've a picnic to have first. Up at this open spot with the bothy?' He showed Finlay on the app. Their destination was greeted with a look of surprise.

'I've heard it's a beautiful view,' Ally threw in, wanting to placate this wild man of the mountains who clearly thought them a pair of dunderheads.

'Beautiful, aye, it is,' Finlay conceded. 'But this park can be deadly for the underprepared. Have ye provisions?'

'Tea and sandwiches,' Ally said, quick as a flash. 'And some of Senga Gifford's drop scones.'

This piqued his interest. 'Senga fi the repair shop café?'

'That's right.' So the woman's baking really was famed the whole park over? Wait until she tells the old crow about this; her head will swell even bigger.

Ally was already untying the drawstrings on Jamie's backpack and pulling out the plastic tub Senga had forced upon her this morning, saying Jamie would need sustenance if he was hillwalking. She'd been positively starstruck at the thought that the local hero might be saved from starvation and exposure by *her* baking.

Finlay looked at the pack with furtive interest, like a squirrel sniffing out nuts.

'Would you like one?' Ally shoved the tub closer.

'I couldnae...' Finlay began, but as Ally stripped the plastic lid off, revealing the golden discs, he weakened.

He reached for one. Immediately biting into it, taking a moment to look at it in his hand as he chewed.

'Nice, right?' said Ally.

This was enough to draw him back to his job.

Fixing a Broken Heart at the Highland Repair Shop 201

'Get that back in his backpack,' he snapped, gesturing to the box of drop scones. 'If you stumble, you need your hands free to catch yourself. Ever had a broken wrist on a mountainside? Nae fun.'

'Oh! Right.' She quickly obeyed and packed their provisions away.

Jamie hoofed the bag higher onto his shoulders and clipped the support straps across his chest. 'Well, it was nice to meet you. I think we're ready for our wee daunder now, up to the picnic stop.'

'A daunder?' echoed Finlay. 'A *daunder!*' He shook his head at the audacity. 'Be sure to keep an eye on the weather closing in. I'll give it an hour before the cloud cover sinks doon upon us.'

'Got it,' said Jamie, chastened.

Finlay knew his warning hadn't landed. 'If I end up having to leave ma dinner and come oot to find yous pair after dark with one of yur legs snapped in twain, you'll be mair feared o' me than any doctor wi' a stookie!'

'Um?' Jamie looked to Ally in confusion.

'Thanks for the advice,' Ally told the exasperated ranger. 'I promise we'll be safe.'

Yet the man still wasn't convinced. 'You've your phones charged fully?'

'Yes,' Ally and Jamie answered as one.

'Well, turn one off for now. Nae point draining twa at the same time. There's no telling when you'll need to ring rescue services.'

'Good point.' Ally dived into her trouser pocket and swiped her phone off.

Observing them with world-weary derision, Finlay tapped at his temple before turning the same finger on the walkers. 'Stay alert.'

'Wow,' Ally whispered as the ranger went on his way. 'Didn't know we'd meet the man who owned the actual mountains!'

Jamie laughed as they moved up the path once more and it felt good and conspiratorial, but that deep seed of sympathy planted in him as a kid was still present.

'I'll bet he's seen some awful things out here. He's probably scared to bits every time he sees a bunch of people messing about on the hills like it's a day at a theme park.'

They were so close to accessing the mountain pass, Ally felt the air change. She didn't know if it was the altitude, or the draw of the granite, or this guy always thinking with his heart that was doing it.

'That's fair. So many people have got on the mountain and never made it down again.' She shivered like she always did when she thought of the stories, impressed in her all her life, about tragic school and scout groups, lone hikers and lost children. They'd put the fear of the mountains into her and it had never left. 'But does he have to be quite so dramatic?'

This raised another gentle laugh.

'Did you grow up scrambling these paths?' Jamie was growing a little breathless. Ally was glad to know it wasn't just her finding it harder going the higher they ascended.

'Not so much as you'd think. Dad was always working, pretty much, and Mum had a lot on her plate with me and Murray, and for a long time she was looking after our granddad too. We'd come out onto the paths now and again...' she shrugged.

'But you weren't bagging Munros every weekend?'

'Hah! With Murray in tow? Hardly. He's always preferred a coffee shop or a beach, or a big city.' This stopped Ally. 'In fact,' she said, turning back to point into the wide vista. 'Over there somewhere is a loch with a pink sandy beach.' Jamie stopped and peered too. 'You can't see it from here, the mists are

Fixing a Broken Heart at the Highland Repair Shop   203

obscuring it, but we went there for days out, more often than not.'

'Visibility's not as good as it was,' Jamie said. 'Should we have our picnic and head back down?'

'What? No, we're almost at the bothy. Just a bit further.' The truth was she wanted today to last as long as possible, now that she was enjoying herself.

He checked his app once more and they turned and followed the ever-decreasing red dotted line tracking how far they still had to go.

There were a thousand things she wanted to ask him as they walked. Was he excited at the prospect of returning to Edinburgh? Would he continue volunteering there until he heard one way or another about whether he'd been selected for the intake of rookie regulars? She guessed he would. He was born for the street beat. Other things she wanted to know clamoured in her mind as she placed down her boots, step after step. Would he miss her? Would he ever come back to visit? Had he looked at the Edinburgh to Cairn Dhu train timetable any time lately? Like she had last night, trying not to hope for things.

To shut off these thoughts, she landed on something safe. 'How's your dad been?'

'Uh, well...' Had she asked the wrong thing? His face was set and serious. 'He's gone quiet again.'

'Again?'

'Yeah, he doesn't mean to. It's something he's always done. It's like he loses all his words. Karolyn says he's shuffling round the house like a sleepwalker. He's doing all the usual stuff; picking up the newspaper, doing the online shop, loading the dishwasher, but he's barely talking.'

'Do you think it's depression, maybe?' Ally didn't want to be too presumptuous, but she'd seen the man with her own eyes and there was a lurking sadness in him that day at the shed, even though he was doing his best to support his son.

'It comes and goes,' Jamie said, like there was nothing that could be done.

'Has he ever had any help? A doctor? What about bereavement counselling?' She reined it in before she turned into Little Miss Solution Finder. It was in her nature to try and fix things for other people, but she knew hearts were a tricky thing to repair.

'Those aren't things he'll talk about. He's got that *keep calm and carry on* thing going on, like loads of dads. Can't say it's worked for him so far.'

Ally was imagining Jamie's childhood, putting together the puzzle pieces from the little she'd gleaned. No wonder he'd been so sad when they first met.

On impulse, she put her hand in his once more. Touching him again was enough to cast a new kind of spell, something bigger than the dizzying mountain mood, something alive and electric, stronger than childhood memories and present worries.

'You should talk with him,' she said, and not without some difficulty. She felt herself getting breathless as they fell into a slow, matching stride, their arms rubbing together. 'Now you've got some perspective on home.'

He thought about this.

She caught him plumping his lip pensively.

'Reckon I could. I need to do *something* before I head back there.'

The rocky boulder-strewn path was opening up to rough, scrubby walking. As they stepped inside the wide mountain pass between the great walls of Mount Cairn Dhu, the temperature fell sharply. The air was damp. What little sunlight was making its way through the white-grey cloud cover suddenly

Fixing a Broken Heart at the Highland Repair Shop   205

dimmed further. They were getting deeper now. Getting drawn in.

Their eyes fell upon a low drystone wall sitting oddly alone in the middle of the scrub. Ally recognised its purpose, but allowed Jamie to approach it, wondering if he could work out what it was.

She watched as he stepped around and inside the strange snail-shell curl of stones, some of its top stones had fallen and were strewn on the ground of dry grass and alpine plants so flattened by weather and boots it was like a dense, tough carpet.

'It's a storm shelter?' he said, squatting down inside it so the top of his head disappeared from view.

'It is.' Ally approached the wall, following its curve until she found Jamie crouched inside its protective arms. 'Walkers caught unawares can pitch their bivvy inside and, hopefully, emerge unharmed when the storm passes.'

He looked oddly at home inside the little curve, already stretching his legs out before him. 'Good spot for a picnic?'

Ally looked deeper into the pass. 'Hmm, if you aren't afraid of adders.'

Jamie sprung up. 'Adders?'

'I didn't say there were any. I just mean, you'd have to poke about a bit with a stick in case there are some in there.'

'Maybe we'll keep walking,' he said decidedly, and Ally followed him on up the pass, their laughter getting lost in the dampening air.

Ally wished they were still holding hands as they climbed up towards the bothy, its white walls and grey roof just visible at the top of the curve of the pass, but the walking was getting harder and she had to pick her steps alongside a shallow spring that had come from nowhere and was making the walking soggy underfoot.

'So...' Jamie said from a few paces behind her. 'Any news of Switzerland?' The question made her heart soar as high as the buzzards.

He'd remembered. She'd not mentioned it since the night at the Ptarmigan, but he was still thinking about the possibility of her leaving. That had to mean something.

'Well, when you were recuperating, I had a second interview,' she called over her shoulder, wishing she could see how that news landed. She didn't dare glance back in case he thought he was being tested, observed for signs of distress.

She told him in a jolly way all about how she'd presented the glamorous Andreas Favre and Barbara Huber, as well as someone from HR, with her plans for growing the repair shop and café as a shared space with the aim of repairing their community, sharing skills at risk of being lost, bringing people together and combatting loneliness. She told him about how meeting up with her girlfriends had been the deciding factor. She'd seen how isolated and lonely they were, just like she'd been, and how tough things were, and she'd come up with her strategy. He'd listened as she outlined all the suggestions the repair café experts had come up with to help her make it a reality too.

'And I presented all that stuff to Future Proof Planet, along with how you helped me bring people back to the repair shop after the whole stolen jewellery thing.'

There was admiration in Jamie's voice when he said, 'I hope you took credit for that yourself and didn't mention me.'

'Of course I mentioned you in my presentation.' It was getting harder to walk and talk. She gulped for breath. 'It was a collaboration. Fifty-fifty as far as I remember? You were running around knocking on just as many doors as me. And you got snooty Carenza on side. I couldn't have done that without you.'

Fixing a Broken Heart at the Highland Repair Shop   207

The bothy was getting bigger and the clouds grew lower. Ally had to swipe droplets of moisture from her face as they walked deeper into the mountain mists.

'We made a good team,' he said.

The words hung amidst the suspended rain droplets as they walked the last few yards to the squat little stone cottage, one of many all across the Highlands, left unlocked for walkers needing rest and shelter.

They did make a good team. Ally couldn't deny it. Jamie was calm and firm and persistent. He saw the good in everyone. She'd learned recently how tenacious she really was, and she had an innate appetite for fixing things and a curiosity about the world that had only recently been re-ignited, in part due to the man who was now coming to join her in front of the door of the bothy, his hand reaching for the handle at the same time as hers.

Somehow, he was reading her mind because he said the exact thing she was thinking at that moment.

'I hope there's nobody else inside. I want it to ourselves.'

His hand on hers, they turned the handle and pushed the door open.

21

Peat-scented and low-ceilinged, the bothy slouched tiny in the grand landscape, waiting to welcome them. They clomped inside, Ally wondering aloud if she dare take her boots off, the backs were rubbing at her heels, and she was sure her feet had swollen. But would she get her boots back on if she did?

Jamie sat on the low bench at the door as Ally sealed them inside. She slipped the thick wooden latch, knowing he'd notice.

He was throwing his running shoes off in a careless way. 'Get cosy!' he said. Then, thinking better of it, he immediately reached for them, placing them neatly side by side.

There wasn't much to the little shelter: stone walls and a fireplace, a threadbare rug, probably seventy years old by the looks of it, spiderwebs and a small window under the eaves.

'A hobbit house,' Jamie said, delighted with the place, now unpacking their picnic.

'I wonder who was here last?' Ally said, lifting an old jumper off the back of the only chair in the place.

'Whoever it was, I love what they've done with it.' Jamie was

Fixing a Broken Heart at the Highland Repair Shop 209

about to unzip his jacket but thought better of it. 'Are you cold too?'

Together, they lit the fire with kindling and the smallest of the dry logs from the pile by the hearth. It was slow and smoky but better than nothing.

'We need to make sure that's extinguished properly when we leave,' Ally said, not remotely wanting to think about leaving.

She lifted the lid on a polystyrene storage box in the corner and found sealed bags of dry pasta inside. On the floor stood a container of fresh drinking water, ready for an emergency and a long stay if needed.

Jamie had unpacked their picnic and Ally passed him her bottle of handwash.

As the fire tried its best in the hearth, the world beyond the little window under the eaves grew duller and further away.

'I could live here,' Ally announced, fancifully.

Jamie didn't seem to think it was such a silly thing to say. He handed her a sandwich and they set to eating, their bodies both drained and somehow invigorated from the walk.

'So will you come to our skills share and societies festival on the ninth?' she said as they ate.

He seemed to think for a long time before saying, 'I think so, but that's round about the time for me to be going home. I'll let you know.'

She didn't push it further. If they hadn't just walked for an hour and a half she'd have felt her appetite wane.

As they ate they became aware of the cloud shrouding the bothy from the change in the air alone. Everything felt suddenly dampened, the way it does when heavy snow falls and everything becomes muffled under its weight. The strange quality of the silence outside was enough to get Jamie on his feet and pulling the door open to investigate.

'Ah!' he said, standing aside to let Ally see the wall of wispy white beyond the door. 'The clouds have come down.'

Oddly, Ally didn't panic. Neither did Jamie. He stepped right out of the door in his socks to take a better look and, after only three steps, he was gone in a wash of white. *That* alarmed Ally; Jamie's absence. Even the few brief seconds while he was shrouded in watery vapour and diffuse mountain light felt like an alarm jolting her awake. She got to her feet just as he came back inside and shut the door once more, telling her, 'Whole mountain's gone.'

'Good,' she said.

He smiled too.

His phone worked, miraculously, and he rang the station to report themselves safe at the first bothy on the pass, and he asked for Finlay, the ranger, to be reassured they were fine and that they had plenty of supplies, as well as a fire going. They'd come down when the cloud lifted.

He dropped a pin on his GPS app, so everyone else would know where he was and then he checked the weather report. The low pressure was due to lift by evening. Rain was already breaking over on Ben Macdui, and the wind was set to rise. Theirs was only a temporary confinement, he was sure of it.

Ally used his phone to ring home and she repeated to Murray everything she'd just heard Jamie saying. Murray made some remarks about making sure she used their time alone wisely and she hung up as he sang her a smutty version of 'she'll be coming round the mountain,' and she had to stifle a laugh and pretend to Jamie nothing had happened.

'So,' Jamie said, pocketing his phone now that everyone knew they were safe. 'We sit it out?'

* * *

Fixing a Broken Heart at the Highland Repair Shop   211

They focused on the fire. Someone had collected pinecones in a basket and left them by the hearth for fuel. Every so often Ally threw some into the flames and they watched them spark into brief, blazing light. As they talked about all of Ally's plans for the skills share and they made short work of Senga's drop scones, they shifted their bodies until they were toasting their feet against the hearth, their arms wrapped round their knees. The tea was soon drunk, and the world outside forgotten completely.

'Have you... been in many relationships?' Jamie asked, not quite out of nowhere, considering the unspoken buzz between them.

'*Hmm*, not so much. Gray was the longest I was ever with anybody. Never anyone at school. Some little things at college.' She shrugged. It was all true. There'd been guys and some not very good hook-ups and lots of teen angst and crushes, but relationships? She didn't have much to say about those. 'How about you?'

This made Jamie take a deep breath and he looked into the fire. His brown eyes shone bronze in the hot glow. 'A few. A big one when I was seventeen, lasted until I was nearly twenty-one.'

Ally raised her brows at this. It made sense, actually. From what she'd gleaned, he'd been a lonely kid, the sort who might commit to someone early.

'I'm glad you had somebody,' she said. 'What happened?'

'Oh, the inevitable. She met somebody else in her final year at uni, in Brighton.'

A devious little part of Ally registered that this guy had navigated a long distance relationship between Edinburgh and Brighton, and for a long time too. He was a walking green flag. Not that this was relevant to their friendship in any way, of course.

'Was that it?' she said.

'*Hmm*, there were others after that, kind of short-lived things, but all pretty amicable when they ended.'

'Why did they end?' she said, when what she wanted to know was why would anyone let Jamie Beaton go? She couldn't fathom anyone breaking up with him.

'I guess some relationships are just a mismatch and there's nothing you can do about that.' He said this with an easy shrug.

'A mismatch?'

'Yeah, you might spend time trying to change yourself for them, or they might try to change you in small ways, but in the end you both have to face facts; it's not that there's something wrong with either of you – you're both basically good people – it's just a mismatch.' He said this with a lift in his voice like it was so simple.

'When you put it like that, breaking up sounds easy.'

'Relationships don't have to be dramatic. I've been called to enough domestic disturbances and street arguments between couples to recognise relationships that aren't going anywhere. Sure, things can get tricky sometimes and you need to work together to fix stuff, but generally, I think if you're mismatched it's never going to be good.'

Say it! Ally's brain was up to no good. *Say it!* it prompted her. But nothing, not even the smile on Jamie's lips and the way he was leaning his folded arms on his knees and his head on his arms, blazing eyes fixed upon her, would bring her to blurt out the question. *Do you think we're a good match?* She kept the words inside.

'Ally, I'm... glad I met you,' Jamie said, and Ally got the impression it was only one tenth of the words he really wanted to say. She'd take it though. She felt the same.

'All my life, I've liked to take things apart to see how they

Fixing a Broken Heart at the Highland Repair Shop 213

work,' Ally found herself musing aloud, eyes on his. 'Even when I was a kid. And after I found myself stuck at home and left behind, and ever since breaking up with Gray, I've done the same thing with people. Looking for the fault.'

He was steadily observing her in the firelight, the bothy walls shadowy and indistinct around them, only ghostly whiteness beyond the glass.

'I did it with you as well,' she confessed. 'I wanted to think you were bad, that day we met. And then, later, I wanted to think you had a girlfriend...'

'What?'

'I did!' she confessed, laughing. 'I saw you with your sister and I jumped to the wrong conclusion. I just didn't want to think you could be this...' She gestured to him with her hand, taking in his whole body. He waited with his eyes widening. 'This... good.'

'All to keep me at arm's length?' he anticipated.

'Exactly. I've had faulty instincts. I've not known how to read people, like Gray. And after him, I've assumed ill intentions even when there were none, all because I'd stopped trusting myself, stopped trusting other people. I wanted to find fault wherever I looked.'

'But you came running to me when you needed help, so what does that say? Your instincts might be better than you think.'

She heard the words, let them seep in, but she wasn't really thinking any more. If she did, she'd have to think about him leaving soon, and how she had so much work to do helping the repair shop evolve into its next form. She had friends to work on cherishing and sharing with. She had a messed-up brother who'd fallen right off the career ladder and landed with a bump back home and had been hiding out in his bedroom ever since: so many people to help and things to fix.

Right at that moment however, there was only this man in front of her and a warm fire and the feeling of being lost in a cloud with real life on pause, and all she wanted to do was kiss him and see if it really was as good as she remembered.

Jamie reached the same conclusion only a moment before her, and turned himself to face her, lifting onto his knees. She closed the space between them in an instant, joy bubbling up where before there'd been churning feelings.

'Can I?' she asked, pausing an inch from his lips, waiting for him to kiss her as confirmation, before pressing herself closer to him, nothing holding her back.

His mouth, tracing down her neck, sent her nerves sparking like the fire in the grate as they struggled out of their jackets, laughing and kissing all at once.

He kept his mouth to her throat as they tumbled messily onto their strewn coats, his hands catching her head before it bumped the floor. She was safe, she was warm, she was happy.

Mouth to mouth, hard then soft, alternating lip pinches, sharp and tight, then wider, deep opened-out moaning kisses, her tongue softly swept between his parted lips, making him gasp, the sound of his breath building and hitching and sending her dizzy.

She'd pulled off her T-shirt before her brain could fathom what was happening, and he'd mirrored her, the sight of his broad chest and the fading bruises at his ribs filling her up with astonishment and pity.

He asked if touching her was all right and waited for her reply before he'd lowered himself in the slowest, most careful way over her, his bare chest and stomach against her skin. The sensation loosened any grip she had on herself.

Fixing a Broken Heart at the Highland Repair Shop   215

She pulled him nearer, hands spread over the pockets of his trousers, the material crisp as she gathered it, high-altitude kisses starving them both of air, switching off every polite inhibition within her.

They were still laughing, amazed, as they kissed, shucking off socks and trousers, him moving his lips to her bra, moving the thin fabric aside to take her into his mouth.

It was agreed between them that he should search out his wallet and the condom, which he did without dragging his eyes away from her, without taking his mouth off her skin.

With a hungry-eyed, devilish pause where he kneeled over her, rolling the protection into place, showing her his whole self, she couldn't wait any longer and pulled him close to kiss him again. Body to body, and in the blaze from the fire, they kissed and ground and held each other closer than they'd ever held anyone in deep connectedness, not caring about the cool floor, not feeling the shifting air pressure from the clouds lifting as the sun broke through again, forgetting everything but one another as they shared the deep shuddering burst of pleasure together, holding each other tightly until it subsided into a softening glow.

* * *

Jamie woke from the sleepy bliss first, thinking he'd slept for hours but finding it had been a matter of minutes. Still, he felt curiously rested. It was broad daylight outside, the Cairngorms really delivering on its promise of throwing four seasons in any given day at the unsuspecting traveller.

The bothy was close and quiet. No one needed anything from either of them. Nothing needed to be done, other than watching the fire, delivering soft kisses to Ally's closed eyelids as she too awoke, running his hands over the smooth curve of her shoulders, and contemplating with wonder how they'd been so incredibly good at this, and on their first time together too, then remarking with laughter what would the next time be like?

Jamie, however, knew more keenly than Ally that they'd better find their clothes and get down the mountain before the heavens chose to hail or snow, yet still he submitted a little longer to the longing to lie still, his body mirroring Ally's, curled like bears in their winter den, happy to hibernate, not thinking of the world waiting for them when they emerged into the sunlight once more.

Sadly, reality has a bad habit of not knowing when to keep its nose out of innocent lovers' business, and today was no exception.

There came the sound of a fist hammering at the bothy door. Jamie guessed from its agitated insistence which grumpy, camo-clad survival expert stood outside.

'Ranger service,' called the cross voice, trying to peer in at the steamed window under the eaves. 'Open up! Let's get you down off my mountain!'

Finlay Morlich escorted them home without a word. Jamie couldn't help but think of the officer who'd brought him back to his dad's that night when he was a wayward kid an inch away from going right off the rails. Only now, Jamie wasn't wracked with squirming shame and powerlessness, wasn't eaten up inside with grief and missing his mother. He'd come a long way in recent years, and most of that distance he'd covered in great strides since meeting Ally McIntyre.

He quirked an eyebrow at Ally when they reached the car

Fixing a Broken Heart at the Highland Repair Shop 217

park at the foot of the slope next to the ranger hut. Finlay unlocked the doors of a beaten-up old jeep and gestured impatiently for them to get in. He was set on driving them to their doors, apparently.

Ally hadn't taken the interruption to her bothy escape quite so easily as Jamie. She was still squinting against the light now, looking ethereally tired and more beautiful than he'd ever seen her with her hair messy at the back and her cheeks blushing pink with embarrassment after the heated scramble for underwear while Jamie, amused, had curbed the bothy fire and laced his boots. Ally didn't think it was funny, so he didn't push her to see it that way.

In the back of Finlay's jeep as they bumped their way down the road to town, Cairn Dhu Mountain shrinking in the rearview mirror as though it wasn't some magical place up in the clouds where they'd excursioned in heaven itself, Ally hurriedly switched her phone back on.

Finlay, who'd been seemingly oblivious to their embarrassment – as though he hadn't even suspected what they'd been doing – didn't fail to notice Ally had followed his advice on relay running their phone batteries. He nodded approvingly to himself now as he drove not one mile an hour over the speed limit.

Jamie, who had nothing to fear and not a drop of awkwardness or tension left in his body, reached a hand over the space between them, thinking Ally would take it in hers. He wanted to squeeze her fingers, take that preoccupied look from her brows, make her smile again. But Ally was reading from her screen, engrossed.

'Oh!' she said, and Jamie caught the flush bloom in her cheeks.

'Everything OK?'

She handed him the phone so he could see it for himself.

Future Proof Planet are delighted to extend you an offer of twelve months' employment in the role of Blue Sky Thinking Technician based in our Zurich office.

He scrolled a little further over the details of salary, benefits, the included flat share, and all the rest of it; the promise of a wonderful opportunity for Ally.

A glance told him she was about to burst with excitement and something else, something regretful, something anxious, preventing her from enjoying her success fully. He knew the cause, the fly in the ointment: it was him.

Thinking fast, he had precisely one second to get his response absolutely right or he'd risk blowing this whole thing. It had to be pitch-perfect. Too sorry sounding, and there was a risk she'd turn this dream job down to stay with him or if he seemed sulky she might think he believed he had the power to stop her going and would hate him for it. Too cool and she'd think he didn't care about her now he'd got what he wanted.

She hadn't spoken at all since Finlay's arrival at the bothy, and she wore a startled expression like she couldn't quite process what they'd done. Gently was the only way to go now. A show of unwavering support. So he wet his lips, set his face in a delighted smile and began.

'Ally! This is... this is wonderful! Congratulations!'

He took her hand and squeezed it on the seat between them, like he'd wanted to a moment ago, only now he was sort of patting it too.

Her eyes flew to his, questioning. 'Really?'

'Of course, really! I'm thrilled for you! Switzerland? You're going to have the best time!'

Fixing a Broken Heart at the Highland Repair Shop   219

She didn't look sure.

'Aren't you happy?' he asked her.

'Uh, of course I am.' She took her phone once more and set her eyes on the screen, scrolling absently like she couldn't make out a word of the job offer.

'You should be. Did I say I was delighted? Because I am, truly.'

'Yes, you said that.'

Why did she look close to tears? What was he getting wrong?

'You should reply right away, tell them you accept!'

She looked blankly back at the message. 'I should?'

'Heck yes, you should!' *Heck, yes*? Since when did he say heck anything?

He rubbed the back of her hand with his thumb.

Finlay flicked the indicator for the turning into the McIntyres' mill house and the repair shop driveway. The sight of it gave Jamie the feeling astronauts must have when they splash down in the ocean having spent weeks in orbit. Everything looked the same and yet nothing was the same.

Finlay cut the engine, turning in his seat with an arm over the passenger headrest. He looked ready to deliver a steely message about irresponsible behaviour and the deadliness of mountain terrain and the brainlessness of the pair of them, but surprisingly even he seemed to get the measure of the mood in the back of the jeep and he kept his mouth shut.

'I've got a lot to do,' Ally said, gesturing at the phone in her hand.

'Of course. You crack on!' Jamie's cheeks hurt from the artificial grin. 'I'll see you in a bit.'

Finlay waited impatiently for her to get out of his vehicle as though he had other silly people to save from themselves.

Jamie leaned across the seat and kissed her. She let him do it.

'You've got this. Don't think, don't panic, just get ready for the trip of your lifetime.'

She nodded like she was on a slower setting than him.

'Right,' she said. 'See you in a bit.' With a look of bewilderment, she hesitated before opening the door. She turned again, preparing to say something, but Finlay was getting tired of whatever this was.

The ranger handed Ally a leaflet as a parting gift. 'There's yin for you an' all,' he said, giving another to Jamie.

Staying Safe in the Cairngorms, the cover blazoned. Jamie wanted to laugh at Finlay's hard headedness but when he looked to Ally he was met with the swinging shut of the door.

Finlay fixed his eyes on the windscreen and pulled away once again.

The last Jamie saw of Ally that day was her standing on the gravel outside her house, her phone in one hand, the leaflet in the other, her face frozen in astonishment.

Jamie sunk in the seat as Finlay barked something over his shoulder about whether he was still belted up in the back.

Visions of their morning, shrouded in white, replayed in his head now. Neither of them had been aware in the slightest they'd been striding headlong into danger. Something told Jamie as the jeep hit the high street he wasn't quite out of the fog even now and his mind raced trying to work out why he still felt so lost.

22

'Salopettes?' said Ally. 'Really?'

'Yep, trust me, you'll need 'em.'

Murray had been more animated than he'd been in a long time since his sister's announcement on Friday that she'd accepted the Zurich job. He'd not disappointed, proclaiming, 'We need to get you to a mall!' So that's where they were now, on a sunny Monday morning, looking for Alpine sportswear, apparently.

She hadn't had a moment to think about Jamie and what happened at the bothy since she set foot in the mill house just before tea time on Friday and told everyone her news. Her mum and dad had insisted on popping Prosecco and ordering Chinese food from the takeaway in Stranruthie, and they'd chattered and fussed all evening and in her dazed state she'd let them. Then she'd helped at the repair shop all of Saturday and she'd spent Sunday composing her resignation letter for work, and sorting out her Swiss visa, buying insurance and returning her signed contract, all with Murray's help.

The world around her had changed unrecognisably in the

space of a few days. And now, according to her brother who, 'knows about these things, trust me,' she needed a whole new wardrobe too.

'No, none of these are any good. Let's try another place. You have to be Zurich-ready!' he was telling her now, hustling her out of the store as if he didn't have all day to shop. 'Besides, you won't be able to afford *a thing* in the stores there. Not on a temp's wages.'

Murray was determined to help her, and part of her was grateful. She hadn't a clue what kind of thing she needed for twelve whole months of living in another country. He didn't have to be quite so brisk though.

As soon as they'd arrived at the mall, they'd stopped for coffee in one of the big chains, and she'd watched as her brother downed a cortado standing at the counter, right in the face of a totally bemused barista. He'd tapped the cup down like it was a tequila-drinking competition. 'Ahh! *Real* coffee! I've missed this.'

'Has it been that bad, drinking instant at home?' Ally had said, thanking the barista for her caramel iced latte and dragging him out of the café.

So far, he'd made her look at merino base layers, '*essential* for winter' and 'decent boots, none of your misshapen thrifted stuff.' He'd thrashed through the rails, dismissing garment after garment, pulling out white and beige things in linen and cotton. 'Think layers, lots of layers, but smart casual, leaning towards the smart end of the scale.'

She'd let him bundle her into changing rooms with armfuls of clothes and waited for his infrequent nod of approval when she came out to show him.

She used to love shopping with her brother, years ago, but she didn't remember him being this manic.

'The men will all be in sports jackets, of course, and shirts

Fixing a Broken Heart at the Highland Repair Shop 223

and sometimes ties,' he continued in his whirlwind way as they went into another store she wasn't sure she could afford to even look in. 'You can't have them showing you up, so try these.' He'd bundled dresses and jackets upon her, and shoved her into another changing room.

When she looked in the mirror under the harsh lights, she barely recognised herself. She rejected all the long black tubular dresses that somehow made her look both gothically terrifying *and* frumpy, probably not what the designer was going for, and told Murray she'd borrow her mum's green suit jacket for her trip, it had been good enough for her interviews, making him gape in exaggerated horror.

Murray dragged her into the sunglasses store next door, telling her not to 'even *look* at the prices because you *will* need a good pair. Just be sure not to leave them by someone's bedside or...' and he'd tailed off, remembering something unsettling.

'What bags were you thinking of taking?' he wanted to know as he shovelled a bacon double cheeseburger into his mouth in the fast-food lunch place. 'God, they don't make dirty plastic burgers like these in Switzerland, honestly! Eat up.'

Ally only picked at her fries. She hadn't had much of an appetite since coming back down to ground level on Friday. Her brother had forbidden her usual ketchup and ordered mayonnaise, telling her she'd better get used to it.

Ally informed him she'd planned on carrying her stuff in 'a book tote or something' and he'd dropped his hands, burger and all, in heavy disappointment onto the plastic table.

'All right,' she groaned with an eye roll. 'What kind of bag are you talking about?'

After he'd gulped his way through a McFlurry, he trailed her around a painfully expensive shop which claimed to sell handbags but had only about eight of them on the starkly bare shelves.

'This one?' he tried, examining a mulberry-coloured thing with short, hooped straps and a tiny flap on the front with a big gold catch. 'Mind you, if you *are* planning on shopping for luxury goods while you're away, you can't do any better than a trip to St Gallen, lovely little stores, all the designers and...'

'There's no price tag on this,' she said, interrupting his weird travel blogger monologuing.

Who was he trying to kid? This was Murray McIntyre, the boy who'd devoured *Heat* magazine for celebrity gossip and made her go with him to see Harry Styles in Glasgow, where they'd worn matching outfits and they'd both screamed themselves hoarse when he sang 'Kiwi' as an encore. He might try to hide his insecurities under this pretentious act, but he was still her twin brother and he couldn't bluff his way out of telling her what the hell was wrong.

Having had enough, she snatched the – admittedly very nice – bag from him, dumping it back on the shelf and, even though he was mortified, hauled him from the store under the cool glare of the shop assistant.

'That's it!' she snapped, when they hit the bright lights of the concourse. 'What is *up* with you?'

'I'm totally fine.' He leaned back on the glass barrier with a crooked arm, glancing down at the shoppers and fountains on the floor below. He tried crossing a sockless ankle but failed entirely to pull off the pose of 'unbothered and fabulous', appearing only slightly daft and utterly transparent to the person who knew him best in all the world.

'Is it because I've accepted the job? I did say if it made you upset in any way, I wouldn't touch it.'

Fixing a Broken Heart at the Highland Repair Shop 225

'I know, and I told you not to be stupid. Of course I'm not upset about that. I promise.'

'You've been acting strange ever since you got back, and I just *cannot* with you right now. I need Murray, not this bougie international playboy thing you've got going on.' She held up the fancy shopping bags he'd forced upon her – all lovely stuff, but she'd have been happy travelling in her old faves from the charity shop.

His face fell. Good. She was getting through to him in his delusion.

She aimed her last shot. 'A playboy who's been sleeping all day and prowling between the fridge and the telly all night, and who's putting away mall snacks like they're about to be banned! Just, stop. Breathe. Tell me what's wrong. Please.'

His expression cycled through affronted, then irritated, before landing on defeated.

'Tell me.'

With a heavy sigh he mentioned in a sorry voice that he'd spotted a Krispy Kreme on the way in and she should probably follow him.

Back in their mum's car in the multi-storey and with an hour left on their ticket, having returned all the unnecessary clothes he'd charged to a shiny gold credit card for her, they lifted the lid on the original glazed dozen.

'Thing is,' he told her between chews, fully dropping any charade of being dignified at this point. 'There's some stuff you should know, about Switzerland. My life there... it's not quite as high-flying as you've probably imagined.'

'What are you telling me?' she said gently, biting her own donut, her legs curled beneath her on the driver's seat. 'Your luxury life in Switzerland has been a big swizz?'

'Well...'

'Oh my God, it has?'

'It's true I had an apartment and everything. That came with the contract.'

'Right?' She waited.

'Only, I shared that flat with three other guys and, I don't know if you've flat shared with a bunch of straight Dutch and German environmental engineers before, but there was a lot of bro behaviour. Crunches on the living room carpet, that sort of thing? Squats and hundred litre bottles of water downed all day long, and *so* much sliced cheese for breakfast and 6 a.m. before half marathons and, oh my God, the sports kit tossed everywhere!'

Ally was beginning to see his problem. 'Bro overdose?'

'It was too much! I just wanted to crash in front of *Love is Blind* and eat my snacks in peace.'

'Okay, so what happened?'

'Well, I got friendly with someone.'

'Andreas?' Ally said matter of factly. 'I know. He was the one ringing me looking for you, remember?'

'Well, he asked me to move in with him and of course I jumped at the chance. He has a seriously nice apartment.'

'The one you sent us photos of? Pretending it was yours?'

He hid his shame in another bite of donut. 'We should have bought some tea to go with these. They're so sweet.'

'Can we stay on topic, please?'

He threw his sister a look like a man who knew he was beaten. 'Okay, okay! We were together for a while and things were great. Better than great. But he didn't want anyone in the office to know about us, and I respected that, you know? Workplace romances aren't good for his reputation.'

'He wanted to keep you a secret?' she said, trying to keep the dryness from her voice.

Fixing a Broken Heart at the Highland Repair Shop   227

'Secret, and casual. Except we weren't casual any time we were alone together. It felt serious enough then! We even stayed with his sister in Lucerne for a week. I babysat her kids, for Pete's sake! Anyways, Andreas would leave the apartment half an hour before I left in the mornings; he'd take his car and I'd cycle to work, and he didn't acknowledge me once I got there, acted like he barely knew me, when the night before he'd have been promising me the stars.'

'I get it.' She knew great big red flag behaviour when she heard about it these days, now that she was wiser.

She wasn't, however, used to counselling her sophisticated, cool-hearted brother about these things. How had this role reversal happened?

'So you couldn't help catching feelings for the boss man?' she asked.

'You've seen Andreas, right?'

Ally had to admit he was beyond handsome. She couldn't blame Murray for falling headlong into a messy situation with the guy.

'He promised he'd make it official once my probationary period was up, like it might ruin my chances with the charity if it got out beforehand. But that time came and went, and still nothing. Things carried on the same, and I'd sneak into his building round the back, and the next day he'd ignore me in the coffee line but then grab my arse at the back of a packed elevator, straight-faced and bold as brass.'

Ally could see how that might be kind of exciting for a while, but the sugar glaze on Murray's face told a different story.

'He was running hot and cold on you,' she said.

A solemn nod from her brother. 'After a while that kind of thing gets to you. When I was last in Zurich, he had to attend a fancy evening event for work, a big do for all our corporate and philanthropic donors, and I happened to be invited too, and... there he was, with *David* on his arm.'

'Who's David?'

'Some old billionaire tax-dodging hunk with, like, three yachts and fingers in multiple aerospace programmes. He's one of the charity's biggest private benefactors – big as in there's a whole wing of our building named after him. Everyone loves him. He's always hosting parties and he flies colleagues out to his homes all over the place for holidays, you know, as perks?'

'Sounds like a good person to be friendly with! And he and Andreas were...' Ally didn't know how to put it. 'Involved?'

'Yep. And they were out together in broad daylight, in their tuxes, adjusting each other's ties, and all our colleagues were smarming over them like they were the cutest thing they'd ever seen. Ugh! And I knew I shouldn't say anything...'

'Oh no!' This couldn't be good. 'What did you do?'

'I couldn't stop myself. I marched right over there and asked Andreas what the hell he was playing at. He tried to laugh me off and be all charming and blond and smiley. He even tried introducing David to me, like I didn't already know who he was.'

'Ugh!'

'Exactly! And I told him to cut it out. That's when Andreas excused us both and walked me outside. Man, he was furious! He said I was making a scene, which I barely was, honestly! He reminded me we were only ever a casual thing, whereas he and David went way back and he thought I, of all people, should understand that.'

'What's that supposed to mean?'

'As his side piece, is what he meant.'

'What a creep.'

'Yeah.' Murray's enthusiasm for telling the story waned.

Fixing a Broken Heart at the Highland Repair Shop

'When I went back to his apartment my key card had been de-activated and my bags were waiting for me by the dumpster.'

Ally held a hand to his arm as Murray dropped his half eaten donut into the box and shut the lid, sick of himself.

'What did you do after that?'

He shrugged. 'I went back to the bro pad for a while, watched them high-fiving each other over bench presses and mixing their kale and protein powder smoothies, but I couldn't show my face at work. I had to get away. So now I'm here.'

'So, you didn't quit?'

'Not as such.'

'And you didn't get picked to go to Mali?'

'Would you pick the guy everybody now thinks had some kind of embarrassing, jealous crush on his senior colleague and made a twat of himself at a work event in front of all the rich donors?' Murray's voice cracked. 'The thing that hurts most is that David is actually a really sweet man, and Andreas probably does like him a lot.' His voice dropped an octave. 'Liked him more than me. And he wasn't ashamed to be seen out with him, unlike me, the lowly employee.'

'What? *Lowly*?' Ally wasn't letting that slide. 'You have no idea how much I admire what you do.'

'You really don't have to say that, sis.'

'I'm not kidding. You do such important work. You change lives. And so what? Maybe you weren't getting paid the mega bucks, and you didn't have a lake view penthouse and live in the lap of luxury... but I'd still have killed for a job like that.' She was riled now, couldn't help herself. 'You've seriously no idea how hard it is to have a walking talking *double* of yourself out there in the world doing all of this amazing, planet-changing stuff when you're stuck at home and can't seem to get moving.'

Murray turned in his seat to watch her, like he was learning something for the first time.

'And I know I was lucky to have a job at all,' she conceded, 'but I can't tell you how *bored* I was with it all. The same customer service script every day. The same clocking in and clocking out and scheduled bathroom breaks and those customers who really, really should just write their logins down somewhere and maybe they wouldn't keep getting locked out of their own systems! God, I was so sick of the whole thing.'

'Wow!' Murray's eyes had turned very big and round.

Ally didn't mind that she was scaring him a little. She had to share what she'd been going through all alone while he was living his phoney Insta-perfect life in Switzerland.

'I was left wondering why I was stuck. *Why me?* I kept thinking. And if I couldn't blame good old-fashioned sexism, then maybe I had to face the truth. The problem was me, not being good enough.'

'Och! That's some nonsense, right there,' Murray interjected.

'It didn't stop me getting all in my head about it. For a while I felt like everyone else had moved on and forgotten me. All my friends, you, everybody.'

'We were all just busy, doing our own things. Having our own problems, some might say *disasters*.' Murray offered a wry smile.

'I know that now. I saw it when I met the girls. They're all struggling too, in their own ways. Life is just hard for people our age. We have to do it all, and maybe without the same support structures or as many chances of success as some older folk had. And in this economy!'

Murray nodded like he'd never heard a truer word spoken. 'So you figured out for yourself that you weren't actually behind. You're exactly where you ought to be.'

Ally settled back into the driver's seat, uncurling her legs and slipping her feet back into her shoes before taking another donut and giving it a pensive bite. 'I suppose I did.'

She chewed, and for a moment things felt like they used to, Ally and Murray, a little like chalk and cheese, but still undeniably twinned forever.

'Jamie helped too. I think I'd have gotten there on my own eventually, but there's something about him that brings out the best in me, fast-tracking me towards wanting to try new things and see things from a new perspective.'

'Huh.' Her brother was looking at her, thinking. 'And you spent the other day with him, trapped in a bothy?'

Ally took another bite, hoping if she chewed hard enough he'd miss her reddening face. Not likely, the way he was examining her, a salacious smile dawning.

'And you're planning on seeing him again?' he said.

This made her pause. The uneasy feeling she'd had saying goodbye to him on Friday came flooding back now.

'What does he think about you going off to Switzerland?'

Ally was the one in the hot seat now, but there was no getting away from the fact that she hadn't a clue where she stood.

'When I told him I'd got the job, he was delighted for me.'

'Okay? You say that like it's a bad thing.'

'You don't get it, he was *so* happy for me; there wasn't even the slightest hint of realisation that it meant I'd be nine hundred miles away from him with a full-time job for twelve whole months.'

'Longer if they like you.'

Ally's heart made a pained little jump.

'Oh yeah,' Murray went on. 'If they're impressed with you, they'll probably offer to extend your contract at the end of it.

That's what happened to me, remember? I was only supposed to be there to oversee one project.'

'Right.' Just what she didn't need, even more bombshell surprises to process.

She'd barely known how to respond to Jamie's voice note on Saturday morning. She played it for her brother now, since all hope of retaining any dignity was gone and they may as well both wallow in the misery together.

'Listen to this,' she said, clicking play.

'Hey, Ally, it's me. Jamie. Jamie Beaton. I mean obviously it is. How many Jamies do you know? Actually, scrub that, you might know a few. Who am I to say? It is a common name. Oh God, let me start over. Hi! I had a great time yesterday. I'm here till the ninth, it turns out, umm... Of course, you'll be busy, preparing for your new job. Which is great, by the way. In case you think I don't think it's great. It is, really great. I'm, uh, not very good at these messages. OK, I should go. Umm... OK. Cheerio. And congratulations again. Bye... OK bye.'

'Someone needs to tell that man how to handle the Day After Phone Call, jeez!'

'I'm glad you think it's funny,' winced Ally.

'So what are you going to do?'

Ally exhaled hard. 'He's leaving soon, you heard him. A couple of days before I head to Zurich, as it happens. What can we do? Other than go our separate ways and be glad we knew each other for a while.'

'You're not going to be happy with that.'

Murray was right, of course, but what choice did she have?

'Our timings were just off,' she said, injecting as much maturity into it as she could. 'Right person, wrong time. It's a mismatch.'

Just like Jamie had explained. There was nothing wrong with

Fixing a Broken Heart at the Highland Repair Shop 233

either of them, nothing she'd change about him, nothing she needed to change about herself to make them a better couple. Only they were on different paths. A mismatch.

'We really should have bought some tea,' Murray said, inspecting his sugar-coated teeth in the sun visor mirror.

'Totally should have,' Ally agreed, trying to pack away the sorry feeling in her chest. 'So, what happens now for you? Don't you still have a job to go to?'

'I have no idea,' said Murray.

'There's only one way to find out.' She buckled her seatbelt and turned the engine over, before tapping his phone through his shirt pocket.

He looked down at it like she'd pulled the pin from a grenade. 'What?'

'Call Barbara Huber, *our* boss. She's in charge, remember? Not Andreas bloody Favre.'

'I can't. What if she knows about us? I've no idea what Andreas told her.'

'You don't have to tell her anything. Assume she's got some idea what her office workers are up to in their private time. And you know, maybe a secret affair reflects badly on him, and not you, the innocent party in all this? You didn't do anything wrong, as far as I can tell.' She let the handbrake off and pulled out of the parking space.

'Can't I just drown myself in donuts for the rest of my life?'

'Talk with her. If not for you, do it for me.' They made it out of the multi-storey and onto the ramp for the main road. 'I'm flying out there in a week. You don't want me answering awkward questions about your whereabouts when you've not had the chance to explain your side.' She hazarded a side glance at her brother.

He thought for a moment before dialling. As the ringtone

sounded he hissed out of the side of his mouth, begrudgingly impressed, 'Since when did you have all the answers figured out?'

Ally's smile withered away as Murray spoke with Barbara, the uncomfortable reality sinking in fully; there was still one great big glaring aspect of her life that was far from figured out and she had no idea what the answer was.

Following her feelings for Jamie was impossible, what with her European escape on the horizon, and Jamie was only too thrilled that she was leaving, or at least he wasn't upset that she was. Besides, he had his all-important transition into the regular police service to focus on, and his family to deal with.

She told herself again that theirs was, unfortunately, a mismatch. Only, every time she remembered the heat of the bothy fireside and the way Jamie had said her name in staggered gasping breaths, his back arching, the silvering scar on his brow flashing in the flames, she couldn't help thinking how they'd seemed, briefly, absolutely perfect for one another.

23

'Who's going to say what?' said Jamie furtively, the worry on his face reflected back at him onscreen next to his sister's, wearing a similar frown, inside her own little frame.

'Maybe a Zoom call isn't the best way to do this?' Karolyn said.

'I'll start, shall I? Tell him it's an intervention?' he suggested.

She shifted uncomfortably on the edge of the sofa seat. 'You can't use the word intervention. He'll run a mile. Just say we've been concerned... oh God, he's coming now.'

Jamie watched as she broke into a smile. 'Hi, Dad, come and sit down a minute.' She patted the spot beside her. 'Jamie's here too.'

His dad lurched into shot, looking more than a little confused. He was still holding his newspaper and pint of semi-skimmed.

'Aye? What's all this in aid of?' He obediently sat down, just as Jamie knew he would.

'Well, we're...' Karolyn began, before tailing off. 'We've been...'

'This is an intervention,' Jamie blurted like he was reading someone their rights.

'Jamie!' Karolyn protested.

'A *whit*?' said Samuel Beaton, even more perplexed.

'Listen, Dad,' Jamie softened. 'You know how I'm coming home on the ninth, just as soon as I complete my required volunteer hours here?'

'I do, aye.' He waited expectantly.

'And you know how things have been...' he paused so he could swallow, 'since Mum passed?'

Samuel glanced from the screen to Karolyn then back to his son.

'We've been talking, and it's time a few things changed,' Jamie went on bravely.

'Moved on,' suggested Karolyn, 'a wee bit.'

Mr Beaton's face remained hangdog. His eyes had the glisten of tears behind them.

'*We've* both made steps to move on with things,' said Karolyn, doing what Jamie wished he could do and taking her dad's arm. Their father had to surrender his shopping to the carpet at his feet so he could reciprocate and hold Karolyn.

'I'll be home soon enough,' Jamie tried again, 'and I want us to try talking to somebody.'

'Talking? To who?' their father croaked.

'A bereavement counsellor,' Karolyn clarified. 'Jamie found her online.'

The news sank in. Mr Beaton cleared his throat. 'You want me to talk to a strange woman, about your mum?'

'We'll all talk with her,' Jamie put in. 'Or, if it's easier, you can do it on your own at first. But we thought we could all do with getting some of it out in the open.'

'You did, did you?' Still noncommittal and not impressed,

Fixing a Broken Heart at the Highland Repair Shop   237

Samuel shifted back on the sofa, just an inch but enough to show he wanted to get away.

'It was Holiday that did it,' said Karolyn. 'And hearing Mum's voice. Did you know Jamie's been visiting all the Cairngorm tourist spots we went to when Mum was alive? Some of them with his new friend, Ally!' She turned wickedly laughing eyes on Jamie as she said this, and he fought hard to ignore his sister's teasing.

He hadn't talked much about how their date had gone, but Karolyn had always been able to read him like a kids' picture book, so he hadn't really needed to. He'd mentioned that he'd left her a voice message as soon as he woke up on Saturday morning, to check things were still OK, and to re-iterate how happy he was for her getting her new job.

He worried he should have re-recorded the thing. Had he sounded nervous? He'd been fine right up until the point he started to speak and the shaky, unsure feelings had hit him. Was she regretting what had happened? Or was she annoyed about how they'd left things? Bloody Finlay the ranger getting in the way of a proper, romantic goodbye. They'd been so rushed. He just knew he was already making a big mess of this.

He hadn't told his sister how he'd left the ball firmly in Ally's court as to what happened next, and that had been days ago. She'd replied with her own voice note message, just a few cheery-sounding words, telling him she was 'super busy' sorting things out for her trip and the skills share event which was, she'd been sorry to realise, the same day Jamie was planning on leaving town. She said she hoped they'd 'bump into each other soon' and left it at that.

Deep down, he wasn't entirely sure how anything much could happen next, given their circumstances.

How he wished he hadn't wasted time avoiding the pull of

her, heeding Edwyn's vague warning, when they could have been spending the best summer of their lives together. At least then, they might have had a solid foundation to leave things on before she flew away for a whole year. As it was, she was unlikely to want to wait for him.

He'd done the only thing he could think of. He'd celebrated her achievement, made sure she understood he was proud of her. The last thing he wanted was to be the person spoiling her excitement about her new life, especially after everything she'd been through with her ex and all her insecurities about not being as worthy of as great a career as her twin.

She deserved this job and she deserved to be happy and carefree. He wasn't going to be the stone dragging her down, not when she was finally taking flight.

Only now, it felt like *he* carried a great dragging weight in his chest, but if that's what it took for Ally to launch into the life she wanted and needed, he'd bear it for her sake, even if it meant letting go of the very best thing to happen to him. He'd have to toughen up and take it.

'What do you say, then, Dad?' said Jamie, thinking he might actually cry, and not just because of the intervention. 'It's been a long time coming, but I think it'll help you get some things… unstuck.'

Samuel Beaton hid his face. His hands sunk into his lap.

'Don't be upset, Dad. It's OK. We'll do it together,' Karolyn soothed, her arm on his back.

Samuel's shoulders bobbed. Was he crying?

Maybe this was a mistake? Maybe he wasn't ready after all? Maybe he never would be?

Yet, when their father lifted his head they saw he'd been laughing. There was a gleam of pride in his eyes, a smile, belea-

Fixing a Broken Heart at the Highland Repair Shop   239

guered and harangued, but not defensive or upset as the siblings had feared.

'You pair have cooked this up yourselves, have you?' he said looking between his kids.

They nodded.

'I could talk to someone,' he said. 'If you want me to.'

'It'd do us good, I think,' said Karolyn.

More silence followed, and the man put his arm around his daughter and kissed her forehead, looking at her like he couldn't quite believe he had a grown-up woman for a child.

'I...' Samuel began, but his feelings took over. A tear rolled down his cheek, and he didn't swipe it away. 'I had to be strong for you two. You were babies. Tiny wee things. And I hadnae a clue what to do with yous. Your mum, she always knew the right thing to do and say. Knew where everything was kept! I swear, it took me two weeks to find the loo rolls after she was gone! And I'm not proud of myself for having left so much to her, no, I'm not.' He shook his head, silently admonishing himself. 'I learned as best I could. But there was so little time! No time for thinking or feeling anything. I had school concerts and the school run and chickenpox and all those bloody clucking mothers in the schoolyard who thought I couldn't do it, but I *did* do it.'

Jamie's own tears fell, remembering his stoic hard-faced dad, determined to get it right, a man who never sat down for a second, he had the work of two parents to do and he'd be damned if he was going to let his Lucy Jayne down, even if he did occasionally forget how to do the softer side of things.

'We know you did,' Karolyn's voice was barely there.

'That day, when we picked up Holiday,' Samuel smiled at the memory of it. 'Something changed in me.'

Us too, Jamie wanted to say, but he couldn't speak for the lump in his throat.

'I've been thinking a lot, about your mum and us, and... all of it really, ever since.'

Karolyn nodded, swiping at her face. Her dad kissed her forehead again.

'OK,' their father said with a deep breath. 'Let's talk with this wummin. See if she can help us a bit.' He wiped his nose. 'It'll be nice to talk about your mum. I've been remembering so many things about her recently...'

'Me as well,' Jamie managed to say.

'Me too,' Karolyn echoed.

'There was this one time, she'd been determined to get you these wee Furby things for your Christmases,' he said, some great, straining floodgate weakening. 'And she needed to be in the queue for Jenner's opening first thing in the morning. She'd heard somehow they were coming back into stock in the toy department. Well...' his words tumbled on... 'your mum insisted on being at their gates for six in the morning, camped out she did! Took a flask of coffee and a deckchair! And yet, she was the only person waiting when they opened at nine!'

'But she got them,' Karolyn said, smiling, remembering unwrapping the thing, while a new core memory unlocked in Jamie's head.

'That was the Christmas she wanted to try goose instead of turkey, and oh my goodness, you've never seen such a thing. It arrived from the butcher, feathers and all! And that's why we have nut roast every Christmas, kids.'

He talked on while his children listened, adding in their own scant memories, even before the counsellor had been booked. This was good practice.

With the relief of releasing words unspoken for far too long, the Beaton family took another big step towards healing.

24

He'd left his packed suitcase zipped and upright by the door of his flat. He'd cleaned the place until it gleamed in the August sun streaming through the window. There'd be no deposits lost to landlords for the fastidious, disciplined Jamie Beaton.

He'd returned his high viz Highland Police vest and key card, badge and all the rest of it to the station, shaking hands with Chief Inspector Edwyn.

'You've been a credit to us, Special Constable. Lothian and Borders will be very fortunate to have you.'

Edwyn had rocked on his heels, hands behind his back as Jamie said his thanks and was presented with his whip-round single malt and a handshake from the Mason brothers and all the others who'd come, belatedly, to recognise the contribution he'd made. All of them admitted he'd be much missed. He hadn't been able to give much of an answer when they'd asked if he'd come back to visit any time soon.

'We'll see,' he'd mumbled, thinking how for now he'd no real reason to return. He'd carried the bottle out of the station and into the street.

His police fitness test was due to take place at half four in the east end of Edinburgh, his train was at ten to eleven. He'd need to be quick.

He made his way down the high street that had seemed so provincial and poky when he arrived here, not expecting much; he'd hoped for some collegiality at the station, maybe, some learning opportunities, a closer insight into the systems, that kind of thing. He'd trusted that seeing how another constabulary operated would be beneficial for his CV. And he'd dreamed of walking in his mum's footsteps, retracing the holiday he'd only the vaguest memories of.

Looking back, it hadn't been all that bad, his three months in the Cairngorms. It had started out tough, and he'd faced the challenges of being the new kid at the very bottom of the pile, but he'd risen to them and even harder ones too; foiling a gang, finding his mum in the landscape – and unexpectedly finding a way to reach his father too. Then there'd been the discovery of just how beautiful the place was: mountains and open valleys, the community paths and the little villages, chimneys that smoked even in the summer. He'd fallen a little in love with all of it.

He was finding, as he made his way through town this morning, that near enough everyone had a word of greeting for him. That was new too.

It came about after news of the other raids had hit the papers. Properties all across the region and into the lowlands had their hinges busted and unsuspecting inhabitants cuffed. Even wider networks shifting drugs and stolen goods had been uncovered and stopped in their tracks because of Jamie collaring Francie Beaumont and his men, millions of pounds worth of contraband and stolen property seized. The court cases

Fixing a Broken Heart at the Highland Repair Shop   243

were already underway, the charges stacking up for Francie and his networks.

He wondered what had become of Livvie Cooper, but there was no way of finding out; the systems for hiding people from harm were impermeable, even for his superiors. Her whereabouts, and that of her daughter and elderly mother, would remain shrouded in mystery for their protection. This brought him the strongest glow of pride. He'd done that.

Though, as he looked up at the hunched back of Cairn Dhu mountain, the vegetation on its lower approaches already turning copper and orange as the first hints of the season's end touched the park, it struck him how Livvie and her little girl would surely miss this scenery? He knew that he would.

As he came to the long curving wall that led off the high street and onto McIntyre land, he tried to tell himself that the mellow pink and grey granite of the Cairn Dhu houses was nothing compared to the dirty brick and cobbles of Edinburgh. The eagles and buzzards nesting in the snowy peaks of Ben Macdui paled in comparison with the chattering house sparrows in Princes Street Gardens or the puffed-up pigeons perched around the town's distilleries and docks. Try as he might, he couldn't even begin to convince himself.

He tried to take it all in, one last look around. He wanted to preserve these memories but he grew interested in the busy scenes before him. There were an awful lot of cars lining the street today, were there not?

He joined a slow-moving crowd milling on the gravel and clogging up the doors to the repair shed which today were held open and letting out a cacophony of fixing sounds, grinding and planing, tapping and tinkering, mixed in with the clinking of teaspoons and crockery, and music playing, and voices lifting.

He checked his phone: half an hour before he'd have to make a dash for the station. If he could just get inside.

* * *

The Cairn Dhu Repair Shop and Café skills share recruitment drive and societies soft launch wasn't going quite how Ally had imagined it would during her brainstorming sessions, or when she'd presented the vision to the other repairers, or even when she'd put together the sleek case study justifying today's event with which she'd impressed her new boss, Barbara, at her second interview.

It was in fact, going far, far better than she'd hoped.

Early that morning she'd worried she hadn't made enough noise on their new social media platforms, or that the new website she'd built hadn't had enough hits, and that fifty-eight email newsletter subscribers wasn't much to show for its first week of sign-ups. But she'd been wrong.

She hadn't counted on the way news spreads from house to shop to classroom to business premises around here. She hadn't bargained on every one of the people turning up today bringing an entourage of curious pals and nosey neighbours.

Even though she'd talked the talk about how events like these big community projects require 'buy-in' from the locals, she hadn't banked on the extent to which folks from all across the park were invested in her idea.

Yet, here they all were.

Ally watched from her spot behind her repair bench, taking it all in as she wiped an old laptop and re-installed it with Office so it could be donated to the repair café cause.

'Someone will be able to make use of it,' Mr Meikle the Minister had said when he brought it in at ten, just as the doors

Fixing a Broken Heart at the Highland Repair Shop   245

opened, and sure enough, it had pre-emptively been claimed by one of the primary school teaching assistants who had a family in mind for it.

Sachin stood behind his triage desk directing the repair clients, his music spilling everywhere, putting a bounce in everyone's step.

A photographer from a local paper was here capturing the first of the repair café's sessions, a demo by Peaches and Willie of embroidery to give old clothes, that would otherwise be scrapped, a new lease of life. A few people had brought favourite garments for them to work on and were watching delightedly now as Peaches's deft, simple darning needlework covered over a little stain on a white T-shirt with a red heart made of only a few stitches, while Willie efficiently disguised a worn patch on a denim jacket with what he called 'Scandi-inspired' crosshatched embroidery. They made it look so easy. People applauded and said they'd try it at home themselves, now they knew how.

Between repairs, Cary Anderson worked away making a little workbench, explaining to visitors how he'd soon be running his junior carpentry sessions for bairns and their grown-ups to learn some basic woodworking skills.

Senga and Rhona were run off their feet but keeping cool heads as they dished up chocolate crispie cakes and coffees, and invited kids to try their hand at icing and decorating biscuits in the shape of the repair barn. Three little ones sat in a row on the stools in front of the café counter, their heads bent, piping bags moving, and sneaking just as many dolly mixtures and jelly tots into their mouths as they stuck to their cookies. Senga pretended not to notice, and Rhona happily topped up their wee bowls.

McIntyre and Roz had a long line of repairs come in and had only stopped when the man from the local newspaper asked for some quotes on their new venture and they'd pointed them in Ally's direction, saying how none of this would be happening without her.

Ally, however, found that even in the midst of all her success she couldn't quite celebrate yet. Even though Carenza – still trying to make amends – was setting out the chairs and beanbags, building blocks and puzzles in the far corner by the doors for the 'carers and kids cuppa and play' session that was going to take place over lunchtime with her friend, a practitioner from the Speech and Language Therapy service on her day off from her clinic, who she'd managed to convince to come along today to listen and to advise.

Mhairi Sears had arrived for it early, bringing a wide-awake Jolyon in his buggy and, after hugs and a quick catch-up with Ally, the mother and son had taken their cakes from the café out into the courtyard where right this second Jolyon was sitting in the cushioned seat of Pigeon Angus's little red vintage tractor, which was decorated with colourful bunting for the occasion, his feet kicking ecstatically as he screamed and clapped and bit into chocolate crispie cake, Angus and Mhairi delightedly watching on.

Yes, it was all bustling and beautiful and the jar was already half full with donations, and the chalkboard repair totals were jumping up another few notches, but Ally couldn't help scanning the room, waiting for Jamie and what she hoped was going to be a decent goodbye.

* * *

There she was at her workbench. Red hair gleaming purple in the glow from the pink neon sign. Eyes deep green. Even from

Fixing a Broken Heart at the Highland Repair Shop 247

all the way over the heads of the crowd he could see their emerald shine.

His resolve weakened. How was he supposed to do this without dissolving away entirely? He caught her eye and shifted through the people, a smile fixed on his face.

* * *

'You made it!' Ally cried. He looked good. The scar was silvering nicely against his summer tan. She hadn't seen him in over a week since that day at the bothy. They'd both had the excuse of being extremely busy and distracted; Ally had been co-ordinating the skills share plans, and Jamie had his volunteer hours to complete. All this busyness had meant staying away from her and the repair shed. They'd both chosen to believe this was for the best, in the circumstances.

'I said I would.' Jamie was looking around at the people milling about, his hands in his pockets. 'You did it then. All this. Amazing, but not surprising.'

He'd always been able to make her flushed and bashful. Today the pride in his voice made her eyes want to stream. She fought the feelings back.

He seemed to think for a moment before propelling himself forward to kiss her swiftly on the cheek. 'Congratulations.'

'Thanks. So... all set to leave?'

'Yup.' He checked his phone screen. Ally knew it meant they had minutes only. 'And you're all good? Packed for your flight and everything?'

Ally nodded. 'We're leaving at six on Monday morning for the airport.'

'Your mum and dad taking you?'

Another nod. Ally wished now they'd made time to meet up

since the day on the mountain. Ten minutes might have settled things in her mind. But there had been too many loose ends to tie up and plans to make, and Ally had prioritised spending precious time with her family and her old friends.

Plus, Jamie hadn't actually asked her to meet up, and she hadn't suggested it either. He'd made it clear he was pleased for her and he was letting her go without a hint of possessiveness or making her feel bad for chasing her dream of launching herself into adult life at last.

'Dad and Karolyn say hi, by the way. They wanted me to tell you good luck.'

'They'll be looking forward to having you home.'

He smiled a flat smile, nodding.

'They said you were welcome to come and visit, or... stay a few days, if you were flying back for Christmas, or...'

She shook her head as soon as he started saying it. Ally had to stop him before the hope cracked both their chests open. 'I did consider it, cos I'll have a few days off, but the flights are so dear, double the price of the rest of the year, and I'll not be making much money and...'

'Of course.' Jamie was the one stopping her now. His eyes had lost their lustre. This was beginning to hurt way too much. 'Is Murray going back with you?' He looked around as if to ask where her brother had got to.

'He's not going. He spoke with his boss, well, our boss, and she wanted him there, but he just couldn't face it. Going back would be too hard, or so he says.'

'Wow, what happened to him over there?'

'I think he needs some time to process things. Bit of a sibling trait.'

'But you always get there in the end.' He smiled. It was so simple and so reassuring.

Fixing a Broken Heart at the Highland Repair Shop 249

Rhona appeared with a cake in a bag. 'For your train journey home,' she told Jamie tearfully before hugging him and disappearing back to her little café corner.

'Someone has a soft spot for you,' Ally said, trying to wear a grin, not sure she was succeeding.

She watched as Jamie sniffed a laugh, but as her words hung between them, his face fell and he seemed to want to say something.

She wasn't sure if she should drag him outside, right round the back of the barn and hug him and cry and kiss him hard and promise him everything if he'd just wait for her, for twelve to eighteen months, say?

Part of her wanted him to leave now so he wouldn't see her in agony and she couldn't be tempted to ask him why he was so glad she'd got the job and what had it all meant to him that day they'd got lost in the clouds, and in each other, on the mountain.

Instead she did nothing, her face surely conveying the message that if anyone had a soft spot for him, it was her. The tenderest of spots.

Sachin was directing someone over towards her. *Oh no*, she thought. *This can't be it?* She'd have to fix someone's alarm clock or iPad while he walked away from her, unkissed and confused. After everything they'd been through.

'Laura?' The name jumped from her lips as the grocer, and Gray's girlfriend, approached. 'You're wanting something fixed?'

'You could say that,' she said, shamefaced.

Jamie looked between the two women and made to go.

'Just wait a minute, OK?' Ally stilled him with a spread palm.

'Don't worry,' he said. 'I won't leave without saying goodbye.' He made his way towards her dad, who was re-attaching a spade to its handle under the gaze of its owner.

It was so like Jamie to want to say goodbye to her parents too. The soft spot grew fonder and ached terribly.

Laura was watching all of this, curiosity etched on her face now. 'You two are...?' She pointed between them.

'No,' Ally said, then wanted to kick herself. 'Sort of. Well, we're good friends.' She was annoying even herself. 'Is there something you want, Laura?' She tried not to be tetchy. It wasn't Laura she was upset with, never had been. It was herself all along, the overly cautious, content-to-settle-for-unspectacular, stuck in the mud Ally McIntyre, but that version of her was almost completely gone now.

'I came to say I was sorry,' said Laura.

'You really don't have to—'

'I do,' she cut her off. 'Gray crawled back and I let him in, and...' Laura shrugged. 'It wasn't very sisterly of me.'

Ally fought the impulse to say, that's OK, you're not my sister, but something sad in Laura's demeanour stopped her.

'He's dumped you, hasn't he?'

Laura nodded, unable to look her in the eye. 'There's somebody else, apparently. A new lassie, at his work. I heard one of his pals laughing about it when I delivered the bacon rolls on Friday.'

'I'm sorry.' Ally meant it. 'He wasn't anything special, honestly. You'll see that eventually.'

'I think I already knew, but there's just not many lads around, is there? And you're supposed to be settling down around about my age, and here I am delivering bread and cheese, and I'm single all over again.'

'I know a wee bit about that,' Ally said, unable to stop herself smiling softly. 'You're not missing out on anything, believe me. It's hard *all* the way up. You're exactly where you're supposed to be.' An idea hit Ally. 'In fact, why don't you go grab Senga over

Fixing a Broken Heart at the Highland Repair Shop 251

there. She'd got some ideas for expanding the café, running some baking sessions. It's all part of this expansion of our offering.' She swept a hand, gesturing to the bustling room with Roz at the centre, handing out leaflets asking locals to consider volunteering their time and their skills at the shed, and gathering names on a clipboard of interested parties.

'Aye, I will do that,' Laura said, stepping back, picturing how that might work and liking what she saw. 'It'd be nice to come back to the repair shop again. And... if you don't mind, I'd like to start bringing your deliveries, instead of Keeley doing it. Can I?'

'Of course you can.' Ally decided to let Laura discover she wasn't going to be here come the next repair day in her own good time. 'The Gifford sisters will get you back in the loop.'

Laura smiled, relieved, and was making her way through the crowd to the café corner, when McIntyre stopped everyone in their tracks.

'Can I say a few words?' he was announcing from on top of an actual soap box in the middle of the room. Roz stood by him, supporting him with a hand through his belt loop at the back.

'It's wonderful to welcome you all today, and to the first of our skills share and social events. There's many more to come, just keep an eye on our braw new website...' This raised a little cheer from Sachin who'd been joined by his wife and adult daughters at the triage desk. 'And you can follow us on our...' he looked to Peaches and Willie.

'Socials?' they said simultaneously, before exchanging matching amused glances.

'That's it, our socials! We've had our ups and downs this summer but we've emerged stronger, I think we can all agree?' He was looking straight at his daughter now.

Ally gave him a nod. He wasn't wrong.

A movement caught her eye. Jamie making his way through

the stilled bodies as her father's speech went on, whispering excuse mes and apologies as he went. Ally's heartbeat picked up a new erratic rhythm.

'Someone very clever told me that to make change happen, all we have to do is imagine a world where it's already happened, and work towards that,' McIntyre was saying. 'I can imagine a sustainable world of sharing where we make sure everybody has enough before any one person has too much. I can imagine a world where we're less isolated and we're not afraid of reaching out. And since you're all here today, I believe you can imagine that too.' He held his coffee mug a little higher. 'So, here's a toast. To the repair revolutionaries and the world we're imagining into being.'

Ally didn't want to give in to crying, but the impulse made her chest juddery as she sniffed back tears. The whole room was raising cups and cookies and shouting cheers. She should have been jubilant like them. The photographer from the paper captured the moment, capturing also the look on Jamie's face as he wordlessly conveyed to Ally across the crowded room that he really did have to run for his train if he was going to make it on time.

Jamie fought his way to the door at the same time as the parents and kids and Carenza's special guest, the speech and language therapist, were shoving inside, and it felt like being caught in a tide, but he really did have to get out of here.

Ally was on her way towards him, and together they were like two salmon swimming upriver, fighting the currents. They both burst out of the doors together at the same time, into the fresh, cool air of the very last days of the summer.

Fixing a Broken Heart at the Highland Repair Shop   253

'I'm sorry,' he told her, showing her the time on his phone.

'I know,' she said, urgency in her eyes. What was she going to say to him?

'I've loved every second of this,' he said.

'Me too.'

'I'll go smash the fitness test, with any luck, attend the new intake day tomorrow and...' he spread his hands, 'Ta-da! Regular Officer Beaton at your service! Hopefully.'

She smiled. It looked like pride and sorrow mixed together.

'And you go get 'em in Zurich! Show them some of that Ally McIntyre go-getter magic! Change the world.' *Like you've changed mine*, he thought.

There was only time for a hug, a kiss to her cheekbone. No *I'll miss you* or *I'll call you* or anything. Just goodbye.

He let go of the woman he'd wanted to hold to his heart from the first second he'd laid eyes on her, and somehow he walked away.

Mhairi Sears, with Jolyon by her side holding his mum's hand and eating a great big chocolate cookie, came up behind Ally and caught her just in time before the tears started to fall.

'I've got you,' Mhairi told her old friend, and they hugged in the courtyard while the visitors kept arriving in their droves.

It was the biggest, most successful day of Ally's life to date, and all Ally could do was break down as the best, sincerest, most supportive man she'd ever met walked away to begin the next chapter of his life without her.

25

As the alarm clocks sounded early on Monday morning in the mill house, the Cairngorms National Park was waking up to another day of late-summer dew. An early wave of migrating swifts swept southwards across the clear sky, the first to answer nature's message and seek out softer weather, knowing what was coming to the Highlands: cranreuch cold and all the spartan wonders of autumn at this elevation.

Planes criss-crossed high above them, meeting barely a cloud. On late-season dawns like this, the sun is drowsy in its rising, the summer-warmed soil cooling with every passing hour as the worms dive deeper, crab-apples and russets fatten on their branches in the mellowing valley, and, as afternoon rain showers make their return, the Nithy waters swell a little fuller, flowing beneath the old mill house wheel.

Murray was up early, and sitting at the kitchen table, wearing a gigantic old fleece onesie Ally hadn't laid eyes on in years. He was typing on his fancy tablet.

'I didn't know you were coming to the airport too?' said Ally, dragging her case into the kitchen and pouring herself a coffee

Fixing a Broken Heart at the Highland Repair Shop   255

from Murray's moka pot. Another of the perks of having him home; his expensive new coffee-making equipment and monsooned malabar beans.

'I'm not. I'm finishing this funding application to expand the repair shop,' he said.

'But you worked on it all weekend too. You missed the skills share event.'

The event had run on early into Saturday evening, and when the locals had left, Ally had hosted Jo and Gus, Brodie and Luce, Mhairi and Jolyon, and all the other kids, for fish suppers with the McIntyres at the kitchen table.

Murray had been conspicuously quiet through that dinner, preferring to watch *Batwheels* cartoons with Jolyon on his tablet than chat with the grown-ups.

Murray stopped typing. 'I've never been all that handy with repairing, you know that. At least I can do this. I'll have it ready to send by lunch.'

Ally came round to look at the screen. Murray scrolled to let her glimpse every one of its forty pages. What she saw made her gasp.

'When you said you were asking the council for some of their development money for an extension, I didn't think you were planning on converting the whole place into a... what is that, an eco barn?'

'Go big or go home, right? I've got the funding bid-writing experience, why not put it to good use? Make a watertight application?'

Murray was constructing an appeal for funding for not only another thirty feet of floor space at the back of the shed, expanding its wooden walls and adding, not a corrugated iron roof to the new part, but glazing, so the repair shed could rely more on natural light and less on electricity. He'd also factored in costs for 'planet-friendly' wool insulation as well as solar thermal panels to cover the south-facing side of the old roof and things called 'ground and air source heat pumps', whatever they were, and a small wind turbine which, according to Murray's plan, would go on the little drumlin at the deepest end of the McIntyre garden where, as kids, the twins would play 'I capture the castle' and Ally always had to be the knight and Murray always the lovely, bougie prince in the tower.

Murray was keen to explain. 'With the bid comes my promise to spread carbon literacy using the repair shop's new networks. I'm proposing to hold monthly meetings at the shed on the topics of renewable energy, recycling, that kind of thing. It's all here, page eleven. And I've listed all the other repair sessions and social groups the shed will be hosting too.'

Ally couldn't help but be impressed. No wonder Murray had found work in Zurich straight out of college if he could write such compelling reasons for why people should part with their money to help good causes.

She held his shoulders in both hands as he sat over the screen. 'Sure you're not coming with me?'

It took him a moment to answer. 'Like I said to Barbara, I feel like I've closed the door on that part of my life.'

'You sure this isn't just you hiding?' Ally didn't want to trample his feelings, so she stepped as gently as she could. 'I know a lot about hiding from life. This feels like we're swapping places. I don't like to think of you getting stuck, like I was.'

Murray put his hand on his sister's, lifting his eyes to hers. He looked like he hadn't slept at all.

'I can't face him. And I don't want to go back to being who I was over there.'

'Which was?'

'I don't know, someone's secret boyfriend. I can't help

Fixing a Broken Heart at the Highland Repair Shop   257

thinking I did as well as I did because he was showing me preferential treatment over the others. Was that why I was getting picked for projects overseas, getting promoted?'

Ally hadn't quite figured how much her brother had got into his own head about Andreas. He'd taken a bigger hit than she'd realised, and the awful thing was, she wasn't going to be around to help him recover now.

'No, you got to where you were because you're smart and capable, and you can write about...' she checked his screen '... *renewable energy tariffs and ecological building systems* like they're remotely interesting.'

'Oh, they are,' he assured her.

'See? You got the job because you care, and because you were qualified. You were sent all over the planet because you're a safe pair of hands.'

The last kernel of envy that had made her compare herself unfavourably to her twin all this time disappeared within her. He'd earned his achievements in the same way she was about to go out there and show the world what she was made of and earn hers too.

'I don't know, sis,' he said sadly, leaning his head onto her arm.

Murray patently didn't believe her. He'd lost his self-belief and that little spark of egotism that had propelled him through his career. Now that it was extinguished, Ally missed it, even when it had been kind of annoying before.

She tousled his hair. One thing was for sure, she'd be cautious of Andreas Favre when she was over there. In fact, she hoped she wasn't on his team at all. How could she resist telling him exactly what she thought of him? He'd slowly crushed her brother's self-assurance. She could see that now.

'Somebody needs to look after Mum and Dad,' Murray added, consoling her.

'Be sure to hide Dad's cut-off jorts and vest when summer comes around again, OK?'

He laughed fondly. 'Consider them gone.'

She leaned over her brother, hugging him, the top of his head under her jaw. He hugged back.

'OK,' she sighed after a long moment. 'I'd better get going.'

'Sure you're going to be all right?' he said, not letting go.

Ally knew he wasn't talking about the flight or the transfers or finding her new apartment in a strange city or even meeting the two Swiss interns she'd be flat sharing with. He was talking about leaving Jamie.

Jamie had messaged her last night from Edinburgh, saying he'd passed the physical exam and smashed the recruitment day and how he was already missing her but he knew she could do it. She was to 'have the BEST time'.

'He'll be fast asleep in his old bed right now.'

'Doesn't seem right,' said her brother.

Again, she knew just what he was saying. It didn't seem right not to say a proper goodbye after all they'd been through. It didn't seem right that they'd never see each other again, that they were clearly more than compatible and frankly made for each other, and yet they were both set on separate paths.

'It's *not* right...' said Ally.

'...But it is OK,' joined Murray, smiling at his sister setting him up for a Whitney joke even when she was feeling sorry for herself. 'You're going to make it anyway.'

Ally kissed the top of his head and released him. Reaching for her case, she felt the stretch of that invisible elastic that connected them, and not without some pain. 'Facetime you at eight tonight?' She was walking away.

Fixing a Broken Heart at the Highland Repair Shop   259

'Zurich time,' he said, flashing her a glimpse of his ridiculously fancy wristwatch under his onesie sleeve.

'Be seeing you,' they both said at the same moment before she pulled open the door and stepped out onto the courtyard.

* * *

The door closed upon Murray, leaving him alone at the kitchen table, and he clamped his lips tight to stop himself from crying. What the hell was he doing? He was swapping one kind of loneliness, as Andreas's secret live-in lover in the lap of luxury in Switzerland, for another. He looked around the empty kitchen, the sound of Ally's steps retreating on the crunching gravel outside, and he tried to tell himself it would all work out somehow.

'I'm doing the right thing,' he said out loud. 'Some Me Time. Helping Mum and Dad. Autumn and winter in the Highlands. Sorting out this bid. I've got this.' And, entirely unconvinced and more than a little gloomy, he returned to his screen, forcing himself to get lost in his task once more.

Murray McIntyre was done with crying and he was well and truly done with chasing after cold, reserved men with nothing emotional to offer him.

* * *

Outside, Ally swiped to the boarding pass on her phone. Flight SW757 to Zurich. Her ticket out of here. She'd been dreaming of escape for so long that, now she held it in her hand, it was difficult to process.

Her parents waited for her by the open boot. They'd been

watching the dawn and sharing a hug and a single cup of coffee in a travel mug.

On seeing her approach, McIntyre came for her case and hefted it into the back, before bringing down the boot door with a bang.

'Ready?' he said.

Ally looked around at the dewy morning. Cairn Dhu mountain was capped with white on its highest, northernmost face, the heather below the mountain pass was in its fullest flush of copper and purple. Someone on the high street had a summer fire lit in their grate, casting out a good sooty smell of smoke that would always transport her right back to the winters of her childhood. She let herself take it all in, feeling more than ever how twelve months was a very, very long time.

She looked to the repair shed. Its doors were locked, the tools stilled and silent, the craftspeople, bakers and busybodies all still asleep in their beds. Soon it would be bustling again, alive with gossip and drilling, dauding, sawing, and Bhangra beats from Sachin's radio.

It was her repair shop, her community, when before it had just been something her dad did, something she'd been reluctantly roped into. Now it was as much a part of her as it was stitched into the fabric of Cairn Dhu and its people.

'I'm proud of you, my girl,' said her dad, seemingly reading her thoughts.

'Och,' she smiled this off. 'I'm proud of us.'

'You were the one turned our fortunes around, and got us all back on our feet at the shed. You got *me* back on my feet. All these years it's been my job to look after you and then suddenly, there you were, knowing just what to do when I was at a loss. And now you're leaving, flying away with the summer swifts.'

He hugged her tight.

Fixing a Broken Heart at the Highland Repair Shop

'We should save it for the airport. If I start crying again here, we'll never get away,' she said.

'Come on then.'

He made his way round to the driver's door. Roz delivered a swift kiss to her daughter's cheek, still unable to find the words to even begin to say goodbye, then she made her way to the passenger seat and closed her door.

Ally stood by the car, finding her legs moved stiffly, stalling her. Something wasn't right.

She wanted to go to Switzerland. She was ready for it. She was all packed. She'd prepared for this. Yet, her heart was thumping hard and telling her she needed Jamie.

She thought of him asleep in his childhood bedroom. She'd never even seen him dreaming deeply. Never laid beside him and held him for longer than a few minutes. There was so much she wanted to do with him and they hadn't had the chance.

She'd miss his first day of work as a regular officer, miss seeing him passing out in his uniform. She'd miss autumn walks and crunching through fallen leaves with him. There'd be no wrapping gifts for under his Christmas tree or mistletoe kisses or Hogmanay ceilidhs. In another life, where their timing wasn't off, and where they were better matched, she'd want all of that.

With a hard sigh, she told herself to get moving. There is always some aspect of self-denial and sacrifice in pursuing what you want. Always inconvenience and bad timing. It's a fact of adult life.

Ally was right back where she'd started, with a broken heart. Only now, she had memories of laughing and kissing, plotting and working together, hiking and talking, holding hands, feeling seen and being wanted. Fleeting, brief, summer moments, but they'd been worth it.

She found her legs loosening, and she lifted her head again, reaching for the car door. She'd message him on the drive to the airport. Tell him she was glad for him, passing his physical and getting what he wanted at long last. He'd worked so hard, he deserved happiness. She'd really mean it too. So long as he was happy, she could be glad for him. Her hand on the cold metal of the handle, her breath clouding the crisp morning air. She was really leaving.

'Wait!'

At first, she thought it was Murray, somehow coming at her from the gap in the courtyard walls. The voice turned into the hard crunch of gravel, and a streak of blue and black came thundering into the drive. Jamie Beaton, red cheeked and puffing.

She almost dropped her phone at the sight of him.

'I thought I was going to miss you!' He could barely breathe. 'I ran all the way from the station... early train... Christ!' He leaned over, hands on his knees. 'Surprised I passed that physical!'

'What are you doing here?' She watched him in wonder, catching sight of her mum's face through the car window, beaming back at them both.

He tried to catch his breath, straightening up again. Darkest blue jeans, blue jumper. Like an off-duty police officer.

She knew she was wide-eyed like a woman on the verge of losing it.

'I had to see you,' he gulped. 'We have to talk.'

'OK?' She nodded. That's just what she wanted too.

'I wanted to thank you, first of all,' he said, brown eyes wild and sparkling. 'I should have told you when I had the chance. You see? When I met you, I was stuck. And so was Dad, actually. For a long time.'

Ally nodded. 'I know.'

He took her hand, the words tumbling out. 'I only really

Fixing a Broken Heart at the Highland Repair Shop 263

started moving on when I came here. When I met you. You showed me the Nithy Brig and got something unstuck in me.' He thumbed his chest, right where his heart was beating so hard Ally thought she could see it through his clothes. 'You helped me remember a bit of Mum out there.' His eyes locked fast with hers. 'And you let me hear her voice again.' His own voice trembled. 'And hearing her got something moving inside Dad as well. He's trying bereavement therapy, you know? After all these years. That was you who did that!'

The burst of warmth in her chest made its way to her face. She was grinning wildly back at him. 'It's never too late,' she said.

'Never,' Jamie agreed. 'I think Mum will be watching him and feeling proud, you know?'

'I think she'll be proud of you too,' said Ally.

He was looking right into her, wonder lighting his face. 'It feels like you brought me closer to her than I've ever been. Or rather, you've brought me closer to myself. You taught me to imagine a world where things were better and work towards that. You showed me healing was possible. You showed me...' he stumbled closer. 'You showed me love was possible.'

His hands travelled up over her arms. She answered his body, pulling him closer. It turned into a tight hug.

'Thank you, for all of that,' he said close to her ear.

When he pulled back, he kept his hands on her arms.

'Jamie,' Ally began, wondering if she could express in words this great warmth blooming inside her. She hadn't dared imagine she'd see him again, and here he was holding her. 'Jamie, I have to thank you too. For giving me courage. For making *me* unstuck. *And* for letting me go too. I mean, I don't mean letting me go, exactly; I mean encouraging me to do what I need to do.'

'Me too, I feel the same way.'

'Yes, but...' she knew it was coming, could feel it welling up. 'I've fallen in love with you.' She blinked in astonishment as the words stayed in the air between them. They sounded so good she said it again. 'I'm actually in love with you.'

Jamie, to her surprise, laughed brightly. 'Me too. I fell for you the second I saw you, and that day in the bothy, I was a goner.'

Ally crushed him to her, hugging him so tight she thought they both might pop. He squeezed her and they rocked, laughing like children.

Warmth. Simple joy. This must be what it feels like to get what you need.

Ally pulled back, suddenly sharply aware of the time ticking on.

'What are we going to do?' she asked, dazed. 'Are you going to wait for me?'

'Yes, I am. If you want me to?'

She laughed again at the very notion of not wanting him. 'I'll be gone for ages.'

'I know. I even looked into transferring to the Swiss police!' He laughed too. 'But no dice.'

'Oh.' She wasn't even that deflated. He was talking crazy now. It was all so wonderfully mad.

'But I *am* moving here to Cairn Dhu,' he said, his tone assured. 'As a Regular.'

'You're what?'

'In the new intake. Edwyn's already signed off on it. They need officers here, and I'm going to be one of them.'

'What about Edinburgh?' she said, eyes moving across his beautiful features in fascination.

'Ach, they've got Rebus and plenty other gritty, city cops. I'd rather be a Highland officer any day. And it means I'll be right

Fixing a Broken Heart at the Highland Repair Shop

here,' he pointed at the spot where they stood, 'when you come home. I'll have cleaned up these mean streets by the time you return.'

His lips, saying those words, looked better than they ever had, and she had to kiss him again.

After a long moment, he pulled away a little. 'I thought maybe I'd fly out for Christmas in Zurich, see what all the fuss is about?'

'Oh my God, yes!' More kisses, every one sealing their promises. 'I'd love that.'

'Are you coming to wave her off from the airport with us, or what?' Roz called from the rolled-down window.

Their smiles turned bashful. Jamie raised a hand to the back of his head.

'*Can* I come along?' he asked.

'Hop in,' said Ally, her excitement returning, and they scrambled into the back seat, clicking seatbelts, laughing giddily.

'All fixed?' said McIntyre, glancing at them in the rear-view mirror and turning over the engine.

'All fixed,' chimed Ally and Jamie at once, and their lips met in another quick kiss before their car rolled out of the driveway and into the bright mountain morning.

SENGA GIFFORD'S SCOTTISH TABLET RECIPE

110g butter
300ml milk
900g granulated sugar (yes 900g, that's not a typo!)
1 large can of condensed milk, 397g
Optional vanilla essence and crushed walnuts

Start by buttering a 10 inch tin or lining it with greaseproof paper. Place a glass of cold water in your fridge too.

Grab your heaviest based, largest, non-stick pan and melt the butter with the milk.

Add the sugar, stirring thoroughly, then bring it to the boil. Boil until it reaches 118 degrees Celsius (that's 244 F).

Then add the condensed milk and reboil for approx. 20 minutes (you should be fearing for your eyebrows by this stage, and the pot should look like a volcano erupting – honestly, it's frightening, please be careful of splashes!) Keep beating the mixture with your longest-handled wooden spoon to stop it sticking or burning. Watch out for little hot patches that go dark. This is your sign it's a wee bit too hot. You need to stir those away quickly. Don't stop stirring!

You'll see the mixture thicken and change from creamy to a pale caramel colour when it's almost ready. Now you need to test the set.

Do this bit quickly and off the heat: Grab your water from the fridge (remember the glass of cold water?) and drop a little of the mixture into it. If it forms a blob that immediately holds its shape and that you can squidge between your fingers without it feeling sticky, it is ready. Careful, mind, it's still very hot.

Take your pan off the heat and beat the mixture for 5-10 minutes to help it cool a little. This is when you add the vanilla if you want it. You could also add crumbled walnut like Senga does, which is extremely tasty! You might see the mixture becoming grainy around the pan edges as you stir. Another sign you're going to get a good firm set.

Tip: If you take it off the heat too early you'll get something soft and sticky like fudge (which will still be delicious) but not the brittle texture of tablet which should have a nice firm, crumbly bite (and is so sugary it almost dissolves teeth on contact).

Pour the mixture into your greased/lined tin and, when it's firming up, score fingers across the surface to help you cut it later. When it's cool enough, pop it in the fridge.

In an hour, you'll be able to enjoy a slice of Senga Gifford's Scottish tablet with a nice cup of tea!

Your tablet will keep in an airtight container for a week (or on the display counter of the Highland Repair Shop's Café for about forty minutes on a slow day). Beware! It is ridiculously moreish.

A LETTER FROM KILEY

Hello, lovely reader!

I'm Kiley Dunbar. Welcome to my thirteenth book and the very first in a gorgeous new series, *The Highland Repair Shop*.

I've wanted to write a story with an environmental focus for a while now, one that prioritises community and local action, reminding us that in an ecosystem even the tiniest thing matters. I knew I wanted it to be a romantic story too, and I hope you loved meeting Allyson McIntyre and Jamie Beaton, two kind folks who have big dreams they won't be put off pursuing, even when love comes along.

I hope too you enjoyed the Cairngorms setting, even if I do take a few imaginative liberties with names and places, as well as adapting the Fairy Dog myth.

Cairn Dhu town and the mountain that gives it its name are dreamed up, I'm afraid, though you'll find similar spots around beautiful Aviemore, where I've been lucky enough to holiday many times. The Nithy waters and its brig, and the Garten housing estate, they're inventions too. As is the Highland Police force and other wee aspects of the constabulary and training process, and I considerably lighten some bureaucracy around visa applications for the sake of the timeline, please don't be too cross. Thank you for indulging me in a wee bit of poetic license so the story and its playfulness can shine. The actual landscapes and shifting moods of the Cairngorms region is preserved, and I hope my love for the area shines through (even though I'm a Scottish Lowlander myself, born and raised in East Lothian).

If you've enjoyed your visit to the Cairn Dhu repair shop and café, please do leave a review on your favourite reviewing platform. That would mean the world to me and help welcome a brand-new romance series into the world.

If you want to come say hello and find out what bookish things I've been getting up to, you'll find me (all too often!) on Instagram @kileydunbarauthor

I also have a quarterly newsletter which I'll deliver straight to your inbox if you sign up here on my website: http://www. kileydunbar.co.uk/newsletter/

If you'd like to visit your nearest repair organisation, wherever you are in the world, you can begin your search here: https://www.repaircafe.org/en/visit/ choosing from over three thousand six hundred official locations. You can also find out how to volunteer as well as make a donation to the Repair Café International Foundation.

If you'd like to learn more about repairing, check out the wonderful folks at iFixit, a global repair community of people helping each other fix their stuff: https://www.ifixit.com/

Thank you, lovely readers, for all your support as I pursue the next part of my writing dreams at the Highland Repair Shop. I'll continue to work hard with your encouragement.

Love,

Kiley x

ACKNOWLEDGEMENTS

There are a few magnificent folks I need to thank for making this book happen. First of all, there's you, lovely reader. I appreciate you more than you can know.

Thank you to everyone at Boldwood Books, especially Francesca Best, Wendy Neale and Ana Carter. I'm hugely grateful to Shirley Khan for copy edits, to Rose Fox for proof reading, and to Lizzie Gardiner for her bright and bold cover art. Thank you so much Kirsty Cox for voicing this story's audiobook.

Vicky and Lisa are always there to listen to all my writing worries. Thank you so much for everything.

Lastly, but above all, thank you so, so much to Nic, R, I, and Mouse. I love you all so much.

ABOUT THE AUTHOR

Kiley Dunbar has been telling romantic stories since 2019, including her bestselling Borrow a Bookshop series. She lives in the north of England with her partner, her two lovely Dunbar babies and a beloved Bedlington Terrier, Amos. When Kiley's not writing cosy love stories she is a senior lecturer at The Manchester Writing School.

Sign up to Kiley Dunbar's mailing list for news, competitions and updates on future books.

Visit Kiley's website: www.kileydunbar.co.uk

Follow Kiley on social media here:

Boldwood

Boldwood Books is an award-winning fiction publishing company seeking out the best stories from around the world.

Find out more at www.boldwoodbooks.com

Join our reader community for brilliant books, competitions and offers!

Follow us
@BoldwoodBooks
@TheBoldBookClub

Sign up to our weekly deals newsletter

https://bit.ly/BoldwoodBNewsletter

Printed in Dunstable, United Kingdom